THE BEGINNING OF A
BEAUTIFUL FRIENDSHIP . . .

Duncan looked at what he had in his hand and realized it was the tip of the dragon's tail.

He screamed.

The dragon screamed right back.

"Ah...I...I was trying to get a turnip," he said with a gulp.

"Well then you really have made a huge mistake. That's my tail," the dragon said.

"Yes I see, and I'm very sorry," Duncan said. The dragon cleared his throat and looked at his tail where Duncan still held it. "Ah...sorry. I'll just put this right back where I found it." He laughed nervously, dusted the dragon's tail off, and then gently set it on the ground. "Well, I better be going now." He turned and started to crawl back through the hedge.

"Nonsense," the dragon said, grabbing Duncan by the arm with his tail and dragging him back. "Help yourself to some turnips. Heavens know there are plenty. Mind you, it's not dragon's tail, but that's probably tough and full of fat anyway." The dragon laughed at his own joke, showing off that mouth full of razor sharp teeth. Yet suddenly Duncan no longer felt he was about to be eaten.

Duncan got slowly to his feet then carefully took his sword off his back. When he did the dragon lifted an eyebrow. Duncan gave him a nervous shrug and then started using his sword to dig up some turnips. He reached back through the hedge, grabbed his pack and started stuffing the turnips into his bundle. "I must say this is awfully nice of you, dragon."

"Think nothing of it. Name's Mallory and you are?"

"Duncan..."

DUNCAN AND MALLORY

THE BEGINNING

by **ROBERT ASPRIN, MEL WHITE,**
and **SELINA ROSEN**

WILDSIDE PRESS

DUNCAN & MALLORY: THE BEGINNING

by Robert Asprin, Mel White, and Selina Rosen.
Based on the graphic novel by Robert Asprin and Mel White.

Published by Wildside Press LLC.
www.wildsidebooks.com

One

Sleeping was one of Duncan's favorite pastimes. The young Romancer had been accused of being able to sleep anywhere and through anything, but he was having a hell of a time sleeping through this battle. He wondered briefly why war had to be so loud. Why men had to fight with shields, swords. and all manner of things that rang with loud, percussive noise and made it hard to enjoy a well-deserved nap.

Was all that armor clanging and banging around really necessary? Horses were making hoof-clumping sounds and whinnying in that shrill, feminine way that never seemed to fit something as large as a horse, and men were crying out in pain as they gasped their last breaths.

Had none of them heard of dying with dignity? Had they no pride?

It didn't help that he was wearing segmented metal leggings and knee cops and a fifty-pound chain mail shirt that hung to just above his knees. It wasn't comfortable to walk in or fight in, and it certainly wasn't comfortable to sleep in. As he tried to shift to get more comfortable, his chain gathered in all the wrong places. He cried out in a voice several octaves higher than his own as he reached down quickly to untangle himself.

He thought briefly about doffing his armor, but quickly decided against it. After all, it wouldn't do to get caught out of armor on a war day.

The reluctant warrior felt he just needed a few winks before he joined the war. He was exhausted; besides, his fellow soldiers did a perfectly good job of dying without any help from him. Duncan was in no hurry to die for honor or community or anything else, for that matter. Finally he managed to get into a position where his feet were above his head; it was awkward, at least he was almost comfortable.

Duncan didn't care at all about the war. At one time he'd tried to care, but he'd never warmed up to the idea. Of course he'd never told anyone that. They wouldn't understand. All they cared about was battle and fighting. They ate and breathed war. He ate whatever he could get his hands on, breathed air, and as long as he could keep from dying in the war, he'd go right on doing those things.

Yes, eating and sleeping and breathing were his favorite things—in that order. The only other things he had ever been interested in were chasing women and tinkering. Since no woman would give him the time of day, he'd spent a lot of time tinkering with things—building and inventing them. Most of what he made didn't really do what he'd wanted it to do; and things he tried to fix often wound up just as broken as they'd been when he'd started, but on occasion he actually got something right.

Because of his dreams of being an inventor, he spent a lot of time watching the village blacksmith. Sometimes the smith needed someone who was strong and stupid, and he'd give Duncan some task to perform. Maybe afterwards he'd give him a quick lesson on working metal. More often, he just told Duncan to bugger off and threw a hot coal at him.

When you were a Romancer, your career choices were pretty limited. You could be a farmer and raise food for the army. You could be a blacksmith and make weapons and armor for the army. You could be a soldier and go die in the war. As far as he could see, there wasn't much future in any of those things, least of all in being a soldier.

Oh. Romancers all talked about glory and honor; but what were glory and honor, really? You couldn't bed them. You couldn't stick them in a loaf of bread and make a sandwich out of them. So as far as he was concerned, they were as useless as armor pajamas.

Duncan wanted to be a great inventor, or at the very least a blacksmith. But his father was a major, his brothers had been soldiers, all of his family had always been soldiers, and there was never any question that he would do anything but fight in the war. His heart had never been in it. To tell the truth, he had no natural ability for combat at all. In fact, the only thing he'd gotten good at was running and hiding. His arms and legs seemed too long for his body, and usually, the minute he drew his sword he promptly tripped over his own feet. Oh, he was big enough and strong enough, but with a sword in his hand he was more dangerous to himself than anyone else.

No, a soldier's life was no life for him. Duncan wanted to leave his mark on Overlap in a different way than all his ancestors, by creating grand and glorious inventions. Most of all, he wanted to be alive to enjoy it.

Boats came along the river from time to time and sometimes they stopped for pickups or deliveries. The sailors would go to the local tavern and weave tales of the rest of Overlap, and he would listen intently.

They talked of grand cities and amazing machines even more fantastic than the steam-powered boats they sailed up and down the river. Duncan thought if he could get away from Spurna he could make his mark on the world. He had a lot of ideas and had no doubt that his inventions would make him very rich someday.

In fact, he'd been up till the first lights of false dawn working by lamplight because he was on the brink of creating something that he was sure would make him a household name. When completed, his fabulous invention would put all kinds of pudding into donuts. He was almost finished, too. It just needed a few final adjustments. Duncan could have finished it today; but no, he had to go fight in the stupid war.

Today was a battle day and nothing would do but that he get up minutes after he'd gone to sleep and march off to the front.

Stupid war.

Duncan shut the sounds of battle out, shifted his position again, and drifted off to sleep with visions of pudding-filled donuts dancing in his head.

So sleepy, but he had to get up. After all he had to make the donuts. Pulling his tall, slender, well-muscled body out of bed he took a long look at himself in the mirror. His dark, brooding brown eyes took in his features—a regal nose, bronze skin and a strong chin, longish black hair framing his face. "Damn, I'm good looking."

He didn't get to admire his reflection long because then he could hear them. A crowd stood admiring his machine as it cranked out dozens of the delicious pudding-filled donuts. They made loud sounds of delight as they watched the machine work its magic. Then they began chanting his name in a symphony of praise for the joy and wonder he had brought into their dim lives. "Duncan! Duncan! Duncan!"

"DUNCAN!"

The dream was swept quickly away as he awoke to the shrill, enraged voice of his father. "Duncan, you lazy good for nothing—get up!"

Father's boot landed squarely on Duncan's backside, making his chain mail jiggle. He woke the rest of the way up and tried to stand. He fell down three times because his right leg had gone to sleep. When he finally got his legs under himself and stood at his full height of six-foot-four, his five-foot-eleven father still managed to tower over him. The major had always had this effect.

Duncan's father was a barrel-chested man with arms and legs like tree trunks. His hair was short and grey—as was his mood on most days. His brown eyes seemed to forecast a storm. The major's nose was a hawk's beak, his chin a sharp point. His face and forearms were covered with the scars of numerous battles. The major's mouth was set in a permanent snarl, and his idea of a smile was an irritating smirk.

The major was not a pleasant man at the best of times, and today was clearly not the best of times.

"Ah...hi Dad," Duncan stammered out, shifting his mail shirt and sword till they were hanging straight.

"'Hi Dad?' Is that all you have to say?! Where in the name of all that is unholy were you this morning?"

It's pretty obvious where I was. I was lying under this tree taking a perfectly good nap, Duncan thought, but had the good sense not to say that. Instead, he said, "I was guarding the rear flank."

"Guarding the rear flank!" his dad thundered, and then his lip curled into that smirk. "It looked to me like you were sleeping."

"Sleeping. That's just what I wanted the enemy to think," Duncan said, managing to sound sincere. "They'd think they could sneak around me, but when they tried I'd spring up and attack..."

"You are two miles from the front," the major countered.

"Ahh...well if they were going to try a rear attack they'd want to come way around, or you'd just see them and..."

"I had to kick you to wake you up."

"Part of my plan. It wouldn't do for me to jump up when they were too far away now would it? Where would be the element of surprise in that?"

"We had a war this morning. You were supposed to be there and instead you took a nap!" the major said, pounding his finger into Duncan's chest hard enough to knock his nearly three-hundred pound body back a few inches. He obviously wasn't buying the battle strategy story.

The major's right arm was in a sling and his hand was bandaged up to three times its normal size. It was clear the war hadn't gone well for him, which was, no doubt, why he was in an even worse mood than usual.

"Once again we were counting on you. Once again you promised to take your place in the shield wall. And once again, you were a no show."

You'd think after a while you'd quit expecting me to be there, he thought. He tried another tactic. "Was that today?" Duncan managed to look confused—which wasn't that hard for him on most days.

"Don't give me that bull! You're standing here in your armor."

"I, ah...I... You know me, always ready for action. Why, I'd sleep in my armor, just to be ready at a moment's notice. I was rolling on the ground to loosen it up when you came up. I was..."

"Making up a list of lies to tell me!" Using only his left hand, the major grabbed him by the front of the tabard he wore over his chain and shook him till his armor and his teeth rattled. "The enemy came through the hole you were supposed to fill. Our clan was lucky to escape with our lives. Well, some of us were, anyway."

As he finished speaking he slung Duncan into the tree he'd been sleeping under only moments before. As he did, a clod that had been lodged in Duncan's right knee cop fell out, making a small dirt cloud. Even this seemed to tick his father off.

"We lost the war! What do you have to say about that?"

"Does this mean dinner is going to be late?"

"Dinner! Dinner! Is this all a joke to you?"

Somehow he couldn't hold his tongue. "Let's see. The third Tuesday of every month at exactly ten o'clock in the morning at the banks of the Sliding River on a field chosen by our ancestors over a hundred years ago we have a war with the Centaurs. At the end of a bloody, two-hour battle the bodies are counted, a winner is declared, and the winner gets to claim they own the Sliding River for a month. Gee, I don't know why anyone would think that was funny. I don't know why they would think it was—oh I don't know—completely insane."

The major was shocked speechless. Unfortunately, that didn't last long. "That's what's wrong with you, Duncan!" His father was yelling now, pacing back and forth and throwing around the hand that still worked in grand gestures to punctuate his yelling. "You care nothing about tradition. Why, all my brothers died in the wars. My father, my uncles, all your brothers died in the wars. My little cousin Remy twice removed on my mother's side died in the wars. The problem with you is, you think you're too good to do what the rest of us do. Let me tell you something. Our family has a long proud tradition...."

"Of dying?"

"We're warriors. We've always been warriors and we'll always be warriors...."

"Till we die a horrible death on the end of some Centaurs' spear," Duncan mumbled.

"It's an occupational hazard. There are worse things than dying."

"Really?" Duncan rolled his eyes. "Worse things than dying? I can't think of any off hand. Could you name a couple?"

"Being a coward for one thing, Duncan. Being a coward is worse than being dead."

"That's only one thing and... I really don't see how being a coward is worse than being dead. I can live with being a coward. Really, I can.

But I can't live with being dead." A confused look momentarily clouded his eyes; then he shook it off. "Come on, Papa. The wars…they're just stupid. You're fighting over who gets to say the Sliding River is theirs for a month! Everyone swims in it, fishes in it, boats go up and down it. No one charges toll, whether it's our river or theirs, because everyone knows that the river doesn't really belong to anyone. It can't belong to anyone."

"You make it sound as if all our family—all of your own brothers—have died for nothing."

Duncan looked at his father in mock shock. "Oh, no. They died for the glory and honor that comes from saying the river is ours…for a month. Unless, of course, we lost the month one of them died. In that case, I suppose, they really did die for nothing."

"The Centaurs are our sworn enemies."

"Because they want to say the river is theirs?"

"Yes precisely."

"But it's not theirs, it's ours."

"Nope they won this month," his father said, looking at the ground. "Poor cousin Remy died for nothing." Then he looked up with fire in his eyes and glared at Duncan. "Because some idiot decided to take a nap instead of going to the war."

"I don't see how my dying would have helped. Did it ever occur to anyone that we don't have to fight? Maybe we might settle this whole non-dispute by playing a heated game of tiddlywinks? Or anything else without a sharp point that kills people… Of course tiddlywinks takes skill, but I'm sure we could adapt. Or here's—an idea—we could just let the Centaurs say the river is theirs because it really doesn't matter at all."

Looking back at the confrontation, Duncan was never quite sure which of those things he shouldn't have said had caused the Major's next outburst, but he probably shouldn't have been surprised by it.

"Get out!"

"What?"

"Get out!"

"Out of where?" Duncan asked, confused. If he meant for Duncan to get out of his armor, that seemed like a really good idea.

"Out of my house. You are not my son. You are a clumsy, lazy bum with no discipline, no loyalty, and no honor. A warrior's training and a warrior's rations are wasted on you. Get out of my house, get out of this village, get out of this country. Just get out!"

"But…."

"No buts. You have embarrassed your family for the last time. Pack your things and go."

His father stood over his shoulder while he packed his meager possessions—made even more meager because every time he picked something up to pack it his father said, "That's not yours. I paid for it, That makes it mine."

"Do you expect me to go out in the world with nothing?" Duncan asked in disbelief.

"Dying's looking better and better, isn't it?" the Major said in a gloating tone.

"It's over quick. I'll give you that," Duncan spat back. "You know what? I don't care. Anything is better than being stuck here. I've wanted to go for a long time."

"Then quit whining like a girl and pack faster. I'm meeting the rest of the army at the pub to talk about the battle and raise a glass to the dead." As Duncan went to stick another blanket in the makeshift pack he'd built, his father shook his head. "One blanket ought to be plenty for a self-sufficient fellow like you."

When Duncan left the house and started towards the stable his father ran in front of him and held up his good hand.

"Just where do you think you're going?"

"To get my horse."

His father shook his head.

"Come on, you expect me to *march* out of here on foot?"

"*Soldiers* march, boy. I expect you'll crawl or skip your way out of here. That horse belonged to your brothers before you. He's forgotten more about integrity than you ever knew, and I'll be hanged if your worthless hide will ride him. Now get moving."

The major marched him to the edge of town in utter silence.

Their village was mostly a collection of cut-stone buildings with slate roofs. The fighting arena sat square in the middle of town and dominated it: a circle of columns topped with massive rocks, around a patch of dirt. The town was littered with marble statues of dead warlords. As a child, Duncan was sure they were watching him. As an adult, he grew to hate them because he realized the only way to get a statue was to die and then…well, you couldn't really appreciate it, could you?

As they walked Duncan paid attention to the familiar sights. The blacksmith was busy at his forge making a new sword but he still took the time to raise his hammer in the air, shake it wildly, and holler, "Good riddance!"

Duncan wasn't sure what it meant, but it was no doubt a parting wish for him. He smiled and waved back.

The blacksmith shook his head and turned back to the forge burying himself in his work so he wouldn't have to think about his young, almost-apprentice leaving. It put a lump in Duncan's throat.

They passed the tavern he had so many fond memories of—at least, until the last six months, when he hadn't been allowed in the door. The bar keep had told him it would take Duncan at least two years at his measly warrior's wages to pay off his debt. Warrior's pay got bumped up for every war you fought, every injury you received, every Centaur you killed. Since he'd never done those things, he was still making minimum wage. He'd decided there was no reason to pay his debt if he wasn't allowed in the bar till he'd paid it off. Why pay not to go someplace and not to drink? It made no sense to him.

A crowd had gathered outside the pub. They shook their fists and booed him, no doubt still mad over losing the war. The bartender held up a piece of paper—Duncan's bar tab. The man spit on the paper, tore it in two, threw it on the ground and stomped it. Somehow, Duncan knew this didn't mean the debt was forgiven.

"Good riddance!" the bartender yelled at him, shaking his fist in the air.

Duncan realized it must not be good wishes at all. He started to get a knotted feeling in his belly and a tightness in his chest.

They walked past the market place where he'd spent so much time as a boy. Happy times, running between the carts, occasionally pinching an apple. Several times he'd accidentally upset carts of food, sending fruit and vegetables cascading everywhere. Good times.

The vendors must not have seen it that way. As he walked past they started throwing rotten food and yelling at him. They had good aim, too, because by the time he ran past them he was covered from head to toe in vegetable slime. The major hadn't been so much as smudged.

Wiping a rotten tomato off his face, Duncan walked past the town brothel. The girls standing out front laughed at him, but then they always did.

Not a single person ran out to say goodbye, at least not anyone that didn't seem to be glad that he was going. He'd never been an unpleasant fellow, had he? He'd never been malicious or hateful to anyone. Was there a single person who was sorry to see him leave?

All Duncan's life he'd lived in Spurna. He'd never been much more than a few feet beyond the town's limits. Everyone knew him, and he knew them, but none of them were going to miss him when he was gone. Swallowing the lump in his throat he started to walk faster.

Shaking off the self-pity that suddenly reached to fill him, he thought, *So what if none of them will miss me. There's not a one of them that I will miss either. I'm walking past everything I have ever known, most likely for the last time.* The knot in his stomach seemed to tighten, so he quickly thought, *Good riddance!*

Duncan worked at convincing himself that he couldn't wait to shake the dust—and everything else—of Spurna off himself. He was ready to be done with the place.

Still, he really thought the old man was bluffing. Fully expected the major to give him a brusque speech and then march him right back home.

When Duncan turned to tell his father good bye the old man held up his hand to stop him.

"This is no time for sentimental bull crap, boy. I'm done with you, Duncan. You are a disgrace to our family and to my name. Turn around and get going. All I want to see is you getting smaller and smaller as you walk away. If I ever see your worthless hide again, I'll kick your butt back out of town again!"

"Dad, surely…." The look on the Major's face told Duncan he was wasting his breath but he had to try. "Don't you have any parting words of wisdom for me?"

His father almost laughed then. "Don't take any wooden coins."

"Is that all you have to say to me? I'm your only living son."

"You want words of wisdom to leave with? How about these? I wouldn't trade one of my dead sons for you."

His father might as well have slapped him across the face. He closed his eyes momentarily and swallowed hard then looked the major right in the eyes. "Lovely sentiment. Good bye, Dad."

His father grumbled, looking away, and pointed down the road. Duncan gave him the raspberry, swung around and took off at a quick pace. Part of him kept hoping his father would call out to him, beg him to come back, tell him it had all been a huge misunderstanding. At the very least say he was sorry for those final words.

When the young outcast finally turned around to look behind him, the village was a distant haze of chimney smoke and his father was already gone.

"I don't care! I wanted to leave anyway," he bellowed to the no one that was there to take offense. "You're all idiots, the lot of you. I'd rather be anywhere than in Spurna! You hear me? ANYWHERE!" He started to feel a little ball of pain in the pit of his stomach, so he turned around and started walking again.

He worked hard at talking himself out of being worried and scared. Of feeling unwanted, turned out into the world on his own, but it was hard since that was exactly what he was. *So I'm leaving behind everything I've ever known. So what? It all sucks! There isn't now, and never has been, anything for me in Spurna. I will miss my horse, and I'm sure the more I walk, the more I'll miss him. But no one was sad to see me go. Everyone who ever cared about me is dead. My mother ran off with some sailor when I was just an infant. My father hates me.* Surprisingly, that last one was the one that stung most. *My father hates me.*

Well, that hurt more than he wanted to admit.

His father was a cruel, heartless man who wasn't interested in him or what he wanted from life.

The local girls weren't interested in any man who hadn't killed half a dozen Centaurs and didn't have at least three bad scars. He hadn't killed anything bigger than a rabbit in his whole life, and the only scar he had was one he got falling off a bike when he was five and couldn't really reach the pedals.

As if he ever would have had the time to learn to ride a bike, much less anyone to teach him. The major made him spend all day, every day, training for the insane ritual of war with the Centaurs.

He'd never understood it. As long as he could remember, it had seemed idiotic to him. The other kids had all been excited about growing up to be great warriors and go die in the war. But even as a child, Duncan had never been the least bit interested in war or weapons, much less dying.

In Spurna a young man's life was military drills. And so he'd had lessons on every weapon, on the use of shields; fighting on foot, on horseback, and in formation—and he'd never been really good at anything. Maybe if he had been, he would have wanted to go to war and die like everyone else. Maybe his father was right that he was just a coward, afraid he'd be mere cannon fodder.

To fight with no skill, in a war he believed was pointless, would make him as mad as the rest of them. So not wanting to fight in that war must mean he was smarter than the rest of them.

That's what Duncan thought, anyway, and now that he was on his own, what other people thought didn't really matter.

Thinking about everything he'd just left behind, wondering where he was going and how he was going to get there, he didn't notice the sun setting. It was almost too dark to make camp before he started looking for a suitable place.

A small clearing just off the road seemed as good a place as any. Duncan quickly found wood and built a fire using the flint and steel that rattled in his pouch—along with a small piece of twine, five spent rivets—and two coins. He'd have to make do with that.

As if he didn't already know he was unprepared for a journey, he realized as he brought up an armload of wood that his father had sent him off with no food. Not even a stale loaf of bread.

His stomach twisted and grumbled its disapproval. He tried drinking some water. When he got desperate, he took his tabard off and tried sucking at a dried stain where a rotten vegetable had landed. It not only tasted bad; he felt pathetic.

Being kicked out of his home really started to sink in. He was alone in a world he didn't know, and he had next to nothing.

Duncan grabbed his canteen again and started to take another drink, but it was only about half full. That wasn't a real problem because he could hear the river in the distance. He'd walk down first thing in the morning and fill his canteen. So he took another drink to try to fool his stomach into thinking it was full.

No food was a going to be a huge problem; his stomach already felt like his throat had been cut.

Duncan put the wood down and went to check his pack. Some pack. It was nothing but an old blanket stuffed with what his father had let him take. He'd rolled it up and tied it with rope on both ends to make a shoulder strap. He had some trouble untying his own knots, but he knew what he was going to find, so he shouldn't have been quite as surprised as he was.

The pack held a change of clothes and a cloak that was really too small for him. It held a small whet tone, a large knife, a ball peen hammer, a small pair of blacksmith tongs, and a tin cup. He had the clothes and armor he was wearing, and his sword hung in a tattered sheath on his back. That was it. His belly was empty except for water and whatever he'd licked off his shirt, and it was getting dark.

Suddenly any joy he had felt about leaving Spurna left him.

The small pile of items in front of him was all he had to show for his life. His father hadn't let him take any of the things he'd made—not even his pudding-filling pastry machine. Then his stomach rumbled, and he got incredibly depressed.

He kept poking at the items on his blanket as if they might magically turn into food. Or at the very least something that would give the last twenty-five years of his life some meaning. Even a spoon might be nice, something that at least had touched food.

I could beg, I guess…That is, if I knew how to beg. He threw another piece of wood on the fire and sat down on the corner of the blanket to take his leggings off. His belly grumbled again. By now it was pitch black except for the area right around the fire, and it was getting cold fast. Summer was just over, and fall was quickly bringing cold weather.

He took off his sword and chain mail, grabbed his cloak and wrapped it around him. He stacked the rest of his belongings on his chain and leggings. Then he brought his sword close to him and rolled himself in the blanket and sat watching the fire and thinking how eerily quiet it was.

Alone, miles from home and as far as he knew miles from any human or not-so-human being; he'd never been truly alone before. He certainly had never spent a night alone in the woods. In the silence that surrounded him he could hear small things moving about in the leaves under and around him.

Suddenly the woods weren't quiet at all. Things he couldn't see now seemed to go out of their way to make spooky noises.

Duncan decided he didn't want any of the things crawling in the leaves to be near him. He got up quickly and scuffed all the leaves in the area to the edge of his fire.

Wrapping himself in the blanket better and moving closer to the fire Duncan tried hard to think about pleasant things. He was afraid that something was going to sneak up on him from the dark. He put more wood on the fire, making the flames dance high into the air and sending embers flying. Duncan didn't give it too much thought. In fact, he didn't give it any thought at all.

He put his mail shirt back on—just in case something did come up behind him in the night. It wasn't like he hadn't slept in it before. The night was cold so he put all the wood he'd gathered on the fire, rolled up in his blanket, and tried to get comfortable. He tried hard not to be afraid because then…. Well, that went back to his father's accusation of being a coward, didn't it?

Duncan fell into a fitful sleep dreaming first that he was sleeping naked in a snow bank. Then the snow all melted and he was way too hot. Then he was just right, and so he slept peacefully the rest of the night.

He woke up the next morning to the smell of smoke. He opened one eye carefully and peered at the fire which looked to be nothing but dead coals.

"Hum." Duncan mumbled and started to go back to sleep but then his stomach started rumbling again and the hunger wouldn't let him go back to sleep. Sitting up he stretched, and that was when he noticed the clouds of smoke above him. Looking around quickly he found that the woods around him had burned during the night. Oh, large trees were all right since there had been a good share of rain lately. But small trees, brush, and all the deadfall had burned to ash—except what was still on fire.

Duncan was puzzled. He looked around him. *What is this? Some spell gone wrong? A lightning strike without rain?* Then he looked around at his small camp. He looked at his fire and cringed. He remembered kicking the leaves out of his camp into a ring all around the fire.

"Oops," he said out loud. It was obvious what had happened. His too-big fire had ignited the ring of leaves he'd raked up. The entire countryside had caught fire while he'd been asleep. He had been lying on the ground so the smoke hadn't reached him and…well, he was damn lucky to be alive.

He took off his chain mail and rolled it and everything else he owned up in his blanket, then tied it into a pack again. Slinging his sword and his pack over his shoulder he hurried back to the road. On one side of the road everything on the ground was burned and the trees charred, on the other was a normal forest.

"At least it didn't cross the road. That's worth something, right?" he mumbled, trying to make himself feel better as he started walking.

He wanted to put some space between himself and his camp. It couldn't be good to be start a forest fire, especially if it had burned someone's house or crop or worse.

Duncan's shoulders slumped and he tried to console himself. "It probably just burned some leaves and a few scrub trees. Probably did more good than harm really. Killed a bunch of ticks and fertilized the earth and such and…"

That was when he smelled it. He sniffed the air again to make sure and then he found himself walking towards the smell, unable to stop.

His nose and the stomach it was attached to brought him to a still-burning hollow tree lying on the ground and in the hollow what was left of the groundhog that had been living inside it. Duncan drew his sword and pulled the animal from the fire. He felt bad about the groundhog for only a second, and then he gutted it, skinned it, and held it over the still-burning log to finish cooking.

Sitting on a soot-covered rock Duncan ate the whole thing till he was sucking the bones. Then he started looking around for more unfortunate animals his fire might have killed and mostly cooked for him. He found three rabbits and a squirrel. He skinned and gutted them, wrapped them in his fighting tabard, and stuck them in his pack for later.

He'd been happily checking for other edible things when he realized he was lost in the forest with no idea where the road was.

Also…he'd forgotten to fill his canteen and it was almost empty.

The young arsonist was working very hard at not panicking, when he finally came across a road again. Looking up and down it he had to admit he had no idea whether it was the road he'd been on before, much less which way to go. He looked to his right and to his left and decided it was easier to walk downhill than up. So that was the way he went. When he reached a spot where the forest was burned on one side of the road but not the other, he turned around and went back uphill—which was really was as tiring as he'd thought it would be.

He didn't see another living soul most of the day. That made sense because his village was in a very sparsely-populated part of the world. That was one of the reasons for walking with the flow of the river instead of against it. Up river there was less and less civilization, down river more and more.

As he drank the last drops of water from his canteen he listened. He could hear the river, so he walked toward the sound till he came to the bank of the Sliding. Filling his canteen he thought about camping along the river. If he waited for a boat, he might get a ride. But the river seemed almost as untraveled as the road, and he decided it was best to keep walking on the road where he didn't have to fight the underbrush for passage.

As he got back to the road, it was getting late, and he knew he should pick a place to camp for the night, but he thought he'd walk just a little further. Still, he was hungry, so he decided to take a break and eat. He sat down by the side of the road and opened his pack, making a face as he unrolled his tabard. The oils from the animals along with the smoke made it look and smell like…well, like burned, dead animals. The animals didn't look nearly as appetizing as they had when he packed them. Still, beggars couldn't be choosers, so he took his knife and scraped the fur off the meat and started eating. It wasn't much to look at but as his father had always told his picky younger brother Edger, "Food isn't for looking at. It's for eating."

Poor Edger. He'd been run through with a sharp stick during a drill.

Duncan became thoughtful. How great a fighting tradition could his family claim? All but his father seemed to have died without fighting many battles. Some, like Edger, had died without even getting to the battlefield. Maybe he wasn't any worse a fighter than any other member of his family. Maybe he was just the only one smart enough to admit he couldn't fight.

He was about to eat his last rabbit when he heard the familiar sound of a horse-drawn wagon heading his way.

He put the rabbit down on his tabard and stood to get a better look. Pretty soon it came into view, two men driving a wagon full of hay bales pulled by two horses.

"Hey!" Duncan started jumping up and down waving his hands in the air. "Hey you there, stop!"

"Whoa, there! Whoa," the thin man driving the wagon said, pulling back on his reins. He stopped his team then looked down at Duncan. "Why?"

"What?" Duncan asked confused.

"Why stop?"

"I ah…I need a ride and…"

"We'll give you a lift for that rabbit there. Looks like it's done just the way I like it. Right, Zeb?"

"Done just the way you like it, Roland," the other guy said with a grin, looking about as hungry as Duncan had been when he'd found the groundhog that morning.

"Sounds fair." Duncan handed the man the rabbit. "Where are you fellows headed?" he asked.

"Triad. The stables there pay the best price for hay," Roland said.

"Best price yep," Zeb said. He was a big man with a quick smile.

"Good thing, too. Damn fire burned up everything was left in the field while we were sleeping last night," Roland said, scratching his head.

"Burned up while we were sleeping, yep," Zeb said, throwing his hands in the air in a dramatic gesture that didn't match what he'd said.

"You wouldn't happen to know anything about that would you?" Roland asked Duncan.

"Would ya?" Zeb added.

Duncan looked at his feet. "No." He shrugged. "I didn't see any fire. Sorry. Maybe freak lightning or something."

Roland turned to Zeb. "Ha! Go figure. Not a cloud in the sky but it must be like this fellow says, a lightning strike."

"Yep, lightning strike," Zeb said. He seemed to just repeat what the skinny guy said, which Duncan thought was sort of odd.

Duncan knew nothing about Triad. He didn't really know much about Overlap past his own village except what he'd heard the sailors say, but he had to go somewhere, didn't he? "Could I maybe hitch a ride with you fellows as far as the next town?"

"The next town?" the thin guy said. The two looked at each other and smiled. "Be happy to."

"Happy to." Zeb chuckled.

Duncan grabbed his pack, took his sword and scabbard off, and started to crawl up front with the driver and his friend.

"Sorry, bud, no room up front. You'll have to ride on the back."

Duncan nodded and walked to the back of the wagon. There, he found himself sitting on about six inches of wood holding his pack and sword on what little lap he had in front of him. Every time the wagon hit any sort of rut he was thrown about six inches in the air and the bales shifted and threatened to push him off. Trying to keep his seat he nearly lost everything in his hands. And the wagon wheels seemed to go out of their way to make dust to choke him.

The fellows driving the wagon kept laughing, and it put a lump in his throat. He'd never really had a friend or anyone that he laughed and joked so easily with. So recently shunned, Duncan tried not to get in a funk. It was hard, what with eating dust and bouncing around on the back of that wagon while he hung on for dear life to the small bag that held everything he had.

He was alone in the world without a friend or home to call his own and no idea at all where to go or what to do. It was exciting and terrifying at the same time.

He fell off the back of the wagon at one point, and had to run to catch up. He barely got back on without losing his stuff. Duncan thought about trying to crawl on top of the hay but the bales were stacked six high, too high even for him to climb, and... Well, if he was bounced off from up there, it was a lot further to fall.

At one point his butt hurt so bad he thought about jumping off and walking again, but considering how hard it had been to catch up with the wagon, he realized he was making a lot better time this way.

He thought of his night alone in the woods and shuddered. He hadn't been thrilled before he'd burned up a huge part of the forest and these guys' hay field but now... Well it really wasn't safe for anyone for Duncan to be alone in the woods.

As he thought of the woods—the burned and unburned ones—they drove out of them into a sparse land. The earth was so dark it was almost purple. The few plants that dotted the landscape were dark green, magenta, or yellow. In the distance he could make out the river and could see that the road was following it. The wagon stopped bouncing so hard, and when he looked down he saw that the dirt road had changed to a smooth, black surface. He was suddenly filled with excitement because, though he had known all his life that Overlap was made up of many different towns and he had on occasion seen peddlers and entertainers of different species in his village, Duncan had never actually seen anything but woods, hills and valleys, the river, the lake, pastures, and fields. This place was completely different.

Night was falling quickly but since he was riding on the back of the wagon and would be in a city soon he wasn't worried in the slightest. Besides, here in the open, the night wasn't as dark as in the woods. In fact, the moonlight made it possible to see the alien landscape for several feet in any direction.

The ride was smoother and there was no dust and soon he'd be in a city he'd never been to before. Duncan took in a deep breath and let it out. He was on an adventure. All that lay ahead of him was a bright and brilliant future filled with new things and new places and people like these two men who were only too happy to help a stranger.

His tranquility didn't last long.

The few animals he saw were reptilian, brightly colored, in different sizes and shapes. He saw three that looked like a cross between a lizard and a house cat that had little green spikes on their purple and turquoise-striped bodies. They were sort of cute. They just ran away afraid of the wagon and the humans no doubt. But then there was another creature about the size of a dog that was red and orange and bright-yellow spotted. It hissed and snarled and chased the wagon, its long, thin tail whipping the air behind it with an ominous sound. The thing had a mouth full of sharp yellow teeth and its breath—which easily reached the young Romancer on his perch—smelled like death.

All six-feet-four-inch, two-hundred-fifty pounds of Duncan managed to drag his feet up and sit sideways in the six inches at the back of that wagon. He hung on for dear life to the wire on a bale with one hand, and swung wildly at the animal with his pack and sword with the other.

All his attempts at self preservation seemed to make the animal more determined and aggressive. It wasn't until his pack actually connected with the creature's head and sent it head-over-tail into the ditch that it stopped chasing them.

Even when the creature was gone from sight Duncan stayed perched with one butt cheek on the wagon. There was no way he was going to let his legs dangle over the edge where something might chew them off.

He started to rethink the adventure thing.

The moon went behind a cloud and it was suddenly much darker and three times as cold. He wanted to dig his cloak out of his pack, but there was no way he could do it and stay on the wagon. Just then, the last thing he wanted was to be on foot in the dark in this strange place filled with Duncan-eating monsters.

No he'd deal with the cold and cling for dear life with one hand to his things and with the other to the baling wire. He'd thought only for a moment about what might happen if the wire broke or worse yet the bale it was attached to came loose and fell.

Just as he was sure that he would freeze to death at any moment, the wagon stopped suddenly. It was all he could do to peel his fingers off the wire. He had to open his fingers with his other hand before he could let go and get off the wagon.

"Town is about a fifteen minute walk that way," Roland said. Zeb was now driving the wagon. Duncan's eyes were drawn to the wagon's lights. He had assumed they were oil but could now see that they must run on some sort of generator system from the wheels because they were dimming as the wagon just sat there.

"Fifteen minutes that way," Zeb said, and pointed in again a much more elaborate hand gesture than what he'd said needed.

Duncan's teeth were chattering so hard he could barely speak. "Aren't you going?"

"We're going to Triad. This is the first town we've come to. You could ride on with us if you'd like," Roland said. "But I have to tell you the road's about to get a lot rougher and Zeb's driving. He's not a real careful driver."

"I like to go up," Zeb said laughing.

Duncan thought about being folded on the six-inch platform on the back of that wagon bed, freezing as he was tossed up and down. He then weighed it against a bunch of those lizard-dog things attacking him somewhere between here and the town, the lights of which he could make out in the distance. It wasn't far. They were right. Maybe a fifteen minute walk—tops.

"I'll stay here, thanks."

Both men laughed then and Roland said, "I bet next time you make a fire you'll be damn sure it doesn't get away from ya, Romancer."

With that, Zeb whipped the horses and moved away fast, taking the light which grew in intensity with their speed with them. Both men were laughing loudly.

Duncan drew a deep breath and let it out slowly. So…they'd known all along he'd caused the fire. Probably because they'd seen his camp in the middle of the burned area. Then he was the only one on the road and he was eating scorched meat out of his smoke-stained tabard but said he hadn't seen any fire.

In retrospect he probably should have played that a little differently.

Then he frowned. So they'd purposely perched him on the edge of hell and then proceeded to give him the roughest ride ever.

It didn't matter. He guessed he deserved some form of punishment for burning up their hay crop. Besides, he could see the lights of the town clearly, and his butt would stop hurting eventually. He was still better off than he had been before he'd hitched a ride with them.

He'd go and see if he could find a warm place to sleep for the night. Maybe he had enough money to buy something to eat. Then in the morning he'd look for work. It didn't have to be a good job just something to pay for room and board till he could finish his invention and find fame and fortune.

It was still freezing cold so he opened his pack and feeling his way through the contents, pulled out his extra shirt, the cloak, and even the tabard that still smelled of cooked meat and made his mouth water. He carefully made sure he still had everything then tied the pack up tight and slung it and his sword over his shoulder.

"It's black as pitch," he mumbled to himself. "Still how hard could it be? All I have to do is go towards the lights." He found the road under his feet and started walking. It was even easier than he had thought it would be. He was in a straight line with the town and any time he stepped off the paved surface he could immediately feel the difference. "The joke's on those guys. I'm close to town, and now that I've got all my clothes on and I'm walking I'm even warm again."

No sooner had he said it than he heard something growling at his back. He doubled his pace, but so did the growling whatever-it-was. When he heard the whipping noise the tail of the lizard dog had made— only times three—he started running as fast as his legs would carry him towards the town.

He had hoped that the things wouldn't come into town but there was no such luck. Duncan kept running looking for somewhere to run to. The town was filled with large, well-kept, one-story wooden buildings. There were big signs that glowed in the darkness in bright greens and blues in a language he didn't know. He was starting to run out of steam without seeing any place he could escape from the merciless beasts when he saw the one place that looked more or less the same no matter where you were. After all a bar is always a bar.

Whatever was after him was nipping at his heels even as he ran in the tavern door and slammed it quickly behind him. The bar wasn't well lit—bars never were—but after total darkness the lights seemed blinding to him and it took a minute for his eyes to adjust. In fact, he still couldn't really make out the room or anyone in it when he heard a deep voice say, "Well would you all looky what we got here?"

Another voice, just as deep added, "It's a Romancer, ain't no doubt. Look at that tabard."

"And covered with the soot and blood of the recent battle."

"Come to avenge your kind, little man?"

And that was when Duncan could plainly make out the pin-up girl on the huge poster hanging over the bar. Up front all woman—from the waist down all horse. Duncan looked around at the tavern full of Centaurs. That's right. He was in a Centaur bar, in a Centaur village, wearing a Romancer's tabard less than two days after a war.

The blue and green lights should have been his first clue. Blue and Green were Centaur battle colors.

Now Roland and Zeb's laughter made sense. The rough ride had just been the beginning. Their real revenge was to dump him in a village full of the enemies of his people.

Duncan smiled nervously. "It's really a funny story."

"Really?" A big Centaur with a red coat and beard, wearing the blue fighting tabard of the Centaurs, turned to face him. "Let's just hear this funny story."

"I, ah, well, I didn't fight in the war. That's why I'm here…"

"Come to slay us in our own home?! To break all the rules of our war," the red Centaur roared and his fellows gathered around him.

"No, not at all. I was thrown out of my home because I wouldn't fight in the war. See I don't like the war," Duncan said quickly. "I think it's stupid."

"The war is stupid!" all the Centaurs thundered as a single voice.

"Ah…I mean to say… It's your river."

"Yes, because we won the war yesterday." They cheered, so it was worse than he thought. He wasn't just in just any Centaur bar. No, he was in a bar full of warrior Centaurs celebrating their victory.

"As far as I'm concerned you can just have it all the time. I'm not a fighter. I'm just dirty. Seriously, I would like you to just keep the river."

The Centaurs looked confused and the red one said. "You mean… you would give us the river without a war?"

"That's right. It's stupid to fight over it," the terrified young Romancer said.

"Did you hear that?" the red Centaur said in a rage. "We're stupid."

"No! Ah, no, I didn't mean you're stupid. Just that the whole thing is stupid," Duncan said quickly.

"So, what you're saying is that all of our people who have died fighting the war died for nothing?"

"No, no," Duncan said, remembering how mad it had made his father the major. "I'm just saying that no one has to die. You can just have the river."

"This man has no honor!" the red Centaur shouted out. Duncan heard several swords clear leather. Realizing he was talking himself into an ever-widening chasm, he turned and ran back out the door he'd come in.

Straight into the three lizard dogs that had been chasing him. To his surprise, all of them sank their teeth into his tabard, and started trying to rip it apart.

As the angry Centaurs boiled out of the bar, Duncan took off running with the lizard-dog things hanging all over him.

Fortunately Duncan had learned two things from his warrior training his tutors hadn't intended to teach him. No one could run or hide as well as he could. Of course it was hard to do either of those things with a pack of hungry lizard dogs attached to his chest. He ran down a dark alley and slung himself into a large, square box that—from the smell of it—was filled with garbage…and something worse. Making a face he realized that what he was standing ankle-deep in and was *totally* disgusted.

The lizard things now seemed content to just hang on his tabard and snarl at each other as if they were fighting over a bone. Duncan realized they hadn't actually been after him at all. They smelled food, no doubt they scavenged around the town, so they were used to eating scraps. He smelled like scraps. Carefully he took off his pack, sword, and cloak, dropping them into the mess at his feet. Then he removed his fighting tabard with its attached lizard dogs. He was about to place it carefully on the ground outside the container he was in when a Centaur screamed out from the end of the alley, "There he is!"

Too late Duncan realized that when he stood up he was no longer hidden.

Duncan quickly changed plans and slung the tunic and its attached lizard dogs in the direction of the coming Centaur army. He slung his pack and sword back on and jumped out of the garbage bin. He headed for the end of the alley slinging trash, crap and gods alone knew what else behind him.

He thought for a minute of drawing his weapon, then remembered he wasn't very good with it even against cloth dummies. The reluctant warrior decided to live to not fight another day. He ran as fast as his legs would carry him. When he saw the end of the alley and the fence that blocked it he started to despair because the Centaurs were close behind him—and gaining.

Then he remembered one of the lessons he'd only half listened to. Centaurs couldn't climb. He doubled his pace, hit the fence hard, and climbed over it easily—the speed and agility of his climb no doubt motivated by the impending death at his heels.

When his feet hit the ground on the other side, there was nothing but darkness to greet him, and he ran into the night. He was still running long after the last of the Centaurs had no doubt gone back to their bar to finish their beers and laugh about how scared the Romancer had been.

Finally he stopped, vaguely surprised that he hadn't tripped over anything. When he felt around with his foot there was nothing but sand under his boots. And when he started to walk again, he immediately tripped over something that put stickers in his leg. As he was dancing around he tripped over something else and landed on his butt.

Sighing heavily, he rolled over on all fours, looking for a clear area where there was nothing but sand. He was a little surprised to find that the sand was as warm as the air wasn't in this strange place. Another night alone in the dark but this time with no fire, still, all things considered, maybe that was for the best.

Two

Duncan was showing a beautiful woman just how his pastry-filling machine worked when she suddenly bent over to get a better look—and he did, too.

Then she was running her finger across his lip and it was tickling him.

"Quit." He grinned and giggled and then to his dismay he woke up. Though the sand had kept him warm through the night, sleeping on it had put sand in unthinkable places. He opened his eyes slowly and saw a small purple lizard crawling across his face. "Hey you." He laughed. "Find your own bed."

Still grinning, he pulled back his blanket and froze. He was covered with more than sand. Hundreds of lizards and snakes in a multitude of colors and sizes had slithered in around him during the night. For a moment he stayed very still, trying to think of what he should do. Then before he could form a rational thought—much less think of a plan—he jumped up in one fluid motion and ran screaming across the desert. He left a trail of sleepy, disgruntled reptiles in his wake.

When he was several feet from the last lizard to drop off, he shuddered and said a loud, "Yuk!" It echoed across the otherwise vacant valley. He turned around in a big circle, and in the distance he could just make out the town he'd been chased out of the night before. Behind that he could make out a tree line that could only be the Sliding River. Back in the direction he had just run from his stuff was scattered on the ground. He could still make out several lumpy reptilian bodies slithering around over there.

The only plus seemed to be that the mad dash to disperse the scaly varmints from his person had also gotten rid of most of the sand. He headed back to his "camp," happy that he hadn't taken his boots off to sleep till he felt something twitching in his left boot. "Ahhhhhh!" he shrieked, and flopped on the sand. He jerked off his left boot and threw it. A snake crawled out. It turned, gave Duncan a dirty look, and slithered away. The would-be adventurer then pulled his right boot off and threw it. There hadn't been anything in there, but he didn't care.

Struggling to catch his breath he looked down at his hands only to find them covered in what had been all over his boots last night. He rubbed his hands in the sand to remove it, but when he brought his hand up to his nose for a quick check, he quickly pulled it back. Then he got a whiff of his feet and couldn't decide what smelled worse.

Suddenly he felt filthy, and given what he'd been through in the last couple of days, it was more than a feeling.

Duncan retrieved his boots. As he put them back on—careful not to touch the bottoms—he thought about the river, a bath, and clean clothes.

It wasn't that far away but once he got there he'd have to go downstream away from both his people and the Centaurs. One thing was sure, he was going to stay off the road for a while. He didn't want to tangle with the Centaurs again. If he followed the river he should get…somewhere. Eventually.

He picked up his sword and used it to shoo the remaining creepy crawlies away from his things. They slithered away, and he started to wonder if any of them were good to eat. His belly was rumbling again. As if recognizing his hunger, the reptiles doubled their pace before he could pick one to go after. In seconds all of them were gone as if they hadn't been there at all.

Wrapping his belongings in the blanket, he threw the rope strap around his shoulder and put his sword on. He started towards the river wishing for some kind of cover. Duncan was a big man. Bushes with hardly any leaves, spaced twenty or thirty feet apart, and no more than three feet tall, weren't going to cut it. He took a wide berth around the town. Finally, in an attempt at camouflage, he cut a small bush and held it so that it was between him and the town. It wasn't very good cover, but beggars couldn't be choosers. He hoped if anyone saw him they would kindly pretend they didn't. Or at the very least not come kill him.

A couple of the lizard dogs appeared on his right. He drew his sword, but they didn't even try to approach him. In fact, they cowered away, not even bothering to growl. He realized that they probably wouldn't have come after him at all if he hadn't been wearing what was basically a meat-scented shirt. Now they kept their distance then turned tail and ran, and he never harbored the notion that they were afraid of him or his sword. They wanted food. Now that he didn't smell like any food they'd ever eaten he wasn't worth messing with.

It sort of added to his sense of worthlessness to think that scavenging lizard dogs didn't think he was worth eating.

When he came to the road he ran across it quickly to duck behind a clump of bushes. He looked around to be sure he hadn't been spotted by the Centaurs before he moved on again, gripping his bush more tightly than ever.

His mind turned to the guys who had dropped him off in the Centaurs' knowing full well what he was and how they would react to him. Duncan started to get mad at them, but then he remembered he had burned up most of their hay crop. However any remaining guilt he might have about that left him. They were even now.

Still, Duncan would be sure he never accidentally burned anything again.

The walk to the river was longer than it looked. He had run out of water and it was as hot during the day as it was cold at night in this strange land. He wound up taking off everything but his boots, his underwear, and his tunic—which was fine because it was a long tunic after all.

Duncan was enjoying his adventure less and less. He was tired of freezing at night, burning alive during the day, starving, being thirsty, having lizard dogs eating his clothes and Centaurs trying to kill him. And his seat still hurt from that wagon ride.

He was sure he would die of thirst before he reached the river. With every step he took, the river seemed to get farther away instead of closer. Was there actually sand on his tongue, or did it just felt that way because his mouth was so dry? The sun was baking his skin, so he wound up wrapping his trousers around his head and holding the legs out in front of him to keep the sun off his face. Of course doing this made his arms cramp.

He was almost starting to wish he'd just gone up to the front line and died like his father wanted him to.

"It wouldn't have been so bad. A quick, mostly-painless death. Nothing like this," he mumbled to himself. "All I had to lose was my life and looking at it now it just isn't worth that much. Maybe death isn't so bad. Like an eternal nap."

He finally reached the river. He didn't stop; he just walked right in and started drinking off the top. Who would have ever thought that water could taste so good? His decision to follow the river seemed like a better one by the minute.

He'd be in the shade. There would be plenty of places to hide and he wouldn't run out of water again.

When he got out and started walking again he wished he hadn't worn his boots into the water. He'd emptied the water out of them and wrung his socks out, but he still squished when he walked and his feet were starting to hurt. He kept walking because he needed to get out of the Centaurs' country and he wasn't really sure where it ended. He was guessing it would be when the dirt wasn't purple.

He walked till the sun started to set and found a nice, flat spot not far from the river. He cut the small trees and shrubs away with his sword, and then he took a branch and carefully raked all the leaves into a pile.

Gathering rocks, he built a fire pit around the leaves and brush. Using his flint and steel and after several tries he managed to start the leaves on fire. He carefully added wood, only leaving to gather more after he had a small, steady fire going. When he returned he put the wood he'd gathered a good, safe distance away from the fire.

While getting wood he had found some berry bushes and he gathered the berries in his cup. He ate while he picked, and when he'd filled his cup he went back to camp. Sighing he unpacked, washed his clothes out in the river then hung his stuff on branches to dry. He could almost hear what his father would say if he knew Duncan had gotten his chain mail, leggings and knee cops wet with anything but sweat or the blood of their enemies. He started to move the chain mail closer to the fire so it would dry quicker. Then he held it up, looked at it, and smiled.

The want-to-be inventor found several big rocks down by the river moved them into a semi-circle about three feet from his fire pit. He ate the rest of the berries. By now, his clothes were mostly dry so he put them back on—all except his boots, which were still soaking wet.

He was still hungry, but no longer starving. His sunburn was bad in places but it could have been worse, and he had water and a good fire. Hopefully, the rocks had been absorbing the fire's heat—maybe they would block some of the wind and help keep him warm through the night.

He threw more wood on the fire, and then he threw one of his leggings over the rocks, resting on each side across the fire. He then carefully draped his chain shirt over it to make a little chain-mail tent over his fire. It wouldn't smother the fire but it would stop any embers from blowing out of it. Feeling very clever he lay down, covered up and went to sleep.

When Duncan woke he could just make out the first lights of false dawn peaking through the trees—which weren't all burned up. Sitting up he pulled his blanket and cloak around him. He was cold, and his blanket was damp from the dew, but he wasn't freezing and he wasn't covered in hundreds of reptiles, so it was the best morning he'd had since he'd left home.

Of course he hadn't really left home. No he'd been kicked out. His belly rumbled, but he knew where there were some more berries and he was by the river and the river meant fish. Catching fish was something that he could do while sitting, so he'd always been good at it. Of course, he's always had a pole, line and hooks, oh and bait.

Anyway, for the first time since he'd been kicked out of his home he really felt like he could say—if only to himself, "I don't need any of them. I'm fine on my own."

That good feeling lasted till about midday, when learned that eating too many berries and nothing else sent him off to a distant tree where he was forced to squat for half an hour till his knees shook.

Discarding the stack of leaves in his hand, he straightened up with great effort, jerked his pants into place, and then stumbled over to the river to wash. Four fish dashed away as he bent down, as if taunting him.

If I had some tackle I'd have plenty to eat, he thought. Even as he thought it he got an idea. He dug through his pile of stuff to find his knife. He used his sword to cut down a small tree. "Boy would this tick the old man off." He found that whenever he did something that would "tick his old man off" he felt immediately better about nearly everything. Each time his blade slammed into the tree he felt a little thrill pulse through him.

He sat down on his rock wall and hacked the smaller branches off the sapling with his knife. When some of the branches fell where he'd been sleeping the night before, he had another brilliant idea.

"See, they were stifling me. I'm a great inventor. That's what I am. Without them around me to bother me I just come up with one idea after another."

Stripping the leaves from the limbs he piled them up for a bed. It wasn't nearly enough, but there were plenty of leaves all around him. However that could wait till he had a fish in his belly.

He took a piece of the twine and tied his knife to the stick he'd just stripped. Then he quietly made his way back to the spot on the river where he had seen the fish. There were two fish swimming around, so he pounced like a jungle cat…a jungle cat that had bad eyesight, missed the fish, and fell into the river.

Duncan broke the surface spitting out a mouth full of water and splashed around till he found his spear. He crawled out of the water and walked down the river till he saw a school of fish close to the bank. This time he was more patient. Drawing back his spear he waited for the fish to get used to him before he struck.

This time he hit a fish, but it wasn't a clean hit, and the fish was mostly just dazed and swimming funny. Of course while trying to scoop the fish out of the river Duncan fell in head first and lost his spear again.

But when he came up he had that fish in one hand and his spear in the other, so he didn't care about being soaked or anything else. He felt triumphant.

Once again he said out loud, "I don't need any of them. I'm just fine on my own." Then the fish jumped out of his hand and swam away. "I've got to quit saying that," Duncan mumbled. He decided that being in the water might actually make spearing fish easier.

Like a statue he stood very still, his spear close to the surface of the water, and waited for the fish to come back. He was starting to think he'd cursed himself when a fish came right towards him. This time his aim was true. The spear hit the fish and it was a big one. He'd speared it right through the middle. He felt really triumphant again, but this time he kept his mouth shut about it.

Grabbing the fish by the tail, he pulled it further onto the knife, then threw his make-shift spear and its catch onto the bank. He pulled himself out of the river, grabbed the fish, and headed back for his camp whistling a happy tune.

The champion fisherman took his catch off the blade and laid it on his mostly-dead fire on top of the chain mail. He stripped his wet clothes off, wrung them out for the second time in less than a day's time, and hung them in bushes all around his camp. He quickly put on his other pair of pants. Then he cleaned the fish, piling the guts on a big leaf he'd picked for the purpose.

Setting the cleaned fish to one side he removed the chain mail covering from the fire, stirred it to embers, and threw on some wood. It didn't start blazing so he wondered what the fish would taste like raw. He stuck it on a sharpened stick, raised it to his mouth and took an experimental nibble. He quickly decided he could wait for it to be cooked.

The fire finally started blazing and he held his fish over it. It wound up burned to a cinder on the outside and nearly raw on the inside, but he ate it anyway, wishing he had some salt.

When he finished eating he picked up the leaf with the fish guts and the bones he'd added to the pile, carried them over and dropped them into the river by where he'd seen the fish first. It was close but still down stream from where he was getting his water. He was baiting a fishing hole. They'd done it before back in Spurna. If you got the fish feeding in a certain part of the river, pretty soon you could drop in a line and be sure of catching a fish.

His belly was full, and he was feeling really good again, so he started gathering leaves for his bed. He would hold a branch down and strip the leaves off and then go to the next till in just a few minutes he had a nice bed of leaves about six inches deep.

Having done this he decided to go back to the river and catch another fish—which he did rather easily this time. He gathered wood and took care of this fish as he had the first one.

Just before full dark he fed his fire well, put his fire cover in place, put all his clothes—which were gratefully dry—on again and curled up on his new bed. He was full, he was warm, and he was comfortable. This wasn't such a bad life.

Of course he had no sooner thought that than it started to rain. Not a light mist. Not a minor puddle-maker or even a downpour, but what they'd always called on his part of the world a frog strangler.

His blanket, his cloak, and he were all drenched in seconds. His fire died soon after that leaving nothing but smoke. He couldn't see his hand in front of his face, so he sat on his rock wall covered with his wet blanket and prayed for a quick and merciful death.

There was no sleeping. He nearly froze. When the rain stopped and the first light of dawn started to seep through the trees and it was still misting rain he was annoyed that he was still alive.

When the sun came out he wanted to sling a rock at it; by the time the rain stopped altogether he was wetter than he'd ever been in his life. He wrung out everything he owned and tried to find some wood that might burn. But nothing was remotely dry, and there wasn't a single hot ember left in his fire. He stacked the wood he gathered on his rock wall hoping that off the ground it might get dry enough to build a fire in a few hours.

Looking around him at the wetness of everything he felt completely defeated.

The bed of leaves had seemed such a good idea, and it had been so comfortable, but it hadn't kept him dry. Now it was just as drenched as everything else. He bent down to cart the leaves off and that's when he noticed that the ground underneath was dry. The leaves had kept the ground dry.

This gave him an idea.

He chopped down some small trees with his sword and with every chop he was sure his father was getting madder and madder—which made him feel better and better. Then he cut down two fairly largish trees and cleaned them till he had two forked poles about four feet tall. He chose a ridge pole and tied it to the forks with strips cut from the bottom of his cloak—because after all it was already too small anyway.

Putting the "ridgepole" out about four feet in front of his rock wall he then started lashing small sticks to the top to the ridgepole with what was left of his twine. The sticks he ran to touch the ground just behind his rock wall in the back.

Using his other legging as a shovel he started to pile dirt on the sticks at the bottom. "See this, Dad? See this? Now I'm using my armor to move mud. Mud because there is no dirt because it rained. But what's a little rain? Fire, the wagon ride of death, hungry lizard dogs, angry Centaurs, hunger and thirst, too cold and too hot... Wet is nothing. Bring it on!"

It was odd to be fighting with his father when he wasn't there, but it was a lot easier than fighting with him when he was.

He added sticks to his structure till it was quite tight, and then he covered the sticks with six inches of leaves. He covered the leaves with more sticks to hold them down and brought still more leaves to make himself a new bed.

By the time he got done, the surrounding woods were looking pretty bare.

His wood had dried enough that he finally got a fire going and then he went fishing. Even though it had rained enough to wash away all of the fish guts and bones he'd thrown in there was still a bunch of fish hanging out. He speared a couple and went off to make dinner.

This was when he decided that talking to himself made perfectly good sense. After all, even if it was crazy, it didn't matter because no one was around to hear him. If they were... Well they shouldn't be listening to his private conversations.

"Maybe this is what I was born to be—a hermit. Just me alone in the wild with no one to judge me or tell me what to do. I come and go as I please. Who cares what anyone else thinks of me? After all there's just me, and I don't judge. I don't have to work for someone else or meet anyone else's expectations of me."

And it was good he felt that way because he didn't see anyone for the next four days. The river was quiet and he started to remember how seldom a boat actually came to his home town of Spurna.

He spent the days picking and eating berries and catching and eating fish. The more he baited his favorite fishing spot the more fish there were and the easier they were to catch. So the hermit decided that not only were fish very tasty but they were also horribly cannibalistic and really stupid. It was like they ran and told the other fish that there was food, and then everyone came to get the food, and they didn't seem to really notice when one of them got stabbed and pulled out of the water.

Well, they did, because they all ran away but a few seconds later they'd all come back again. He imagined a little fish conversation that went something like this:

"Have you seen Barney lately?"

"Barney? Dude, is that your imaginary friend? I don't remember any Barney."

"Dude, he was married to your sister. He was just swimming around and the next minute he was gone, and I was wondering if you'd seen him lately."

"You're smoking the lawn, man. I don't have a sister, and I sure don't know any Barney."

"Dude, your sister was here just the other day."

"Look." Laughing now. "I want some of what you're smoking. Seriously, dude, you've got some imagination."

"What the hell is that?"

"What, man?"

"That pointy, shiny thing. Ow! Help me! Help me!"

A third fish. "Dude who were you just talking to?"

"No one, man. Are you nuts?"

Duncan wondered if maybe thinking so much about what the fish were talking about was a sign that he was losing his mind, but then figured as long as he didn't actually *hear* fish talking he was still all right.

Of course he really wasn't because the very next day he put two fish heads on sticks and named them Ted and Wanda. He pushed the sticks into the ground on the other side of the fire pit and told himself he wasn't crazy now because at least he wasn't talking to himself.

He caught a glimpse of himself in the water one day and nearly fell in before he realized it was his own reflection. He hadn't even noticed he'd grown a beard. Now he ran his fingers through the length of it. It wasn't very long, but it was every bit as black as his hair. He decided the look suited his hermit lifestyle.

While foraging he had found a stand of wild garlic. After a few days he was getting tired of roast fish, and he thought he'd make himself some fish and garlic soup.

"If only I had a pan," he said to Ted and Wanda. "No that's a stupid idea, Ted. You can't make a pan out of wood. It will burn up… What's that, Wanda? Brilliant! That's exactly what I'll do."

A quick search of camp turned up the legging he'd been using as a shovel. Then he popped the knee cop off the legging and shoved it down into the red hot coals.

"Of course it will work… You know, Ted, I don't think I like your attitude, and you're starting to stink." He grabbed the fish head off the stick and threw it in the fire. "What's that Wanda? Ted? I don't remember any Ted."

While the metal was heating Duncan went in search of a good rock to use as an anvil. He hefted the rock and carried it back to camp. "Yes, it is rather heavy, Wanda. Yes, I do have big, strong muscles… I told you, Wanda, I don't know any Ted."

While he waited for the knee cop to turn the right shade of bright red he dug out his tongs and his ball peen hammer. When the metal was heated to his liking he used the tongs to drag it from the fire and started forming it with his hammer on the rock.

"Any fool can see I'm making a pan, Wanda!" Duncan said as he pounded away on the metal. "You wouldn't want to end up like Ted would you?… What do you mean you knew there was a Ted? Who is this Ted you keep talking about, fish lady?"

He made the ball of the knee cop flat and then pounded and bent and pounded and bent till he'd turned the fin into a handle. Then he did the same thing to his other legging because… Well it looked all unbalanced to have a set of leggings with only one knee cop. Besides, Wanda seemed to enjoy watching him work and this way if he ever had more than one thing to cook at a time he could.

He put aside the leather straps and buckles that had been on the knee cops. One could be used to replace the strap that had been on the legging he was using over the fire—which had burned up the first night. If he ever needed to use the legging for armor again, that is.

He ate some soup and thought it was pretty good. That night it rained and he was dry, so he felt satisfied with his little shelter. But as he watched the flickering flames of his camp fire fighting against another downpour, he started to wonder what he was doing.

"What's the point of me, Wanda? Is it going to be enough for me just to exist? There is a whole world out there with hundreds of different things to see and experience and do. Am I really just going to sit here by the river, fish, eat berries, sleep, and add leaves to my roof? Well of course I care for you, Wanda, and I'm fond of Ralph, too." Ralph had replaced Ted. He wasn't as talkative but he also wasn't as judgmental. "I'm a great inventor. Is this enough for me? And what of the rest of the world? Don't they deserve to be able to use the things I might invent? Wow, Ralph! You don't say much but when you do… You're right. You do never know if you don't try."

By the time he went to sleep the breeze was blowing little wisps of rain into his face. He dreamt a hungry lizard dog was chewing at his nose, hanging on to it like they had hung on to his tabard. They'd torn apart his fighting tabard—the one he'd never worn in a battle—and now the lizard dog was going to eat his face. But he was so young and he really hadn't lived yet. Had he?

The wind started blowing harder. More rain hit him in the face and he woke up screaming. It took him a minute to get his bearings and remember where he was and a moment more to move further back into his shelter so that he wouldn't get wet. Well, not as wet. If possible it was even darker tonight than it ever had been before, and colder…much colder.

Clutching his damp blanket and cloak to him, he prayed for the morning to come. The fire was now completely out and he was sure at any moment one of those lizard dogs was going to find him and start chewing on his face.

"Wanda, Ralph can you hear me?… Yes, it's very dark and so cold. I don't want to live like this. We're barely into the fall, and I'm already freezing every night. I want to sleep some place with a roof and walls. I want to have fun, to adventure, to see things that most people don't see. Mostly I just want to be able to see." He moved his hand back and fourth in front of his face, hitting himself in the nose. "I literally can't see my hand in front of my face… Can either of you? … Sorry I forgot you don't have hands."

He didn't tell them that he was lonely.

When the rain let up and he got over his dream he went back to sleep, determined to pack first thing in the morning and leave.

He was even more determined to leave when he spent most of the day trying to get his fire going again. There was nothing dry enough to catch a spark from his flint and steel. Finally he tore a small corner from his cloak, frayed it, and sacrificed it to get a fire going.

But by the time he'd caught a fish and eaten and told Ralph what it had been like to be hungry and thirsty and have it be just as dark, he'd talked himself out of moving on. It wasn't anything Ralph had said. Duncan remembered what it was like to be attacked by hungry lizard dogs and chased by angry Centaurs. The world away from his camp was a big, scary place full of things that mostly wanted to kill him.

He needed to be prepared before he left. He needed to catch a bunch of fish and smoke them. Dry a bunch of garlic so it would keep. If he packed enough food for the road he should be able to make it to some town where they didn't want to kill him right off.

Ralph wasn't sure it was a good idea to leave at all, he was a simple fellow. Wanda on the other hand wanted to travel, see new places and things.

The would-be hermit found that being self sufficient was a lot of work without much reward. He could see himself getting a job, making money and having a real place to live. Some place where he wasn't cold or wet every time he turned around.

Well, he didn't have the first idea how to go about smoking fish, so he wound up just eating his first few attempts before he got good at it.

By then he'd made a little woven mat out of green cattails to throw over his fire when it rained, and he'd made side walls of the woven mats for his shelter. He made his roof bigger and tighter, weaving green reeds and cattails through it till it was so water tight it didn't leak anywhere.

Wanda vanished in the night. No doubt she got tired of waiting for him to get his act together. He replaced her with Velma—a home town girl with a sweet smile who had no desire to leave.

It really did seem like the fish here were stupid enough to just keep inviting all their friends to the spot in the river where it was easy for him to kill and eat them. In short every day it seemed like a worse idea for him to leave where he was and go anywhere else.

Even after he was sure he'd put up enough smoked fish for a week or more, and at least that much dried garlic, he wasn't in any hurry to leave. In fact, he just kept weaving more cattails and reeds into his roof making it tighter and more solid. He kept putting off leaving even when it started getting colder and colder and he had to go further and further to get wood.

Then one morning when he got up Ralph was gone.

"Where'd he go?" he asked Velma. "Really? Just like that he left. Did he say where he was going?" He would never hear her answer because about then there was a great cracking sound as if the world were being torn in half. Duncan suddenly remembered something he had forgotten. The reason why they call it the Sliding River is that—upon occasion—it moves.

Three

"Crap!" he shouted at Velma, who agreed. Duncan had seen the river slide a couple of times, and he knew he had to think fast. He gathered everything he had, slung it into his blanket, and tied it with his rope. He started to run, then realized there wouldn't be time. He knew he couldn't swim in what was about to hit him. And he definitely couldn't swim and keep what few things he had.

Then he saw his roof. He quickly tied his bundle to it and then jumped on top and hung onto the ridge pole for dear life.

Velma looked at him, her dead fishy eyes accusing. "Return to the river from which you came, Velma. Swim free! Swim free, my dear friend."

The would-be white-water rafter knew a little of what to expect. So he just hung on and hoped for the best. The water hit in a huge wave, and he and his roof went with it. He found himself floating down the angry river, hanging on to the roof as much to hold it together as to stay on it.

Tossed around as he was he had no idea how long he just held on, but by the time he washed up on shore he saw nothing but red dirt and dead trees. For a moment he thought he'd wound up in the forest he had burned down. Of course that wasn't possible because the river didn't change directions even when it slid. Besides, these trees weren't burned—they were just dead.

The ground was baked red clay. He saw absolutely nothing living. The greenest thing in his line of sight was his own roof. Duncan and everything he owned was wet. He had used every ounce of strength he had, and he was frozen to the bone. When he grabbed hold of his bundle and crawled further away from the river he dragged what was left of his roof with him and hardly noticed.

Duncan had thought the river gave him security, but it had turned on him, too.

The air was warmer than he was, so he discarded his clothes and just sprawled, spread-eagle on the ground, soaking in the warmth from the ground below and the sun above. He was completely exhausted, spent, and he fell asleep.

He didn't know if he'd just dozed off or slept for hours when he heard a woman saying in a slightly slurred speech, "Don't worry children, it's just a human. This is what they do. They are often found throughout Overlap sunning themselves in this way to make their skins browner."

"What's that, Mommy?" a child's voice asked.

"Never you mind, Suzy," the mother said.

"I think it's his winky, Mom," a little boy's voice answered.

No man wants to hear his manhood called a winky. That woke Duncan all the way up. He looked down and realized he was completely naked. He hadn't purposely taken his under drawers off. They must have just come off with his pants. He covered himself quickly with his bundle—still attached to his roof—and somewhat disoriented he jumped to his feet and backed away, dragging his roof as he did so. He looked for and found the people who had been talking—except they weren't like any people he'd ever seen before. The woman was only about three feet tall and her children were maybe a foot tall. When he tried to reposition his bundle to cover himself better the little girl screamed.

"Calm down, Carmen, you don't want to frighten it. It might stampede. Humans are more afraid of you than you are of them. Now let's move on and leave him be. We've already woken him up." She took hold of her children's hands and led them quickly away.

Duncan closed his eyes and then opened them, but he could still see the strange little people as they walked away. He dug through his discarded clothes till he found his underwear and pulled them on. They were only a little damp, so he must have been out longer than he thought. He untied his bundle from his roof and propped what was left of it against a dead tree to make it a shelter again.

Going over what he'd heard the little woman tell her children he wondered why he should be afraid of those tiny people at all. Duncan laid his clothes across his roof to dry, then started looking for wood. He didn't have to look far. There were branches from the dead trees down everywhere. He unwrapped his bundle and water ran everywhere. All his smoked, dried fish were now completely rehydrated, as was his dried garlic. He grabbed his flint and steel and worked on starting a fire, which didn't take too long. Then he went down to the river to fill one of his pans with water.

"Traitorous bastard," he spat towards the river. He hatefully removed a pot full of water from the now perfectly calm—if slightly displaced—river.

He threw some of the fish and garlic into the water in the pot and put it on the fire.

Looking around he wondered just where he was, and then he had a sudden thought. "I didn't want to be home or do what I was supposed to do there, but I would never leave because I was afraid of the unknown—so the decision was made for me. I was unhappy being a hermit on the river bank, but I was reluctant to leave because I was afraid of the unknown. and again the decision was made for me."

This gave him food for thought as he laid his provisions out on his roof to dry. His roof looked a little rougher for wear. It had lost all its leaves and half its sticks and if he hadn't started weaving those reeds and cattails into the stick pattern, it probably would not have held through the river's slide at all.

Curiously, he realized that if it hadn't been for the fear of instant death, riding the river in the slide might have been fun.

He wondered if anyone knew just exactly what caused the river to move. Duncan figured it had something to do with Overlap being made up of the many different worlds it was made up of. Maybe the river didn't know where it belonged and just kept sliding around trying to figure out where it went.

It never moved very far, never more than a few feet in either direction, but when it did it always left a bit of a mess somewhere.

Duncan ate his soup, put on his nearly dry clothes, and went right to sleep. He was exhausted and didn't wake up till he heard a man's voice say, "Well there goes the neighborhood." He sounded more than a little disgusted. "I told you didn't I? He's right where they said he'd be."

Opening his eyes, Duncan saw only his flood-tossed roof, light peeping through it everywhere. He didn't see anyone at all.

"Damn," another voice said with equal disgust. "We just got all those trees killed out from the last time there was an influx of humans."

"At least there just seems to be the one this time."

"Come on, Jasper, you know how it is with them. One of them shows up and before you know it there are thousands of them. This one's just a scout."

"You're right. Let's get rid of him before he goes and gets more."

The next thing Duncan knew two small sets of hands had grabbed onto his feet and begun dragging him towards the river. Duncan sat up quickly. "Hey! You two!" He tried to jerk his feet away, but to his dismay found that he couldn't.

"Calm down now," one of the three-foot men said. "You'll find it will be much easier if you don't put up such a fight."

"Now see here…" Duncan started trying unsuccessfully to get away from them.

"Shush, it will all be over soon," the other one said.

Duncan gave up trying to be delicate and started trying to kick them off him, which they didn't seem to notice.

"You know, Jasper, I feel a little sorry for him."

"Don't do that, Meyer. You know how they are. When they get settled into a place they're impossible to get rid of. It will be over soon."

"Oh, you're right, I know you're right."

"No, no, he's not!" Duncan cried out. He tried to grab, even punch the little men but nothing seemed to faze them. When he actually managed to make contact with one of them his fist felt like he'd hit a rock.

"Now quit. You're putting up such a fuss," the one called Jasper said as they pulled him into the water. "It really is quite useless to struggle, and will all be over soon. Don't make this harder than it has to be." They climbed onto his head, and they were so heavy that he was completely submerged in moments and just fighting to get his head above the water—which he didn't seem to be able to do.

Then suddenly they were both gone, and he jumped up and gasped for breath.

"That's what I thought!" a female voice accused. "Poor thing, it looks frightened to death. Now you leave it alone the both of you. It has as much right to live as any other living thing."

"Ah, but Mama," Jasper said, "you know how they are."

Duncan ran out of the water and hurried towards his camp as fast as he could. He dove into his wrecked shelter and came out with his sword. Of course the sheath only pulled half way off so that it hung limp and wet off the end of the sword. He whipped it up and down till the sheath came all the way off. It flipped through the air to land at the feet of the tiny people.

"Look what you've done now," the woman said accusingly to the men. "He's gone on the offensive." She looked at Duncan. "There, there now. No one's going to hurt you. Are you boys?"

"No, no," the two men mumbled.

"Now apologize," she ordered them.

"Ah, Mama," Meyer said. "It's just a stupid animal."

"Tell it you're sorry," she said in a voice that reminded him so much of his own father that it almost had Duncan apologizing for them trying to drown him.

"We're sorry," the two men said together. Duncan didn't believe them for a minute. He was also extremely tired of being wet every time he turned around, and there was something else.

"Everywhere I go someone or something tries to kill me. Look," the Romancer said, and lowered his sword only a little, "I don't want to stay here, and I surely don't want to plant any trees. Even if I'd wanted to stay here before, I certainly don't now. I didn't come here on purpose in the first place. Could you maybe tell me where the nearest human settlement is? I'd just like to go someplace where nothing tries to kill me for a couple of days."

The mother one glared at the two men, who looked at the dirt in front of them. "I'm very sorry for my sons who are grown men and should know better. There is a road about a mile west of here that leads to Tarslick. All sorts of creatures great and small live there—including humans."

"And rats," Jasper whispered to Meyer, but loud enough that Duncan could hear him. Their mother cut them a dirty look, and they both looked at their feet again.

"Our world brought just as many disgusting things, my children. Remember that. Walk that way, young man," she said, pointing down the road. "Soon you'll come to another road; just follow it to Tarslick. You should be safe there, if anyone is ever safe in a big city."

"Thank you," Duncan said, and started breaking camp. He didn't care about wet clothes or anything else. Fate was telling him it was time to move again, and he was moving.

* * * *

Duncan walked most of the day. His fish hadn't quite dried out again, and it was sort of rubbery, but he ate some anyway and kept walking. He didn't want to have to camp in the woods again. But as it started to get dark he still saw nothing that looked even remotely like civilization, so he picked a spot and made camp.

The next morning he was determined to make it to Tarslick, but the sign that said twenty-five miles to Tarslick didn't give him much hope that he'd make it that day, either.

By midday his feet were starting to hurt from walking in boots that had never had a chance to dry out completely. He was about to give up and make camp when he noticed a little side road. Soon there was another and then another. Shortly after that he saw his first ever car. It ran along the road, smoke coming out of a chimney towards the back. Its wheels weren't anything like wagon wheels. They were made out of some black, tar-looking substance.

The creature driving it—creature because it was nothing that could have been mistaken as human—waved and smiled at him but drove right by. Then the dirt road under his feet turned black and was hard and smooth as the road had been in the desert.

He walked only a few more feet when there was another car, and then another, and then another. One machine made a loud noise that made Duncan jump, and then the driver was pointing at him and yelling for him to get off the road.

Duncan realized he needed to get out of the way of the cars, so he moved to walk beside the road.

More roads were crossing the main one all the time, and the closer he got to the city the more crossroads there were. He saw so many cars that they began to be less of a novelty and more of a nuisance because they kept him off the smooth part of the road. When he got to those cross roads he couldn't figure out when the cars were supposed to go and when it was safe for him to cross. He came to the conclusion it was never really safe and started running across as fast as he could.

About the time he realized he should stop for the night he found that he couldn't. There were houses everywhere, but he saw no inns. He didn't know what the protocol was here for knocking on a stranger's door and asking if you could stay in their house for the night, but he had a feeling it wouldn't be a good idea.

His feet hurt, and he was starting to despair that he'd be walking the rest of his life when a car stopped next to him.

The driver put down the glass in his door, stuck his head out and shouted, "Hey buddy, could you use a lift?"

"Well, I have been happier," Duncan answered, walking up to the car.

The man in the car laughed. "I meant, do you need a ride?"

"Yes, yes I do."

The man opened a door on the side of the car. Duncan took off his pack and his sword and got in holding his stuff on his lap. He certainly didn't have much room in this strange wagon. The man reached across Duncan and shut the door. "You look like you're a long way from home."

"Very far." Duncan was busy checking out the inside of the car. There was a wheel the man turned—obviously to steer the machine. There were things on the floor he put his feet on, and the car made a little chugging, popping sound as it went.

"Your first time in the big city?"

"Are we in Tarslick now?" Duncan asked, looking around and hitting his head on the roof of the car as he did so.

"You're a big one that's for sure," the man laughed. "No, we aren't to the city yet. Let me guess—you're from up river."

"Yes, from Spurna. Thanks for giving me a ride."

"We humans have to stick together, right?" The guy laughed. "So what brings you to the city?"

"I'm looking for a place where I can find work and no one will try to kill me."

"Aren't we all?" He laughed again, "Name's Drake, what about you?"

"Duncan."

"Well hold onto your seat, Duncan, I don't think you've ever even imagined any place like Tarslick."

* * * *

Drake hadn't been wrong. Tarslick was a huge, thriving city like nothing Duncan had ever imagined in his wildest dreams. There were buildings that shone with steel and glass, and bright, multicolored lights that reached as tall as six stories. There were roads and streets, some of which seemed to run into and out of the buildings themselves. Big cars, small cars, and motorbikes roared all around, seeming to come in and out of everywhere.

There were horses and wagons, too, and so many kinds of creatures of all different sizes, shapes and colors that he'd lost count. Of course he couldn't really count very far.

Duncan couldn't decide what to look at first there was just so much going on. Lights flashed in numerous languages in a rainbow of different colors. One sign even had a moving picture on it that kept changing. One minute a man was using some strange device to shave, the next a car was racing a horse and winning. Then there was a picture of a bright colored bird. It flew over a house and crapped; the crap soon covered the whole house.

Duncan made a face, "What's that?"

"A really bad ad. It's an insurance company. Their point is that they cover your whole house. I don't think it really works. I keep wondering when they're going to pull it."

Duncan nodded like he understood, which he didn't, because he'd been asking about the thing making the pictures in the first place.

"So. How much money you have?"

"Two coins."

"Really?"

He nodded.

"Well, bro, I hope you get some good work soon." Drake shook his head. "There's only one place in the city where they will do more than laugh at you for that much coin, and it ain't in one of the better neighbor-hoods."

They drove to a part of the city where there wasn't as much traffic and the buildings weren't as big or bright or pretty. Mud brick houses in various states of decay lined both sides of the road. In some places sheets of tin and cardboard boxes had been leaned against the decaying walls of the buildings to make infirm structures. It was obvious that people were living in them. There was a metal barrel in an alley. A fire was in it and a large group of different kinds of creatures had gathered around it for warmth. Some of them were cooking some sort of dead animal pushed onto a stick over the flames.

To Duncan's dismay Drake pulled over to the curb and stopped. "Well this is as far as I can take you, buddy. Good luck."

"Thanks." Duncan reluctantly got out of the car. He looked back inside and Drake must have seen the apprehension in his eyes.

"Big guy like you with a sword shouldn't have too much trouble with the riff-raff."

"It hasn't helped me so far."

"You'll be fine. Just remember that in the city everyone has an angle."

"I will. Thanks, Drake." Duncan waved and watched as the man drove away. He would have liked to take the man's words of wisdom to heart, but the truth was he hadn't understood most of what he said. He spoke the same language as most on Overlap—it having been decided long ago that it was easier that way—but he used words Duncan didn't know and in a way he hadn't heard them used before.

Walking around, a stranger in a new land, trying to take everything in, he looked for someplace that might be an inn. He didn't know what sort of filth he was walking in, but it stuck to the bottom of his boots and made a sticky sound as he walked.

He could feel the eyes of the people inside those hovels watching him. The further he walked down the street, stepping over and around garbage, the more uncomfortable he got. So when he saw a sign he could actually read he walked in without much thought.

The neon sign flashed, "Cater's, bar, grill and lodging."

When he walked all the way into the dimmer-than-usual bar the floor creaked under his weight. The place looked like it was a bad wind away from falling apart, but the fellow behind the bar, the bar maid, and most of the cliental were human, which put him some at ease.

The innkeeper looked from Duncan to the two coins he held in his hand. "Two coins won't buy you much in the city, fellah." He paused to spit some of whatever he was chewing into a funny-shaped pot sitting on the floor, and Duncan made a face. "Boy like you, fresh out of the woods so to speak, you're an easy mark for the sharks in the city. Lucky you came here. I'll tell you what. Since I'm in such a good mood I'll let you have a stall in the stable for a week, but not a minute more. It's my problem, I'm just too nice. Ain't that right Abby?" he asked the bar maid.

"Yeah that's right Austin, yer ah peach," Abby said. Then the large red-headed woman in the flowing pink and purple dress started laughing and walked away with a tray full of beers. Duncan watched the beers as they moved away and licked his lips.

"Here you go, kid." Austin, a small red-headed man with a handlebar mustache and garters to hold up his sleeves, pulled another beer and handed it to Duncan. "See, that's what I'm telling you. I'm just too nice. It will be the death of me yet."

The barkeep took Duncan's two coins and stuck them in his pocket then walked away to serve another customer. Duncan sat down at the bar and drank the beer slowly, savoring every drop.

The stable wasn't in much better shape than the tavern was. There were holes in the walls big enough to throw a cat through. The roof looked like it leaked, and of course the place smelled like moldy hay and horse crap. Still, after living in the wilds the stable seemed like a luxury suite to Duncan. He kicked a couple of horse apples out of where he wanted to make his bed and put down some fresh straw.

The three horses he shared the stable with turned out to be much better company than fish heads on sticks. Still, Duncan was sure it would be a long time before he could forget the haunted look in Velma's eyes as she disappeared into the swirling waters of the Sliding River.

* * * *

The very next morning Duncan went out to look for work. Austin pointed him in the direction of what he called an employment center.

The city looked even dirtier in the light of day, and he found the things he was stepping over and around occasionally moved. He couldn't tell if these creatures were alive or dead or something in between, and he didn't try to find out.

He had a certain unsettled nervousness he didn't remember ever feeling before. As he looked up at the extremely tall building he was walking by he thought, *It's this place, it never rests, never sleeps. Like the city itself is a creature. I feel really small, like I'm something it's eaten and is thinking about spitting out.*

The third building he entered turned out to be the right one. He was directed to sit in a big room full of chairs, most of which were filled with other people—and not-so-much-people—who he guessed were also looking for work.

The people and not-people passed the time looking really depressed and looking at strange slick books with bright pictures which looked like they'd seen better days. Occasionally one of them would look at the clock on the wall and sigh. So he did it, too, just to fit in.

After he'd waited for what seemed like forever, a small, grey woman with tall, grey hair called him into her office. She motioned for him to a chair in front of her desk, and then walked around to sit behind it. She was so small and the desk was so big that Duncan had to stretch his neck to see her.

"Right off I can tell you that we'll never be able to place you unless you take a bath, and wash your clothes properly. Nothing personal…" she held up a paper she had in her hand and read his name from it, "… Duncan. But you smell like bad fish and smoked cheese."

Duncan nodded. That seemed fair. He *did* smell like bad fish and smoked cheese.

"And the beard has to go, too. There is a bathing room in this building for that purpose and a laundry in which to do your clothes. Here at Everyone Needs a Job Employment Agency we believe a clean employee is an easy-to-place employee. Is that understood?"

"Yes ma'am."

"Good. Now before I send you off to clean yourself up, what skills do you have?"

"Excuse me?" Duncan asked.

The woman looked him up and down and summed him up quickly.

"No skills," she said in a voice that sounded like she might have gargled rocks before coming to work that day.

"I have a sword."

"Are you good with it?"

Duncan thought about lying but then thought better of it. "No, no. Not really."

"Don't worry, honey, we shouldn't have any trouble finding you work. Let's face it, the less skilled you are, the less you expect from a job. The less you expect from a job, the less you expect from life. And the less you expect from life, the easier it is to place you in employment."

And the Everyone Needs a Job Employment Agency didn't have any trouble finding him work, either. Keeping it, however, was a different story for Duncan.

His first job was as a singing waiter. They fired him after only three hours, stating that he couldn't carry a tune in a bucket, and that he still carried a tune with more precision than he could carry a tray of food.

The employment agency got him a job the very next day trimming the hedges of a wealthy politician. Two days passed and he was still doing fine. Then on the third day he was paying more attention to a pretty girl walking past the front gates than he was his work. He accidentally lopped the head off of the governor's favorite animal-shaped topiary. He tried to tie it back on with a piece of string, but it wouldn't stay in place. His argument that it made a statement with the head hanging from the string did not amuse the governor, and he was fired on the spot.

Next they placed him in a wolverine obedience school. It seemed that some fools thought wolverines would make good pets and guard animals. Duncan hadn't done well there at all and would have scars for the rest of his life to prove it. He wasn't there a day when one of the clients threatened a lawsuit. Duncan wasn't sure what that was but from the looks on their faces it wasn't a good thing. Duncan tried to explain to them how much better off they were.

"Look, the animal wouldn't behave at all before and now it sits, it stays, and it plays dead brilliantly."

"That's because he's not *playing* dead he *is* dead. You killed him."

"No I didn't. He's just sleeping."

"His head has been cut off and you've just shoved the pieces back together. You killed our pet."

Tying the head back on the wolverine hadn't gone much better than tying the head back on the topiary.

"It's just a nick," he said, shrugging.

"No, it's not! His head's been completely cut off. Don't try to tell me that will heal. I believe you're stupid, I just don't believe you're *that* stupid."

The really bad wolverine trainer decided to change tactics. "He did it himself."

"Did it himself! You really expect me to believe he cut off his own head?"

"It could happen."

"How?!"

"I don't think the real question here is *how*, I think it's *why?* Why did little Beethoven decide he wanted to take his own life? Was it maybe that you expected much too much of him? Let us stop for a moment and ask ourselves where does the fault truly lie?"

Well neither the client nor his employer thought he made a convincing argument, and he was canned on the spot.

The next job the grey woman found him had him stripping in a woman's bar. It had taken him four days to get over the humiliation of prancing around on stage mostly naked. He had just started making good tips when his natural clumsiness came calling. He tripped on a pair of discarded pants he'd started his act wearing and fell off the stage right on top of the club's best clients sending all three to the hospital. To avoid a lawsuit—he wished he knew what those were—the club fired him.

* * * *

The little grey employment lady looked at him over her desk and the stack of accumulated "employment" files she had on Duncan.

She took a deep breath in and let it out slowly. "If I didn't like you, kid, you'd just be out on your fanny, but I'm gonna give ya one more shot 'cause there is this honest look in your eyes." She took another deep, raspy breath in, let it out, then asked again, "Do you have any, and I do mean ANY skills?"

Duncan still wasn't sure he understood the question. "What do you mean exactly by skills?"

"Is there anything that you are really good at?"

Duncan's eyes got bright and he said, "I'm good at fixing things."

"Fixing things?" she said carefully.

"Yes. Well, you know, I've never been trained and I can't build things from scratch like a blacksmith, but I can take things that are broken and figure out how they're supposed to work. I can take pieces of things and make other things, too. Machines that do stuff. I'm a tinkerer I guess you could say."

"A what?" the grey lady asked, and he thought he noted a suspicious tone to her voice, but it was hard to tell since at any minute he was sure she might breathe her last.

"I'm a tinkerer," Duncan said proudly, wishing he'd thought of it sooner. Surely it would be easy to find him a job where he fixed things.

The little grey lady stood up to her full height—which meant Duncan wasn't able to see much but her hair over the desk—her hair and her arm—as she pointed at him and said, "Out! Get out of my office this very minute!"

"Excuse me?"

"I knew there was something crooked in your beady little eyes. Now you get out right now before I have you thrown out and tell the whole town just what you are."

"Is this some sort of joke, lady?"

"Joke! I should think not. How dare you pretend to be normal. Now get out! I'm warning you, I've got mace!"

"All right." Duncan stood up and looked down on her. He didn't see a mace anywhere and doubted she was in good enough shape to hit him with one if she had it. "I'm going. I don't understand why, but then I haven't really understood much of anything ever since I left home."

Duncan walked down the street back towards the pub feeling completely confused. "Crazy old woman…or whatever she was." He wasn't really worried. Austin had pointed him in the direction of the Everybody Needs a Job Employment Agency and he was sure he'd know where another one was.

But as he walked into the bar everyone stopped talking and it seemed to him that they all just started staring at him. He shrugged it off as his imagination, but when he walked up to the bar and ordered Austin glared up at him.

"You!" Austin yelled accusingly, waving a finger in the newly-unemployed man's face. "Get out of my bar! Pack your gear and get out of my stable. In short, just get!"

"But I'm still paid for the stable for two more nights," Duncan protested.

"Consider it a small fee to pay for lying about what you really are."

"Seriously, is all this because I told the lady at the employment agency that I'm a tinkerer?"

"Ha! You admit it. Get out! Get out right now before I have you thrown out."

"People just keep saying that," Duncan muttered.

"I mean it boy! We don' need yer kind hanging round here."

"What is going on?"

"Don't act like you don't know. I run a top-drawer establishment. I don't need ya'll giving the place a bad reputation. Now go and don't let the door hit ya on the back side on your way out."

Some of the customers grumbled in his general direction, too, and Duncan decided fate was once again pointing him on down the road.

He went to the stable and started packing, "Geez, boys, can any of you tell me what I did wrong?" he asked the horses. "I'm going to miss you all. It's been swell bunking with you. I want you to know how much I appreciate how gracious you all were when I brought a date home. I should have asked first but none of you complained… I wish I could say the same about the girl. She was all, *Yuk, you live in a barn. I've dated a lot of scum in my life but never someone who lived in a barn full of horse crap*." He finished packing. "Well I better go before men come after me with lanterns and pitchforks… I'll write when I find work."

The human reject left the barn and started walking. He asked a stranger on the street which way was both down stream and out of the city. The man pointed him in the right direction with a smile since after all he couldn't tell by looking at him that Duncan was a tinkerer.

It took him most of the rest of the day just to walk out of the city. On the outskirts of town just past the last of the houses there was nothing but acres and acres of crop land.

It was pretty, and the tension he'd been carrying since the minute he'd entered the city melted away. In spite of the fact that he'd been run out of yet another town he had to admit part of him was glad to be out of Tarslick. He wasn't sure, but he didn't think he liked big cities. Everything was so loud, and people all seemed to talk at once but never seemed to hear what anyone else said.

No, he decided, city life wasn't for him. But he'd enjoyed sleeping out of the elements and eating regularly. Of course just living there had taken most of the money he'd made, and he only had a few more coins in his pouch now then he'd had when he'd arrived. Drake hadn't been wrong, and now he knew what he meant when he said that everyone had an angle.

Yes, all in all, he had to say he wasn't really very impressed with his whole Tarslick experience. Though he had to admit he'd seen a lot of amazing things that he didn't even know existed till he got there. There were neon signs that flashed words in bright colors and lit up the night. Huge windows filled with displays showing off everything from clothing to small machines that did everything from washing your clothes to mixing your cake batter.

To his ultimate dismay there was even a machine that put filling into donuts. He'd felt robbed when he'd seen it working in the window of a bakery. Ever since he'd seen that he'd doubted he'd ever find a place where he mattered at all. As far as he could see all the really great stuff had already been invented by someone else.

There was a world full of cars and buses and trucks and machines that tore up streets and made them. There wasn't a single thing worth inventing he could think of that someone else hadn't already invented.

Tarslick had in fact been a crash course about the world outside his small village. Of course, most of what he'd learned he wished he still didn't know. And he now had many things to add to the ever-growing list of things he wasn't any good at.

"Maybe I should have eaten something before I left the city. Not in the inn, though, because I'm pretty sure they all wanted to kill me. I still have no idea why," He thought about it for a minute. "Maybe tinkerer means something different to them."

His stomach made an unhappy noise which fit his mood. "So stupid. A city full of places to buy food and I walk right out of it without so much as a sandwich. Now I'm starving and there is nothing to eat, except…" On the other side of the hedge he was walking beside was field after field of turnips. From the look of them he knew it was close to harvest time. "Surely no one would begrudge a hungry traveler a few turnips."

Duncan looked around quickly to make sure no one was coming down the road and that no one was in the field to see him. He took off his pack, set it on the ground, got down on all fours and reached through the hedge. He felt around till he found something that felt right, then he grabbed hold and gave it a tug.

When it didn't give he crawled through the hedge to see what the problem was. He looked from the odd-looking blue thing in his hand up and up at the most frightening thing he'd seen yet.

He screamed before he had a chance to think about it and the thing screamed back. He cringed.

Standing above him was a creature over seven feet tall. Mostly blue except for its white chest and belly, and white tips on its cheek fringes and the tip of its pointed ears. Its long legs, arms, and slender body were covered in scales, and sharp claws tipped its fingers and toes.

Worst of all, its huge mouth was full of razor-sharp teeth.

Duncan looked at what he had in his hand and realized with a lump in his throat that it was the tip of the dragon's tail.

He screamed again.

The dragon screamed right back.

"Ah…I…I was trying to get a turnip," he said with a gulp.

"Well then you really have made a huge mistake. That's my tail," the dragon said.

"Yes I see, and I'm very sorry," Duncan said. The dragon cleared his throat and looked at his tail where Duncan still held it. "Ah…sorry. I'll just put this right back where I found it." He laughed nervously, dusted the dragon's tail off, and then gently set it on the ground. "Well, I better be going now." He turned and started to crawl back through the hedge.

"Nonsense," the dragon said, grabbing Duncan by the arm with his tail and dragging him back. "Help yourself to some turnips. Heavens know there are plenty. Mind you, it's not dragon's tail, but that's probably tough and full of fat anyway." The dragon laughed at his own joke, showing off that mouth full of razor sharp teeth. Yet suddenly Duncan no longer felt he was about to be eaten.

Duncan got slowly to his feet then carefully took his sword off his back. When he did the dragon lifted an eyebrow. Duncan gave him a nervous shrug and then started using his sword to dig up some turnips. He reached back through the hedge, grabbed his pack and started stuffing the turnips into his bundle. "I must say this is awfully nice of you, dragon."

"Think nothing of it. Name's Mallory and you are?"

"Duncan. And thanks again, Mallory. I was getting a little hungry."

"Don't mention it. I'm a giver. It's what I do."

Duncan had just finished stuffing his pack as full as he could get it when an angry human woman wielding a cross bow ran into the field. "You ruffians had best get out of my turnip patch!"

Mallory smiled at him. "Of course it's always easiest to give away things that aren't yours." He made a mad dash for the hedge, tearing through it. Leaves went everywhere. Duncan ran through the curtain of hedge debris following the dragon as the first of the crossbow bolts whizzed past his head.

"You better run!" she screamed after them, "or I'll make a rug out of you, human, and use that dragon for a furnace!"

Mallory had both fists full of turnips, holding them by the green tops, and as he ran the bulbs on the bottom seemed to dance. Mallory turned and said over his shoulder, "Who does she think she's kidding? I'd make a lousy furnace."

They ran till they were well clear of the woman and her crossbow bolts of farming fury and then they both stopped to catch their breath.

Duncan suddenly started to laugh in between gasps for breath.

"What's so funny?" Mallory asked, a hint of laughter in his own voice.

"Well back there I really thought you were going to eat me. Then who tries to kill me? Another human."

"Eat you!" The dragon cringed at the thought. "Revolting! I'm a vegetarian. Eat you indeed. What would that do to my cholesterol level?"

"What! You're kidding me! A vegetarian dragon?" He started to laugh even harder.

Mallory seemed something less than amused. "Yes. Laugh it up, chuckles. My father thought it was quite funny as well. Well, maybe not so much funny as disgraceful. Of course, according to father dearest, every single thing I did brought shame to him and the family name."

Mallory started walking down the road and Duncan followed.

"I'm sorry, I wasn't laughing at you. Mostly I was laughing at myself. Man, the world sure isn't what I thought it was." The human fell into step beside the dragon. "I never got along with my father, either. I, too, was always just a huge disgrace. Nothing I ever did was right. He wanted me to be a great warrior and die like all my brothers, but my heart just wasn't in it—especially not the dying part."

Mallory looked down at him and smiled. "So, did you just leave the scum-sucking city of Tarslick, too?"

Duncan sighed. "Yes. It seems like everywhere I go they either want to kill me outright or run me off." Then he told Mallory about all the problems he'd had in Tarslick finishing with his job as a stripper. That made Mallory laugh. "And when I told the employment lady that I was a tinkerer...."

Mallory laughed louder, getting almost hysterical. "Oh, you didn't!"

"Why is that such a bad thing? Does it mean something different here?"

"It means exactly the same thing, I'm sure. My friend, *no one* likes a tinkerer."

"Why not?"

"You're kidding, right?"

Duncan shrugged.

"A tinkerer is always screwing something up because he doesn't really know how to do anything. He guesses at how stuff is supposed to work and tries to 'fix' it accordingly and usually winds up ruining whatever it was.

"Everyone has had something expensive or something that they really cared about ruined by an uncle, aunt or cousin who swore they could fix it. You might as well have declared to the world that you were a murderer or a tax collector. On most of Overlap tinkerers are despised."

"But I really am *good* at fixing things and building things and..."

"That's great and very useful I'm sure, but never tell anyone you're a tinkerer. Say instead that you are a skilled, trained, fully-licensed and warranted professional."

"But I'm not."

"Why not? Because you didn't go to school or pay for some piece of paper? Listen, just as many *professionals* ruin things as tinkerers do, but do you know what the difference is?"

"Not really," the self-professed tinkerer said with confusion.

"The difference is that if I let a tinkerer work on say my TV and it no longer works, then I have to say to myself, 'I should have known better than to let anyone but a trained professional work on my TV.' But if I hire a trained professional to work on my TV and he charges me a bunch of money and he still doesn't fix it, then I get to say to myself, 'Well I guess it just couldn't be fixed if a trained professional couldn't fix it.'"

"But…that doesn't make any sense."

"No it really doesn't. Welcome to the real world. Remember this, Duncan. No one ever wants to admit that they are wrong about anything, so they're always looking for someone else to blame things on. You never want to be that person."

"Let me get this straight. People would rather pay some guy who says he's a trained professional…"

"Especially if he has a piece of paper to prove it," Mallory interjected, waving a claw in the air flamboyantly.

"…to *not* fix their TV—whatever that is—than have their uncle work on it for free and *not* fix it."

"To-*zact*ly."

"It still doesn't make any sense to me."

"And if you're very lucky it never will."

"Why'd you leave the city?" Duncan asked after a few moments of confusion. He wondered how someone like Mallory could fit in anywhere.

"Ah…I've always found it best not to stick in one place very long. It's better to keep moving. It helps keep things from getting stagnant."

"That's funny. I've found it's best to keep moving as well. Makes you a harder target."

Four

He really wasn't much to look at. Probably handsome enough by human standards, Duncan was big and all arms and legs. His skin was a pinkish-brownish color. He had nice, brown eyes, a nose that was biggish for his face, and black hair that looked like someone had stuck a bowl on his head and trimmed around the edges.

Frankly, in Mallory's eyes the human was ugly as sin, but he couldn't help that, and after all, Mallory was enjoying his company. The truth was, the dragon had been mostly alone since he'd run away from home, and it was good to have someone to talk to that wasn't running from him screaming, "God, please save me! Don't let it kill me!"

They had walked along talking till it was almost dark, then they'd decided to build a camp together without any real discussion.

"I don't usually get this far off the road," the human, said following him.

"Then you're lucky highwaymen haven't beaten and robbed you yet."

"Highwaymen?"

"Robbers who travel the roads looking for idgits like us to roll for coin."

"Isn't there any place on this whole world where there isn't any trouble?"

Mallory laughed. "Not even over the rainbow, my friend."

They both gathered wood, and then as Duncan was dragging out his flint and steel to light the fire, Mallory said, "Allow me." He breathed just enough fire into the wood to get a nice blaze started.

"Wow! I'm impressed," man-boy said.

"As well you should be. It's quite a trick." Mallory picked up one of the turnips he'd dropped on the ground and started rubbing it on his scales to clean it. He held it out and spun it around. Deeming it clean he enough ate it, top and all, in two bites. Then he started on another one. He was hungry. He watched his camping companion peel a turnip with his knife. skewer it with his sword and hold it over the fire to cook it.

"So, the vegetarian thing, is that why you ran away from home?" Duncan asked.

"No, no. Nothing as simple as that. No, the big falling-out was over my failure in the family business."

"Terrorizing villagers?" Duncan guessed.

"Please. Like I couldn't terrorize me some villagers if I took a mind to. No, we were accountants and financial advisors. Boring, right? But believe it or not, on most of Overlap, dragons are as well known for their financial prowess as they are for their terrorizing of villagers.

"Of course there are now just scores of back-to-our-beginnings freaks who scream that we've forgotten our ancestral ways, yada, yada, yada. You know how elders are always going on about the good old days? You know, the days when you couldn't throw a rock without hitting a village that some dragon or other had sacked. "

"Do I ever. So what happened?"

That was a very good question. The truth was Mallory just wasn't up for an office-dress-code kind of life. In fact, if given only the two choices, he would have rather burned villages. And he had *no* desire to do that, either.

One day he couldn't stand to stay in his cubicle crunching numbers even one more day. He'd "borrowed" a bunch of the family firm's money and gone to a casino.

Mallory had been rolling high and making a bundle. Then Lady Luck had suddenly spit in his face and he hadn't known when to walk away.

"I was in line for a junior partnership with the family firm but I made some unfortunate investments and the firm lost money. They all blamed me even though it wasn't my fault, so I left," Mallory said and thought, *It's not my fault the dice kept rolling craps. And I was run out on a rail— that's the same as "left," right?*

"I felt it was wisest to strike out on my own. Help myself to…that is helping out those with financial problems." *You gotta pick a pocket or two, boy, ya gotta pick a pocket or two.*

'So you're a financial expert huh?"

"What is a financial expert except someone who knows how to take a little money and make it into a lot?" Mallory said, spreading his arms wide and almost losing the turnip he'd been eating.

"But you don't have any money right now, right? I mean…it doesn't look like you have anything."

"Thanks for noticing." Mallory frowned. He still had a few coins tucked back but only a few. *Too many bad card games with cheaters better than me,* Mallory thought but said, "Tarslick was filled with too many other financial wizards. There was no work for me, and I quickly ran through my funds so…as I said, it was time to move on."

"I didn't do much better. I worked the whole time I was there and…" Duncan dumped the contents of his pouch into his hand and Mallory's eyes lit up. "…this is all I have. Fifteen coins."

"It's enough for a stake."

"But after you eat the steak, then what?" the human asked in a philosophical tone.

Mallory laughed. "Not that kind of steak, my boy. Ah…a financial stake. Tell you what, Duncan my friend, we should pool our resources. With my brains and your capital our fortunes could be made."

Duncan seemed to think about it for a minute, wavering and unsure. Mallory sighed. "There's safety in numbers and I know a bit more about the world than you do. As they say two heads are better than one. Of course I met a fellow with two heads once. They just kept arguing and head butting each other, and you wanted to look him in the eyes when you were talking to him, but I could never figure out which eyes. I tried looking in one eye on one head and one on the other but that gave me a headache"

Duncan laughed and held out his hand. Mallory looked at it a minute. He knew what the human wanted—a handshake. To a human a handshake meant a deal made, a promise to be kept. Mallory looked at the human's out-stretched hand and now he was the one thinking about it for a minute. He'd never made a deal with anyone, at least not one he meant to keep. Something told him that if he made a deal with Duncan and backed out, he'd have guilt. On the rare occasions Mallory had felt guilt he didn't like it. He didn't like it at all.

But he was tired of being alone, and for some reason he liked this human, felt a bond with him, a kinship of sorts. Just as it looked like Duncan was about to withdraw his hand Mallory grabbed it and started pumping it up and down. "It's a deal then. We're partners."

* * * *

That night Duncan slept with his back against the dragon and he wasn't worried at all about something sneaking up on him. Let them come if they dared.

They made a breakfast of turnips, washed down with a tea made of some lemon grass he'd found in the ditch alongside the road the day before. They drank it from the pans he'd made out of his knee cops.

"These are quite nice," Mallory said, holding one up to check out the craftsmanship. "And you say you made these out of your armor?"

"Yep."

"And your fire cover?"

"It's my chain mail shirt and one of my leggings," Duncan said, smiling. "My father would give birth to a cow if he saw it. How far is the next town?"

"No idea," Mallory said as he chewed on an entire turnip. "I've never been this way before. Which is good."

"Why?" Duncan asked.

Mallory laughed nervously then stammered out, "No reason really, I just like to go to new places and see new things."

Duncan nodded. A few minutes later as they were packing up he, remembered that the dragon had nothing.

He wondered why he'd made a deal with Mallory at all. After all he had only the dragon's word that he was good at anything, and he had nothing in the way of possessions to bring to their partnership.

It wasn't till they started down the road that Duncan remembered why he'd shaken the dragon's hand.

A simple, black, one-passenger, steam-powered car came popping down the road at their back. Upon seeing them the car swerved, giving them a wide berth, and sped away.

Duncan smiled. No one was going to mess with him as long as he was traveling with the dragon.

They hadn't gone far when there was a sign by the side of the road that read "Casia 10 Miles."

"Ten miles." Mallory sighed. "I'm getting so tired of walking."

"Me, too. My feet have never hurt so much in my life. Have you noticed that if you pick something you see in the distance and say, 'I'm going to walk till I get to that rock,' every time you look it's the same distance away…"

"So you quit looking and then you wind up passing it without stopping," Mallory finished.

"Exactly!"

Mallory shrugged. "Nope, never noticed that."

Duncan looked at him in confusion, but shrugged it off as the dragon's strange sense of humor. Something caught his eye and he turned, only then realizing that the road was now beside the river.

"Well I don't like that."

"What?" Mallory asked.

"The river's right there."

"So?"

"Nothing really except the river almost killed me." Duncan found himself telling Mallory everything that he'd been through that he hadn't already told him.

"I can see why the river makes you a little uneasy. Of course this road sticks pretty close to the river. Since the Sliding River goes all the way around the world—several times actually—it's the best way to know where you are in relation to where you were."

Mallory seemed to think about what he'd just said, then nodded his head and went on. "Most towns and cities are built along the Sliding. The river is still the best way to get around. Unless you have a captain with no sense of humor who throws you off the boat and makes you swim ashore... At least that's what I heard."

Mallory started to weave tales of his own travel. He spoke of everywhere he'd been and all he'd seen and done and it was easy to see that he had more knowledge of their world than Duncan did. Especially since Duncan's experience was mostly being nearly killed half a dozen times and run off by everything from Centaurs to freakishly strong little people.

A couple of wagons passed them as did a few of the steam cars Duncan had seen everywhere in Tarslick. All swerved further around them than they had to, and none of them offered to give them a ride.

Every time the dragon stopped in his story telling to jump around with his thumb out asking for a lift it seemed to make the vehicles that passed them in a haze of dust and fumes go faster. As they zipped past, Mallory would wave his fist in the air and say to the back of the vehicle, "Who needs you any way!"

By the time the third vehicle had left them in its dust Duncan joined the dragon in his strange ritual.

"Doesn't that just beat all!? Doesn't anyone want to help out their fellow creature anymore?" Mallory added as yet another car whizzed past them. "It's discrimination I tell ya." Mallory continued in a nearly inaudible mumble, "You know what the problem is?"

He didn't give Duncan a chance to answer.

"Well I'll tell ya. It's that we've been misinterpreted in the press. Just because generations of my kind have sacked villages and eaten their livestock, is that any reason to condemn a whole race? When's the last time you saw or heard of a dragon sacking a whole village? Or even taking off with a single sheep? Yet they show the same pictures over and over again. Dragons torching huts, taking off with some farm animal or other tucked under each arm."

"Look, every race has its problems. Humans are ugly and stupid—nothing personal—yet you don't see me treating them differently from everyone else. A mark is a mark. I don't care what race they are; their coin is all the same to me. I never discriminate."

"What's that you said? Humans are ugly and stupid?"

"They smell funny, too. That's not the point, the point is… Well I sort of forgot… Oh yeah… Would it kill someone to give us a ride!" He yelled towards the back of a green car as it raced past them.

Mallory talked a lot and Duncan talked a little and soon they had reached the outskirts of Casia. It was a medium-sized town with every bit as mixed technologies and peoples as Tarslick had. Dirt roads mostly, with some brick buildings, but mostly clapboard houses with tin roofs. It wasn't very big and there wasn't a lot of anything.

"We need a tavern," Mallory said, straightening to his full height and looking around.

"Why?"

"Why not?"

That made as much sense as anything else, so he shrugged and followed Mallory towards a wooden building with a tin roof and a covered porch across the front. There was a sign that glowed with a pink light. Of course he had no idea what it said since it wasn't written in his language.

"Here's something I don't get, dragon. Why does everyone speak the same language but write it in so many different ways?"

"I asked my father that once."

"What did he say?"

"'I don't know! Get back to work and quit asking stupid questions. I wish you'd died in your egg!'" Mallory yelled, then calmed down. "Dear old dad."

There was a large, pink bird on the sign, so he guessed the name of the place had something to do with the bird. On the door it said plainly in a language he could read, "No one under eighteen years old or thirty-two inches tall." He didn't even have to wonder why after his run-in with the little people in the dead forest.

"All right, partner, here we are. Give me ten of your coins." Duncan was reluctant to do so. He'd worked hard and suffered a lot of humiliation for that money. "Come on, Duncan. I'm the financial brains in this partnership, remember?"

Duncan took off his pouch, counted out the coins, and handed them to the dragon.

As Duncan and Mallory ducked to enter the bar, they could hear the normal noise Duncan had long ago learned to associate with such an establishment, but as soon as they were spotted there was dead silence. Duncan at first wondered why and then laughed to himself because he had quickly forgotten that his traveling companion was a seven-foot-two-inch, blue dragon.

"I'm a vegetarian," Mallory announced, and the whole room started talking again. "Discrimination I tell ya," Mallory mumbled toward Duncan.

He just nodded silently.

They walked on into the bar, and Mallory's gaze immediately fixed on a table towards the back of the bar. Several creatures of different races and species were playing some sort of card game. From the pile of coin in the middle of the table Duncan knew they were gambling.

He'd seen people play the same sort of game in the tavern in Spurna.

Mallory rubbed his hands together and whispered. "Now you just go to the bar and get yourself a drink. This shouldn't take too long."

"I don't know, Mal, I've seen men lose an entire month's pay playing games like that."

"Just put your trust in me, Dunc." Mallory didn't give him much choice. He just walked away.

Duncan shrugged, walked over to the bar and sat down. He took a stool close to the end.

"What will it be?" the bartender, a tall, thin, blue creature wearing only a loin cloth and a tie, asked.

"A beer, please," Duncan answered, trying not to stare at the guy whose face was longer than his body. He looked around the bar. Except for the bright lights everywhere and the wooden floor—instead of packed dirt—and the many different species present at the tables, it could have been the tavern in Spurna. It was just as dirty and loud for sure.

Duncan's eyes were drawn to the one thing in the room that was decidedly different—a large cage in the corner that contained a small spider monkey. There was a sign on the cage that of course he couldn't read. When the bartender handed him his beer Duncan asked pointing, "What's the sign say?"

"It says pin the monkey and win a hundred coins."

Duncan looked at the small monkey. "That monkey?"

"Yep. No one's ever done it."

"That little monkey?"

"Yes, that little monkey," the bartender said with a smile. "It costs you five coins to try. You want to take a chance?"

That was everything Duncan had left after giving most of his money to Mallory. Since they were partners it seemed like he should ask the dragon before making such an investment.

He looked at the monkey again. It sat on a shelf half way up the side of the cage with its back to Duncan, eating something it held clutched in its two hands. It looked like a timid creature. How much of a gamble could it be? Surely he could pin the monkey in no time flat and collect all that money and... If it was that easy why hadn't anyone else been able to do it? Why would the bartender be willing to risk a hundred coins?

He ordered a sandwich to eat and then another beer. He drank the beer, ate the sandwich, and ordered another beer without a sandwich and then another and then... Well, the more beer he drank the smaller and more timid that monkey looked.

The real problem being that if he gave the bartender five coins to try and for some strange reason he couldn't pin the monkey he wouldn't be able to pay his tab.

He looked around the room and found the dragon happily playing cards. He was smiling, so he must be winning. They were partners. The dragon was playing with his money. So even if he couldn't pin the monkey, which suddenly seemed inconceivable, Mallory could cover his bar tab.

Another beer later it became impossible for Duncan to believe for even a minute that he couldn't pin the tiny monkey. It looked insignificant, maybe even frightened. He emptied his pouch into his hand and handed the bartender his five coins. "I'm going to pin that monkey," he announced.

The bartender smiled. Then he yelled to the customers in the bar, "We have a taker! Someone is going to try their hand at pinning the monkey."

There was a small stampede towards the cage as the bartender led Duncan over to it. The closer to the cage they got the smaller that monkey looked.

"There's only one rule," the bartender said. "Whatever you do, don't punch the monkey in the face."

"All right," Duncan said. That made sense. What sort of brute would punch a tiny monkey in the face?

As he entered the cage he heard a familiar voice say, "That idiot."

The dragon's statement did not build his confidence, but it was after all just a tiny monkey.

What happened next happened so fast Duncan would have trouble remembering it in full detail later. That monkey threw down the piece of bread he'd been eating, stood to his full height and screamed at its opponent, shaking its fists at him. All of which he thought was sort of funny till he lurched forward to grab the monkey and pin it and the enraged creature jumped from the perch, popped Duncan in the nose, and landed on the roof of the cage hanging there and screaming at its victim.

Duncan held his aching nose. He couldn't see. His nose was bleeding. As his vision began to clear he could see Mallory through the cage bars surrounded by the other bar customers. The dragon frowned and shook his head. Duncan took that as a very bad sign.

He was going to pin that monkey if it was the last thing he did. He jumped up and grabbed one of the monkey's legs. The monkey let go and as Duncan's feet touched the floor the monkey grabbed Duncan's head, jerked its leg free, and kicked him in the gut with both feet. Then the little sucker began jumping from one side of the cage to the other, punching and/or kicking its victim with every pass until not only was Duncan no longer sure he could pin the monkey, but he wasn't at all sure that he was going to make it out of the cage alive.

The monkey stuck its tongue out at him. It clung to the side of the cage waiting to attack again. It looked bigger by the second.

As far as he could see he had only one option. He had to punch that monkey in the face. Since it was the one thing you weren't supposed to do it must be the only way to win.

He waited for a moment when his back kept anyone in the room from seeing the monkey or what he was doing and then he took his shot. He hit that monkey square in the face. The monkey shook its head and he prepared to grab and pin the beast. But just as he thought he was about to taste triumph that swirling hairball of death jumped right on his head. Obviously unhurt it started trying to beat its hapless victim to death.

* * * *

Mallory had been making a killing playing five card stud. He'd already made five times what he'd come to the table with and was feeling particularly lucky. When he heard the announcement he cringed. Not only were all the other players leaving the table to go watch, but it was his stupid partner who'd entered into the ridiculous bar bet. He wanted to wring the idiot's neck himself. He picked up his earnings and went to watch with the rest of the bar's patrons.

Mallory looked at the sign and the tiny monkey and then he looked at the size of his partner, and just for a second he thought maybe this wasn't such a bad deal. Then as Duncan entered the cage and the monkey challenged him, Mallory knew it was a really, really bad idea.

Mallory was just enough taller than the rest of the patrons that he could see every inch of the cage and he saw Duncan try to win by hitting the monkey in the face which… Well since it was the one thing he was told *not* to do, meant it was the one thing the bartender *wanted* him to do.

Mallory knew it wasn't going to go well for his gangly, clumsy partner. That monkey was now punching Duncan in the head and biting him. The human seemed helpless to defend himself.

Mallory turned to address the tall dark-haired human he'd been playing cards with earlier. "Bilgewater, you wouldn't happen to know just how much money he had to put up, would you?"

"Five coins," he said. "It's a sucker bet. No one has ever pinned that monkey. I'm sure you could, but I doubt seriously they'd let you even try."

"So in other words anyone who might beat the monkey isn't allowed to play." Mallory was thoughtful. Five coins was too much to give up, but his partner was about to be beaten to death by a small monkey.

"If he pins him what does he win?" Mallory asked.

"One hundred coins."

Mallory nodded and moved closer to the cage, careful not to draw attention to himself. He worked his tail through the bars of the cage, quickly grabbed the monkey by its tail, and then pulled the monkey back into the bars. Duncan looked more than a little dazed.

The monkey spun its head around quickly looking for what had its tail. When the monkey's eyes caught Mallory's, the dragon opened his mouth wide to show the full length of his rows of razor-sharp teeth, and the monkey froze.

"For the god's sake, pin the monkey!" Bilgewater screamed.

Duncan grabbed the monkey and Mallory gave the monkey a warning look and quickly released its tail. The monkey lay spreadeagled on the floor of the cage and let the human pin it.

"You cheated!" the bartender screamed.

Mallory was sure that meant the bartender had seen him grab the monkey's tail.

Duncan left the cage quickly as the bartender opened the door.

"How so?" Sadie, a small woman with long brown hair who'd also been playing cards with Mallory, asked.

"He must have hit the monkey," the bartender said.

"You've been running this scam for years. We all know that all punching the monkey does is make him really, really mad," Bilgewater supplied.

"It's still the rules," the bartender said.

"I didn't see him punch the monkey. Did anyone see him punch the monkey?" Sadie demanded.

Mallory was actually surprised by the two gamblers speaking up. After all he'd taken a substantial amount of their coin. Then he realized two things. First, that his card-playing friends had no idea that he and Duncan were together. Second, if they didn't know then neither did any one else in the bar. That being the case they had the upper hand. "Now see here, barkeep," Mallory said. "You give this young man his winnings. He has beaten your con fair and square."

Duncan, bloody and bruised and more confused than usual, looked at Mallory. He quickly cut the young human his very best keep-your-mouth-shut look.

Without another word the bartender handed Duncan two rolls of fifty coins.

"Thanks," the young human mumbled to the blue man. Rapidly swelling lips were hard to talk through.

Mallory motioned towards the door, pointing with his tail, and the battered Duncan nodded and staggered towards the exit.

"Well, back to our game," Bilgewater said to Mallory as the crowd started to disperse, going back to what they'd been doing before.

Mallory smiled, being sure to show plenty of tooth. "I'm afraid I really must be going."

"But you have to give us a chance to win our money back," Sadie said with a sweet smile.

"I'd love to, but I really must be going. I have a prior engagement." Mallory started for the front door but the others followed.

"I'm afraid I must insist," Bilgewater started. The man and his partner were professional gamblers. Mallory knew the type—flashy dressers, more cards up their sleeves than they had on the table, and a line of bull you could hang clothes on. Bilgewater didn't like to lose, and he no doubt had a plan to win back the money he'd lost and then some.

Mallory cleared his throat, making a small growl-like sound and bared all his teeth at him again, letting their full length show. "I said I have to go," he said, and let just the tiniest bit of smoke puff out of his nostrils.

"Well if you just must," Sadie said nervously, and started pulling on Bilgewater's waistcoat as she backed away from the beast. "It was a pleasure playing with you."

Bilgewater seemed reluctant to go but finally nodded and said to Mallory, "Until next time then."

"Yes, next time." Mallory nodded and left quickly. He found Duncan waiting right outside the door for him. "Shesh! Why didn't you head on down the road?" he whispered then added quickly as he kept walking, "Wait a few seconds then follow me."

Duncan nodded and a few minutes later he caught up to Mallory.

"I can't believe they gave me the money. I actually *did* punch the monkey."

"What can I say? When J.P. Mallory talks, people listen. Now just keep moving. The faster we get out of town the better."

"But why?" Duncan asked, and started walking faster to keep up.

"I'll explain when we get out of town."

"But it's dark."

"The moon is full, plenty of light."

* * * *

Sadie lifted her black, floor-length skirt and stepped up to join Bilgewater on the porch of a bed and breakfast. "See? It's just as I told you. Those two are working together," he said.

"How can you be so sure, Bilge? Perhaps they are just talking," Sadie countered. She wasn't buying it. No doubt because they seemed a more unlikely partnership than even she and Bilgewater. "The dragon is pretty slick. Maybe he is trying to talk that fellow out of his money."

"Well, they came together and they left minutes apart. Suddenly that dragon was in a hurry to leave. The cards were falling in his favor all night, so the question is—'why?'" He turned to Sadie and smiled.

"Quitting while he was ahead?" she shrugged.

"They're partners. I'd bet my silver-toed, snake skinned boots on it. Did you know that dragon has a prehensile tail?"

"No I didn't."

"Neither did I till I saw him use it to grab the monkey and pull him into the bars."

"Why did you…?"

"He's a seven-foot dragon. I'd rather not get on his bad side. Besides the money didn't come out of my pocket."

"But the money he won from us at the table did," Sadie said, frowning. "And you know good and well he was cheating because we both were and he was still beating us."

"Pocket change, my friend. I have a feeling those two are going to do much bigger and better things. I think we ought to keep a half an eye on them, see if their good fortune might play into our hands, if you know what I mean."

Sadie's eyes narrowed to slits and she smiled. "Oh I think I do indeed."

Five

Duncan had been laughing for several minutes uncontrollably. "You grabbed the monkey's tail," he said, as if Mallory hadn't been the one who told him.

"I had to. You were about to be killed. Which is, of course, your fault because you punched the monkey in the face," Mallory said, clicking his tongue and shaking his head in a disapproving way.

"I thought it was the only way to win."

"You really are a babe in the woods," Mallory said. "He tells people not to punch the monkey because it's the monkey's trigger. Even if you might wear him down and pin him, you won't if you punch him because then he just goes nuts."

"I don't understand."

"It's simple. The reason you thought you should punch the monkey—that's the reason why he told you not to. You shouldn't have punched the monkey anyway."

Duncan still didn't really understand, but didn't like being talked to as if he'd committed some unforgivable sin because he punched a monkey. "It was just a monkey."

"Exactly! A poor, defenseless monkey."

"Defenseless?! Have you looked at my face lately? That monkey was beating me to death. You said so yourself."

"Only because you punched him in the face."

"No, he was beating me up way before I punched him in the face."

"Because you were in his space. Have you at least learned your lesson?"

"Ahh... don't make bets in bars when you've had a few pints?"

"Well that goes without saying, but I was thinking the greater lesson is that violence never solved anything."

"That monkey was beating me up."

"Because you were trying to pin it."

"Because I wanted to make a hundred coins and more importantly I didn't want to lose my five coins."

"You hit a tiny monkey in the face with your fist. What a proud moment for you."

"I was sure that was the only way to pin him," he defended.

"And you see how well that worked out for you."

"I won one hundred coins."

"No, *we* won one hundred coins and it wasn't because you resorted to violence. We won because I used my wits."

"You grabbed his tail with your tail. How is that using your brains?" he demanded.

"Oh come on, that was pretty slick. At least I didn't hurt the monkey," Mallory defended.

"Well apparently neither did I."

"True. Still, violence never solves anything. I've found there are few things you can't talk your way out of."

"Surely there is something you think is worth fighting for."

"Fighting is idiotic and pointless. Aren't you the man who left home because you didn't want to fight in a war?"

"Well yes, but that war was stupid. I mean, really? Fighting and dying over the right to say the river belongs to…well, anyone?"

"I have found that most wars and almost all fights are started—and continue—over nothing any less stupid," Mallory said.

"When you make that I'm-better-than-everyone-else face and use that self-righteous tone of voice I want to hit YOU," Duncan said.

"And what would that get you? A fist full of sore knuckles and a pissed off dragon," Mallory said, looking at his claws and picking something out from under one of them. "I've never had the need to get violent. Simply talking to people, explaining my position…"

"And being a seven-foot tall, fire-breathing reptile with a mouth full of teeth like a shark doesn't help?" Duncan interjected.

To his surprise this made Mallory smile. "Well it certainly doesn't hurt."

Duncan laughed, no longer angry with his big friend. He was, of course, welcome to his rather silly, nonviolent ideals.

A dragon that breathes fire and could chomp a car in two but is a vegetarian and a pacifist. Mallory isn't anything he's supposed to be… just like me! That's what we have in common—why we get along, because neither of us are anything we're supposed to be.

"Whatever are you grinning about, human?" Mallory asked.

"Nothing." Duncan shrugged his shoulders. He noticed they'd walked out of town a few minutes before. "Shouldn't we have…I don't know…stopped to buy some provisions at least?"

"We couldn't afford to."

"We have plenty of money…"

"Not because we don't have enough money, dunderhead. We couldn't afford for anyone to find out we were working together. They'd put two and two together. It's never really good to get caught out-conning a con man. You win a really big pot like that you'd better leave before they have a chance to get mad and come looking for you.

"There's bound to be another town not too far up the road. Like I said, as long as you stay close to the Sliding, towns are never very far apart." Mallory stopped suddenly and Duncan stopped and looked at him. Mallory pulled one of his feet up, looked at the bottom of it, dusted it off and then pulled a rock from between two of his talons. He sighed as he started walking again. "I think our first order of business should be to find some sort of transportation."

"I can't agree with you more," Duncan said. "Could we maybe find somewhere to camp for the night? After all, that poor, harmless monkey didn't leave a spot on my whole body that he didn't punch, bite, or kick."

"Of course! I'm sorry. We probably need to clean out your wounds, too."

In the woods it was darker than on the road. They felt around for wood. Mallory started it going and then continued to gather wood and get the fire blazing as Duncan made his way to the river. The water was cold and cleaning out his many wounds made him shiver. He was glad for the warmth of the fire when he got back to their camp.

Mallory had already dragged up a bunch of deadfall to keep the fire going. Duncan hugged the fire, suddenly feeling every bite and punch he'd taken. The warmth felt good on his monkey-ravaged body. He looked with a wary eye from the fire to the proximity of the river.

As if reading his mind Mallory said, "Don't worry, Dunc, the river just slid. It won't slide again for a long time. Also, dragons have superior sight and hearing, and I am well aware of the sound the river makes before it slides."

Duncan nodded. "Mallory, do you know if the river has ever moved far enough to take out a whole town? The towns being so close and all."

"That's a good question." Mallory looked thoughtful for a moment. "The river only slides just so far one way and then the next time it slides back, so all towns, villages, and especially cities, are built well above the slide zone. The most I've ever seen it do is take down a tree. However, there is a story—I don't know how much truth there is to it—of a great city that was destroyed.

"The story goes that when Overlap was first created, there was a lot of confusion because… Well all these different places and times and creatures were slapped together at once. They say that one race built a great city to show their superiority to all other creatures. You know, a bunch of know-it-alls. Anyway, their city had very advanced machines and buildings so tall that they touched the sky. It was built right on the banks of the river, which at that time—according to legend—had not started to slide. Well the story goes that one of their great machines malfunctioned and the river to slide that first time. Of course it wiped out their entire city, so that race is now extinct—which frankly serves them right. Now the river slides back and forth."

"Whether it's true or not, it's a great story," Duncan said.

"Most of the best stories are neither all true nor all fabrication," Mallory reflected.

"That makes sense." Duncan sat down and started unpacking his blanket, feeling suddenly very tired. He rolled himself up in it and went to sleep thinking of one of those steam cars with some place to put his stuff. *He saw the two of them zipping along down the road going from city to town to village—seeing the world. Having girls all look at him because he had such a great car. Just having girls…*

* * * *

Mallory stirred the fire with a stick, bringing the coals up; then he threw on some more wood. As the fire started to blaze he grabbed one of Duncan's pans and went down to the river to fill it with water. He found a bunch of sweet, young bamboo shoots and pulled them and a fistful of onion grass. He used Duncan's knife to cut up the vegetation, put it all into the pan and set it on the fire. He looked at Duncan's chain mail and legging where he'd laid it by the fire pit. At one time it had no doubt been bright and shiny. Now it was burned, tarnished, and soot covered.

It gave Mallory the glimmer of an idea but it didn't congeal before it was gone. That sometimes happened to Mallory. An idea came to him in stages. He knew it was a good idea too, just didn't know quite what it was. It would come to him, though. Some ideas were just too big to be thought up all at once.

The soup, such as it was, was starting to cook and Mallory saw Duncan sniff the air a couple of times and then sit right up.

The human rubbed his eyes, and then as if he'd just had a dream about it he asked, "Mallory you didn't say—how did your card game go?"

"I won twenty-five coins," Mallory answered. Actually he'd won fifty, but he never liked to put all his cards on the table.

Duncan looked around then and asked in a curious tone, "Where is it?"

"I could tell you but then I'd have to kill you." Mallory smiled and stirred the soup with a stick.

Duncan laughed then said as he stood up, "Who are you kidding? You can't kill me—that would be violent."

"Then I'd better not tell you," Mallory said with a grin.

It would be telling a trusted dragon secret to divulge the fact that he had a small pouch behind each of his cheek frills. Dragonologists said the pouches had once held a gland that secreted enzymes for digesting the chunks of buildings one would occasionally swallow while raiding a village. Of course when dragons started to develop tool-using skills there was no longer any need to bite through walls. They could simply pull up a tree and beat a wall in, so the gland was gone, but the pouches were still there and open. The opening to them was inside his mouth and most people didn't think to look there. Even if they did, they usually thought better of it.

Still, he needed some place to carry things that wasn't secret. He'd had a really cool black leather vest that had pockets sewed in under the arms and along the bottom on the inside so that their existence was undetectable to the untrained eye. But he'd had a few bad poker hands in Tarslick that he couldn't cheat his way out of, and he'd lost the vest.

He hadn't left anything he cared about in Tarslick. Except the vest. He'd gambled away almost his last coin there—something that he'd promised himself once already that he'd never do—and now he was having to promise himself the same thing again. This time he hoped he was better about keeping the promise.

He decided one of the first things he was going to buy with the money they'd won last night was a new vest …with pockets of course.

"Seriously, where's the money?" Duncan asked.

"Well hidden. Let's just leave it at that. Here's the thing—you have a pouch with a hundred coins in it, right?"

"Yes."

"So we use that and for the time being we keep the twenty-five I have a secret. That way we have some extra. Remember, partner, I'm the financial guru. Stick with me, and your life will be fame and fortune."

"You haven't led me wrong yet, Mal, and you saved me from being beaten to death last night, so I trust you."

The poor fool, Mallory thought. *But he* can *trust me. I wouldn't cheat him. Hide an extra twenty-five coins from him, yes, but I wouldn't cheat him. The question of course is why not?* His eyes fell on the charred chain mail and he suddenly knew why. *Because he's like me—an outcast. He can trust me because I trust him. I trust him because—like me—he has no one else.*

* * * *

Crazy Adam, the transportation-dealing king, no longer seemed happy to have their business. Duncan had wanted something flashy and Mallory had wanted something big. They had test driven a used steam car that landed somewhere in the middle, which neither of them really liked.

Of course that became a non-point because after fussing over which one of the cars they were going to test drive they then told the guy that neither of them actually knew how to operate any of his vehicles.

The human sighed and looked up at them. "Seriously, neither of you can drive?"

Mallory shrugged. "How hard can it be if humans do it? No offense."

"None taken," Duncan said, but Mallory was pretty sure the car dealer did take offense.

After the man patiently told Duncan what to do, he climbed into the back seat as Duncan sat behind the wheel. Mallory sat in the passenger's seat with his head out the window because he couldn't get all the way in the car any other way.

The dragon was pretty sure the whole car thing wasn't going to work out, so he didn't even bother to complain about how uncomfortable he was. Mallory had listened to the dealer giving instructions to Duncan, and he'd seen the blank look on his partner's face.

Duncan hadn't been able to get the car to go very fast but he still managed to run into the back of a hay wagon. It didn't do any real damage to either the car or wagon, but it really ticked off the two guys driving the hay wagon. Mallory, Duncan and Crazy Adam wound up reloading the hay for an hour.

The whole time they were loading hay, the car salesman kept telling them that maybe a car wasn't the right transportation for their needs. Duncan just kept going on and on about how you didn't want to tick off hay farmers because they could be very vindictive.

When they'd finally finished cleaning up the mess Mallory decided to try to drive which... Well, cars just weren't made to be driven by dragons. That was all there was to it.

"It's another clear case of discrimination," Mallory said, giving up and getting out so that Crazy Adam could drive them back to the car lot.

"Maybe we should try one of these," Duncan said of a steam-driven motor cycle.

But Duncan almost got them killed and covered them both in mud when he drove it fifty feet and dumped it on its side in the middle of a puddle, leading Crazy Adam to look at the state of Duncan's face and ask, "So what happened to your last vehicle?"

"Excuse me?" Duncan asked. The man pointed at Duncan's face, his arms, his hands.

Duncan glared at the guy. "I've never owned a car before. If I had don't you think I'd know how to drive the blasted machine? I got this fighting a monkey." And he managed to say that last part as if it made perfect sense.

"It's a long story." Mallory laughed nervously.

Which was probably why Crazy Adam looked like he'd just as soon they leave without spending any money as waste any more of his time. Mallory grabbed Duncan by the arm and led him a little ways away. "Look, I don't think any of these machines are going to work for us."

Duncan frowned and nodded. "At least not till one of us can learn how to drive."

"Tozactly!" Mallory said.

"Maybe it's time we look at horses," Duncan suggested.

* * * *

Duncan found a horse right away, but every one Mallory sat on bucked him quickly off and after the third one Mallory said, "I don't think any horse is ever going to let me ride."

Crazy Levi the horse trader looked at him. "No reason you can't have a horse. I could cut you a deal. Maybe a team with a wagon would fit your needs."

"Could you give us a second?" Duncan and Mallory walked a ways away.

"Another clear-cut case of discrimination," Mallory mumbled.

Duncan smiled to himself. If he was a horse he probably wouldn't want a dragon riding him either. "They're just stupid animals, Mallory. They can't discriminate." *They just instinctively know that dragons should eat horses.*

"Maybe Crazy Levi has a point. If we had a wagon, if I wasn't sitting on the horse…" the dragon suggested.

"Why are all these guys called crazy?" Duncan asked curiously.

Mallory smiled. "Thinking they're insane is supposed to make us feel like we're getting a really good deal."

Duncan nodded though he didn't really understand. "Do we have enough money for a wagon and horses?"

"Probably, but don't forget—if you run out of wood or coal for a steam engine it won't die of starvation. If we get horses we have to take care of them, feed them, water them," Mallory said.

"I hadn't thought of that." Of course. He felt like an imbecile because he'd had horses all his life. It wasn't like he didn't know they had to be taken care of. "There's a lot of stuff besides feeding and watering them. I think it's a bad idea for us."

"What about bicycles?"

"I thought the idea was to have to work less," Duncan said, not wanting to tell Mallory that he couldn't ride a bike. Mallory nodded looking thoughtful. "I guess what needs to happen is that one of us needs to learn how to drive one of those car things."

"That isn't going to happen today," Duncan said, and thought, *or ever.*

Crazy Levi ran after them as they walked away, screaming out deal after deal. They mostly just ignored him.

Mallory said, "Let's spend some of our coin on a room for the night. Then let's find a tavern, get some food, and maybe another card game. Make some more money. Let's face it. The more money you have the more options you have. It's simple economics really.

"In the morning we can buy more gear, some food for the road, and maybe find an answer to our transportation options."

Duncan thought only a second about taking a real bath in a real tub and of sleeping in a real bed before he said, "That's a great idea."

* * * *

The woman who worked at the hotel had been generous with the hot water. Duncan had stayed in the tub till the water was almost cold and his skin was all wrinkly. Then he'd dried off, crawled under the covers, curled up in the bed and gone to sleep.

He woke up to Mallory saying, "Come on, man, let's go get some food. Put on your best clothes and strap on your sword."

"I thought you were nonviolent," Duncan said, rubbing his eyes and wondering if he could just sleep instead of eating. But then his stomach told him no so he got out of bed.

"I didn't say you were going to *use* the sword. It's for show. Besides, if what you say about your sword skills is true you'd as likely kill one of us as anyone else."

"I don't have any good clothes, Mallory. I have really dirty and tattered and not-quite-as-dirty-or-tattered."

"Good. Wear those," Mallory said. He was counting the coins out of what Duncan realized was *his* pouch.

"Hey, dragon! What are you up to?"

"Splitting *our* money. We'll leave half here hidden in our room and bring the other half with us. It doesn't pay to put all your eggs in one basket. There are pickpockets and thieves in even the smallest towns, and it never hurts to have something stashed away safe. "

Duncan nodded. He supposed that made sense.

"Remember, Duncan, I'm the financial brains of this outfit."

"Ah." Duncan scratched his head. "What exactly am *I* in this *outfit*?"

"Well you had the seed money and…" He seemed to be thinking, and then Mallory smiled—a sight Duncan was just getting used to. "You carry the stuff." And with that he tossed Duncan the pouch full of money. The dragon started looking around the room for a good hiding place for the other coins. He finally pulled one of the pillows out of its case, threw the money in the pillow case, put the pillow back in and then put it back on the bed.

Duncan looked at the pouch in his hand feeling pretty unimportant as he tied it to his belt. "Stuff carrier" wasn't a title he felt a man should aspire to much less be proud of.

"But what do I do…I mean besides carry stuff?"

"You watch my back. I watch yours. That's what a partnership is all about."

"But what are we, Mallory?"

"Leave it to a human to have to analyze everything." Mallory sighed. "Why do we have to be anything? Why isn't it enough that we *are*?"

"If someone asks me what I do I'd like to have a better answer than *I am*."

"Fine." Mallory stroked his cheek frill with one long, clawed talon. Then he looked up, his eyes brightening as inspiration hit him. "We, my friend, are men of mystery and intrigue. We're world travelers." His smiled broadly and swaggered a bit. "We're adventurers."

Duncan liked the sound of that. He especially liked it if being an adventurer could include taking a real bath and sleeping in a real bed every once in awhile. He had to admit he was tired of sleeping under the open sky and all that it included.

"When we get to the bar I'll find a game. I'll ask you for all our money. You'll protest and say the last time you did that I lost it all."

"But you didn't." Duncan was more than a little confused.

"So, you're lying to me, and since I told you what to say, it's not really a lie."

Duncan nodded. He supposed that made sense.

"Then hand me half of the money."

"But you said to give it all to you," Duncan said, not understanding at all.

Mallory hit himself in the head with the palm of his hand then tapped his claws against his forehead for several seconds. When he stopped this he just looked at Duncan and for a minute Duncan fully expected the dragon to roar at him or maybe burn him to a cinder.

Finally Mallory took in a deep breath and let it out in such a way that he might as well have said, "Listen, dunderhead."

"Look…let me see if I can explain this to you. Playing cards is as much about what the other players think of you as it is what's in your hand. If you want the other players to bet all they have you have to make them believe you're betting all you have. You never let them see who you really are any more than you ever let them see all your cards. Do you get it?"

Duncan frowned. "Not really."

"It's all smoke and mirrors, Duncan. Smoke and mirrors. You get them looking over here, but the action is really happening over there."

"It doesn't sound terribly honest."

"So you *do* get it. Just do what I tell you to and you'll do fine. I'll ask you for all the money and then you say…"

* * * *

Mallory wondered what the odds were exactly. He looked to the back of the bar suspiciously taking in Sadie and Bilgewater where they sat playing cards with—among others—the jerk who'd won his vest in that ill-fated poker game. To make matters worse and even more improbable, the jerk was wearing Mallory's vest. Mallory stroked his chin thoughtfully. In his experience such coincidences usually weren't.

At his shoulder Duncan said, "Aren't those the same people you gambled with at…?"

"Yes, and I'm wondering why they're following us."

"What makes you think that they are?"

"Because of the man they're playing cards with. I know him."

"I don't understand."

"Odds, my good man, it's all a question of playing the odds. Either he's following me—which I seriously doubt—or they are—which seems more plausible. But the real question is, *if* they are following us, *why* are they following us?" Mallory said thoughtfully. For a moment he started to just turn around and try another bar. Then he thought that maybe he could make this work to his advantage. After all, he'd love to have his vest back. "Stick to the script."

"Huh?" Duncan asked.

"Just say what I told you to."

Duncan nodded that he understood.

Mallory sauntered up to the table where the three he knew were playing with a cyclops who looked like he was already none too happy with the game. "Would you mind dealing me in?"

Bilgewater smiled up at him, "Not at all. Anyone else have any objections?" The other players all just shook their heads. "Have a seat. The game is Tarslick Hold'em."

Mallory couldn't tell from Bilgewater's expression if he was sorry Mallory had found them there, or if he had fully expected that he would. Mallory hoped he wasn't playing into their hands. It didn't matter. Either way Mallory could use it to his advantage if he kept his wits about him.

The jerk wearing his vest laughed and said, "Always a pleasure to take your money, dragon."

"Lady Luck can be a fickle mistress, Humphrey," Mallory said with his own laugh, and settled into an empty chair between the cyclops and Sadie. He looked at Duncan and held out his hand expectantly. "Give me all the money."

Duncan leaned down to him and muttered just loud enough for everyone else at the table to hear. "We barely have enough to pay for our room as it is. You lost so much in your last game."

"Don't worry, Duncan my friend, I will double the money," Mallory replied. "Now give me all the money."

Duncan grumbled but handed him half the coins in his sack just as they had practiced. As he stomped away towards the bar Mallory decided that, despite his protests, Duncan could get good at this.

Mallory smiled and picked up the cards he'd already been dealt. He looked at the man in his vest and smiled. By the end of the evening he planned to have his vest back.

"I thought you guys might be partners," Bilgewater said. Sadie threw him a look that said she didn't think he should have told Mallory that.

"Yes…well, as they say, it's not always a good idea to show all of one's cards," Mallory said in a tone that implied that the fact that they'd figured out he and Duncan were partners didn't bother him in the slightest.

He looked up and caught Duncan flirting with a bar wench. He didn't really understand such silliness. He just hoped Duncan wasn't going to start showing coin to impress the woman. Mallory wondered how Duncan thought he could watch his back and the woman's front at the same time.

"That was a sweet pot. The monkey bet, I mean."

"Unfortunately I lost most of it. Bad night, you know." Mallory could tell by the looks on their faces that neither Sadie nor Bilgewater believed him for a minute, but he didn't need them to. After all, he wasn't after their money. In fact, he even helped them win a hand or two when he had very little of his own money on the table of course.

Finally the Cyclops gave up, grumbled that the game was too rich for him, and left while he still had enough coin to pay his bar bill.

Mallory saw Duncan leave out the back with the bar wench. *So much for watching my back. I'll count myself lucky if he hasn't spent every coin in his pouch by morning.*

Mallory played till the last of the jerk's money and his vest were on the table. He laid out his straight flush with a huge smile, picked up his vest and put it on. Then he picked up all the money and stuck it into his vest pockets. "Very nice playing with you."

Humphrey grumbled and refused to shake his hand. Mallory shook Sadie and then Bilgewater's hand and smiled. "Until next time."

"Until next time," Bilgewater said with a bit of a bow.

They'd made almost as much money between them as Mallory had, so they were happy. Mallory had decided when he first saw them that evening that he'd rather leave them smiling than with light pockets. He'd rather not have them as enemies, especially if they were going to follow him around.

* * * *

Duncan had a fine night and he woke up in a soft, warm bed feeling pleased with himself and life in general. That was when he heard the argument at the door. Mallory was standing in the doorway arguing with someone in the hall that Duncan couldn't see.

"...see here, dragon, I've had the night to think about it and you clearly cheated me," a man was saying in an angry tone.

"Listen here, Humphrey. When you took all I had I didn't accuse you of cheating. You are a sore loser and..." Not wanting to attract a crowd,

Mallory stepped aside and the angry Humphrey followed him into the room, still arguing.

"Clearly you were in cahoots with those other two."

"I can assure you that I am not. Have you talked to them?"

"I tried to, but they have already left town. No doubt because they…"

"Then if anyone was cheating you perhaps it was them. I haven't run out of town have I?"

"Well no, but…"

Duncan had been sleeping peacefully and this altercation immediately annoyed him if for no other reason than it was interrupting his night of sleep in a real bed. He tried just sticking the pillow over his head to cut the noise, but that didn't work. So he jumped to his feet, the pillow in his hand. Still not quite awake he headed for the basin to wash his face and wake himself the rest of the way up. Just in case he needed to save Mallory from this jerk.

He'd slept hard no doubt from a mixture of love and beer. His right leg was still asleep so he tripped over his sword and stumbled around the room trying not to fall. With his right leg full of pins and needles, he was jumping around on his left leg, swinging the pillow around in wide circles in an attempt to keep his balance that—not too surprisingly—wasn't working. He ran right into the man in the doorway, shoving him into the door frame, and the pillow connected with the man's head making a sick, clanging, tingling, thudding sort of sound. Duncan hit the floor.

When he managed to push himself upright the man just sort of flowed down the doorway and onto the floor—out cold.

Duncan looked from the unconscious man at his feet to the pillow in his hand. "What the hell just happened?"

Mallory took the pillow from Duncan's hand and shook it up and down. The coins rattled in the bottom of the pillow slip and he grimaced.

"Oops," Duncan said, shrugging.

"Oops!" Mallory said in disbelief. "*Oops!* Quick. Help me drag him in here before anyone sees." They dragged the guy in the room and Mallory quickly shut the door. The guy was big, even bigger than Duncan was. He was ugly, his head being really too big for his body, and his features too big for his head. His hair was nearly as dark as Duncan's, cut in the same short, flat-on-top style his father had always worn, so Duncan was glad he'd knocked the guy out just on principle.

Mallory paced back and forth then looked at Duncan and said, "We'd best pack our gear and be on our way."

"Why?"

"Why? You just knocked this guy out and when he comes too he is going to be none too happy, I can assure you. He's a big guy. If he goes to the local law… Let's just say I just don't want to deal with all of that. If Sadie and Bilgewater thought it was best to get out of town then I think it would be wise for us to follow suit."

"But I like it here." Duncan sort of wanted to stay awhile see that girl (*what was her name?*) again.

"What is it you said about when you know you should go?"

Duncan nodded and started packing quickly. The dragon need say no more. It was time to go.

* * * *

They went to the store and bought Duncan a real pack to carry their gear in as well as some much-need provisions and a canteen for Mallory. Then they hit the road out of town, at first moving at a near run.

Mallory could tell that Duncan was a little sad about leaving because he was quiet and thoughtful. Duncan was rarely quiet, and Mallory wasn't sure Duncan really thought—at least not on the same level as he did.

"Did you have a good time last night?" Mallory asked.

"Yes," Duncan said with a stupid grin. "She was a nice girl."

"I'm sure."

"Do you have a girl friend somewhere, Mallory?"

"Good heavens no! I'm only sixty-five."

"Sixty-five?!" Duncan said.

"It's rather young for a dragon. I'm not sexually mature and with the way I've seen others act, I have no desire to hurry the process along. Females expect you to spend money on them, and they want things and…I can't imagine liking anyone enough to just give them my money. How much money did you spend last night anyway?"

"Everything I had," Duncan mumbled as he looked at his feet.

And Mallory then felt completely justified in not telling Duncan about the extra coins he had hidden in his cheek frill pouches. "Your problem, Duncan, is that you don't understand the value of money."

Duncan smiled stupidly again and said, "Oh I think I do, dragon. I think I do."

Mallory laughed and decided that from now on he'd never let Duncan carry more than a few coins at a time.

The human moaned. "I can tell you right now I'm not looking forward to sleeping on the ground tonight. One night in an inn sort of ruined all the 'glamour of the open road' for me."

"I hear you. Still, when our fortune is made we'll be able to stay in the finest hotels in the finest cities in this world," Mallory said. They turned a corner in the road. Noticing that here the road was only a few feet from the Sliding, Mallory was glad to see that Duncan didn't flinch, proving the human was putting his trauma behind him.

Suddenly ahead of them on the left side of the road there was a sign that brought Mallory to a complete stop.

"What's it say?" Duncan asked.

"It says boat for sale—cheap."

"Boat?" Duncan asked curiously.

"Don't you see, Duncan? A boat would be the perfect vehicle for us. All the towns are close to the river. We could ride the river, no more sore feet, and no road dust."

"Mallory, the river *slides*," Duncan reminded him.

"So, if you're in a boat you just slide along with it."

"I was originally hoping to catch a ride on a boat. Of course that was before the river slid with me on it. Still I suppose it must be safe or there would be wrecked boats all along the shores. It couldn't be as hard as riding in the back of a wagon." Duncan smiled then and slapped Mallory on the back. "I think I would like to own a boat."

They followed the road a ways. It got further from the river and they still hadn't seen any sort of boat. Mallory began to think that maybe it was an old sign and the boat had been sold long ago. Soon the river was obscured behind a row of thick trees and brush, and then there was another sign. This one also said boat for sale cheap, but this time "cheap" was in huge red letters. It pointed down a small dirt road.

They followed it for about five minutes and then they both gasped as they saw the most beautiful thing either of them had ever seen. It was a not-too-small, two-storied house boat with a big paddle wheel on the back.

They both stopped and just stared. Mallory immediately saw himself as a river-boat gambler with his own casino. Put in a few tables and a bar maybe.

"Imagine," Duncan said, a far away look in his eye. "Me at the wheel, a beautiful girl on each arm, the wind in my face and... There's no way we can afford it is there?"

"It says cheap," Mallory reminded.

"Cheap is still going to be fifty times what we have. It's a river boat for Pete's sake."

"Look, just keep your mouth shut and let me do the talking. Don't say a word."

Duncan nodded, but it was pretty clear from the look on his face that he thought it was a lost cause.

There was a shack not far from where the boat was docked and before they could even reach the door a bright pink creature with little short legs and arms longer than its whole body waddled over. Its arms stuck out of his head where its ears should have been. Its body and head were a rectangle with no real neck. Its eyes and mouth seemed sort of stuck on without anyone having thought about where they should go.

Mallory thought he'd seen about every kind of creature there was to see, but this thing was really different. He accepted one of the outstretched hands reluctantly but shook it.

Duncan, for his part, looked towards the boat, pretending not to notice the creature's out-stretched hand. After a moment, the creature lowered his hand.

"Are you here about the boat? Oh please tell me you're here about the boat," it said with a voice that sounded like it had a mouth full of marbles. Which it didn't.

Mallory was a little taken aback and he immediately started wondering just what was wrong with it. "Yes, we'd like to look at the boat."

The fact that this guy was in such a hurry to unload it meant it couldn't possibly be as clean on the inside as it was on the outside. Mallory tried to think of some clever way of finding out what was wrong with the boat but when he failed to think of anything he just asked, "What's wrong with the boat?"

"Ahh, nothing. Nothing at all is wrong with the boat. Nothing you can't see anyway. It needs to be painted of course, and it needs a good cleaning. That's all. I just need money for my mother's surgery. To tell the truth, I'm tired of sailing. In fact, I haven't had her out in years. Come on; let me show her to you. She's really a nice boat." The creature practically pushed them across the gangplank and onto the deck. "It's narrow, but the deck goes all the way round the living quarters on both stories."

The first story was broken into three rooms. At the stern was the engine room and the paddle wheel was behind that. Mallory noticed Duncan looking the engine over and wondered if he had any idea what he was looking at. He hoped the human did because he sure didn't.

Directly in front of the engine room was a small kitchen, and it looked like the kitchen stove was connected to the furnace that ran the steam engine that made the paddle wheel go. That made a lot of sense.

The kitchen was dirty and had a musty smell to it, but it had cabinets and a counter with a sink. Dirty could always be cleaned.

There was not a single piece of furniture on the ship, but so far Mallory wasn't seeing any reason for the man to want to sell the boat so badly. Surprisingly this only served to make him more suspicious. The man's story about his mother was not a terribly imaginative lie. There was nothing obviously wrong, no pieces falling off, no large holes with water running in. So whatever the problem was, it couldn't be seen and it must be huge.

The other room on the bottom floor was pretty big and totally empty except for a small bar that was bolted to the deck about two and half feet from the wall that separated this room from the kitchen. The bar wasn't much to look at—wooden with a front and top of some dark brown wood. It had a couple of shelves behind it as a back-bar. Still, the sight of it had Mallory once again seeing a floating casino with several tables for cards, maybe even a roulette wheel. Which would, of course, favor the house. But then they always did.

"They used to throw parties here. Go on fishing weekends and such," the creature showing them the craft said. Then it rushed them over to a set of stairs so narrow that Duncan had to walk up sideways and it was a tight squeeze for Mallory, too.

He wondered if the creature was aware that he'd said *they'd* thrown parties and not *he* had. He got the feeling the creature had seldom, if ever, used the boat. And if he hadn't, why not? After all, the boat looked far nicer than the shack the creature lived in.

Stopping on the second floor in a small block-type hallway the creature explained, "This is where all the bedrooms are. There are four of them and a bathroom." There was another set of stairs in the hallway and he started to go up those.

Mallory took hold of the creature's arm. "Wait a minute, my good fellow. Let us look around a bit." The creature looked annoyed but nodded and let them look around.

The four rooms were all small and filthy. The "bathroom" was beyond filthy. He doubted the shower had been used in years. And the "commode" was a hinged lid that opened to a hole that went all the way through the ship to the river below.

Duncan made a face, turned to Mallory and said, "And I was drinking out of the river." He gagged, and for a minute Mallory was sure Duncan was about to add some filth of his own to the boat.

Mallory made a face, too.

The creature then rushed them up to the wheel house, a small room on the very top of the boat. "Pretty straight forward. Stoke the furnace, pull the lever back to back up, push it forward to go forward. Then it's just adjust the speed and steer it one way or the other. This here lever pulls the anchor up and this one drops it down. So make me an offer I can't refuse."

He was in too big a hurry. Duncan must have realized it too because he asked, "Does the engine work?"

"Sure it does. You don't take me for a crook, do you?

"Not at all sir, but a shrewd business man can make fools out of simple folks like me and my friend," Mallory said, and made his way down the stairs. The others followed. "Could you give us a second to talk it over?" Mallory asked.

"Not much more than that," the fellow said, and he started tapping his foot as Mallory took Duncan into one of the bedrooms which—like the rest of the boat—lacked any actual furniture.

"What do you think?" Mallory asked.

"We're never going to be able to afford it," Duncan said.

"I don't think that's the real rub. Truth is, right now we have a lot of money and he's in an awful big hurry to unload it," Mallory said. "I don't think money's going to be a problem. I am a bit worried about what's wrong with the thing. It's too good to be true and I never trust things that are too good to be true."

"If we can really get it for what we've got, and if it doesn't sink, who cares?" Duncan said excitedly. "It's everything we need—transportation and a place to live."

"And see, Duncan my boy, that's why I'm the financial genius in this team. You leave it up to me. He's in a hurry to sell. Unless I get the sense that he's selling us something worse than the nothing we have now, I think we'll have us a boat. Go on out and look around the deck. Look forlorn and uncertain."

"How will that help?"

"For one thing it will make him think we aren't really that sure. For another... I'm not so sure we shouldn't be forlorn and uncertain."

The guy tried to get more money, but when Mallory told him the amount he offered was all they had—which it wasn't, but it was closer than he liked to play it—the guy had immediately yelled out, "Sold!"

He didn't even try to haggle after that, and the dragon's gut twisted because he knew, just knew, there was something seriously wrong with the boat.

He wanted the boat so bad he just made the part of his brain that kept telling him he was being cheated shut up. He paid the guy and took the title and receipt.

* * * *

Duncan looked down at the waves lapping against the side of the boat and day dreamed about everything they'd do and everywhere they'd go. He didn't know why he had no doubt that Mallory would get them the boat. He wasn't sure he approved of Mallory's methods most of the time, but this time he just didn't care as long as it meant sailing away the proud owners of this river boat.

Mallory joined him on the deck a few minutes later, and the look on his face told Duncan they'd not gotten the boat—which Duncan found surprised him more than a little.

"It was too much money?"

Mallory pulled a piece of paper out of his vest pocket and waved it in the air. "It's ours. He insisted we leave immediately." Mallory didn't look or sound happy, which puzzled Duncan more than a little because he was sure Mallory wanted the boat as much as he did—maybe even more.

The boat needed a lot of work, but so what? Most of it was as simple as sweeping and mopping. Anything beat sleeping out in the rain and cold.

Mallory hadn't quite finished folding the deed and putting it back in his vest pocket when the creature brought a wheelbarrow load of coal up and dumped it in the engine room, and then they could hear him making a fire. Mallory answered the puzzled look on Duncan's face.

"Before dark. Part of the deal is that we have to leave before dark. That couldn't be good. Something's definitely not right. Still, you roll the dice; you take your chances."

Duncan agreed it was strange that the creature insisted they be gone by dark. He even shared Mallory's belief that it couldn't be a good thing, but he didn't share Mallory's sudden lack of enthusiasm.

"Maybe he doesn't really own the boat," Duncan suggested.

Mallory shrugged. "Maybe. Why don't you go help him? Make sure the engine really works? Ask some questions and find out all you can about how it works."

Duncan nodded and headed for the engine room. He helped the creature stoke the fire in the boiler and then listened carefully as he told him how the engine worked. He started to leave and Duncan grabbed him by his shirt. "Wait a minute. You have to show us how to drive this boat."

"I already did. It's simple, self-explanatory really." He started to leave the boat again and this time Mallory, who had walked back in to the boat, put a hand on his shoulder.

"I'd still like you to show us," Mallory insisted.

Grudgingly the creature started up the stairs to the bridge. He showed them what did what and told them when to pull or push what. Then he started going down the stairs while Mallory and Duncan were still asking him questions.

Mallory looked at Duncan. "Do you know how to operate this boat?"

Duncan shrugged. "I'm not sure." He started to go after the guy, and then the boat lurched backwards and nearly knocked both of them off their feet.

Mallory looked out the window to see what had happened and it was clear that the creature had already lifted the gangplank and cast them off from the shore.

"Well you better get sure in a hurry because we're adrift," Mallory said, looking over his shoulder. "Well, don't just stand there! Do something."

"Why me? You were here too when he was telling us how to run the thing."

"Are you kidding me? I wasn't listening to him. Frankly I was way too busy trying to figure out why he was in such a hurry to sell this boat. You know, like he's in such a big hurry to be rid of it that he untied us from shore without so much as a 'Bye! See ya later.'"

Duncan looked at the pressure gauge—it read fifty percent—so he hit what he was sure was the reverse lever for the paddle wheel. He then pulled on the lever he believed put the steam power to the wheel and said a little prayer. The boat started backing away from the shore and soon he was pushing the lever forward and they were chugging down the river.

Duncan was glad it was as simple as it had seemed because otherwise they would have been lost without a clue. "Luck is smiling on us, Mallory. This thing is easy to sail."

"I don't know," Mallory said at his shoulder. "I'm afraid we just got hornswoggled. Look," he pointed out the window at the creature, who was dancing on the shore as they floated away. "That can't be good. There has to be something seriously wrong with this boat. Something we just haven't found yet."

"Quit saying that. You're just cynical, Mal. Maybe he's happy he has the money to save his sick mother."

"Yeah and I'm a house cat," Mallory mumbled.

Duncan didn't completely disregard what Mallory said, but he couldn't imagine anything was seriously wrong with the boat. The engine seemed to be chugging along fine and though they checked a dozen times, they didn't find any leaks. What else could possibly be wrong?

They made it quite a way down the river before it started to get dark. "You know what's odd? I haven't seen another boat all day."

Mallory nodded. "That is odd." He shrugged then said, "If there's any oil for the running lights I didn't find it, so we best get as close to the bank as we can and lay anchor for the night."

Duncan chuckled. "That's weigh, Mal."

"What?"

"It's *weigh* anchor."

"I don't see where that makes any more sense than lay."

Duncan nodded, thinking he had a point, and steered as close to the bank as he dared. Then he cut the power to the paddle wheel and dropped anchor for the night.

"How far do you think we got?" Duncan asked the dragon, who was busy trying to figure out how to use the stove in the galley.

Mallory shrugged. "No idea. Tomorrow we should look for a town. Go ashore and find out where we are. Maybe get a map of some kind."

"It wouldn't hurt to get a broom and some cleaning supplies. Maybe some cots and bedding and…."

Mallory stopped him, raising his hand. "We can't even buy a map until we find a game and get some more capital."

"You mean… You really gave him *all* our money?" Duncan said, not because he didn't think the boat was worth it but because he couldn't believe the dragon would allow himself to be penniless again.

"I have five coins left. What can I say? He asked for four times what we had which… Well, the fact that he went down to what he did without even arguing means there really is something badly wrong with this boat."

"You just keep saying that, but we haven't found anything yet. I still say maybe he stole the boat and the deed's no good," Duncan said.

Mallory laughed. "Then the joke's on him because I don't care about the legalities of the deed. However that would explain why the boat has no name on the hull." Mallory quit laughing. "It's not our problem. We didn't steal it and as they say, possession is nine tenths of the law. We have the boat. We have a deed that looks legal. No, my fear is that it's nothing that simple, Dunc."

"I think today was our lucky day."

Just then a huge rat jumped out of one of the cabinets and ran across the floor. Duncan jumped, landing with his arms around Mallory's neck and his feet on Mallory's left shoulder. The rat ran all the way across the kitchen and climbed through a hole in the wall. Then looking out the window they could see it run across the deck, jump into the water, and start swimming for the shore.

"See, now that couldn't be good," Mallory said, untangling Duncan from him.

"The…the stove made it hot in here. He's cooling off," Duncan suggested.

"Yes that's it. He got too hot in this galley, which is merely warm, and dove into the ice-cold river to cool off," Mallory said, shaking his head.

"He was probably afraid of us, that's all." Duncan straightened himself in an effort to find the dignity he'd just lost, and then said, "Well I for one am glad he's gone. I hate rats."

"Really? I never would have guessed. I'm not all that fond of them myself but the fact the rat didn't want to stay on the boat isn't a very good sign," Mallory said as he put a pot of water on the stove and added some dried peas to it.

When they first heard it—a low moaning sound like the wind only not quite—they looked at each other and both decided to ignore it. It was starting to get really dark and the only light was the fire coming through the narrow slits around the cook stove door.

Duncan remembered how insistent the creature that had sold them the boat had been that they leave before nightfall and now he started to worry. "I saw a couple of oil lamps hanging in one of the bedrooms. I'm going to go get them and see if there is any fuel in them."

"Good idea," Mallory said as he stirred the peas in the pot.

Duncan found three lights and brought them to the galley. He carefully dumped all of the fuel into one lamp. It was only half full and he had no idea how long the oil would last but he hoped a long time. He glared at the dragon. "Can you see in the dark?"

"Lots better than you can," Mallory gloated.

Just as they lost the last rays of the sun, Duncan got the lamp lit and the wick set so that it didn't smoke. Outside the night was as black as coal; inside, the little bit of light shining through the holes in the stove and the pathetic light from the one lamp did nothing but cast eerie shadows everywhere.

They had settled down on the floor to eat when that moaning sound came back. Only this time it was much louder. It didn't go away, either. Every minute it sounded less and less like wind, and more and more like some dead thing come back from the grave to eat their faces.

At least that's what it sounded like to Duncan. "I don't like the sound of that," he said.

"Probably just rigging rubbing with the movement of the boat and such," Mallory said, but Duncan was pretty that wasn't all there was to it.

Then there was a loud, piercing scream and he jumped, dumping half his pea soup down the front of his shirt. He looked at Mallory expectantly.

Mallory took in a deep breath and then let out a long, exasperated sigh. "See, I knew it. I knew it was too good to be true. Didn't I say that?"

"What on Overlap is that?" Duncan asked in a whisper.

"It sounds like a water demon—nasty, pompous little creatures with just enough magic to make themselves really annoying. They attach themselves to boats or docks, cause nothing but grief, and are impossible to get rid of. If that weren't bad enough, they're always tearing stuff up. That's probably why there is nothing left on the boat. If the previous owner had left anything in here, the demon would have torn it up."

"Is it dangerous?"

"Probably."

"Have you…have you seen one before?"

"No, but I've read about them and heard lots of stories. Face it. Most of the life on this planet lives on or near the river. It was just a matter of time till we ran into one. Of course it might have been nice to have had to deal with one on someone *else's* boat."

Duncan carefully put his pan of soup down, gulped and looked at Mallory. "What should we do?"

"Hope it lives on rats," Mallory shrugged.

"Seriously, Mallory, should we abandon ship?"

"How? Jump in the ice cold water and swim to the shore? And let us not forget that we just sank every coin we have into this boat." Mallory looked up then and lowered his voice. "I think the best thing is to just ignore it." The next shriek was louder than the first, but Mallory just kept eating his soup.

Duncan couldn't even think about eating, which showed how terrified he was. "You spent all my money on a boat with a demon living on it!"

"Our money. We're partners, remember?"

"My money, money I worked for. I was beat up by a monkey, I danced mostly naked. I trained creatures that wanted nothing better than to tear my face off…"

"It's a perfectly good boat."

"With a *demon* on it! We're doomed. It's all over. I was so young!"

"Quit being so dramatic. I don't know why you're making such a fuss. I told you there had to be something seriously wrong with this boat.

You're the one that said, 'How bad could it be?' Well it could be this bad."

The thing screamed again and this time the hair stood on the back of Duncan's neck. He found himself scooting closer and closer to Mallory until he was leaning against his right side.

"When you say little, Mallory…how little?" Duncan asked in a whisper.

"Oh not more than a couple of feet tall at the most."

Duncan started to relax then remembered that he'd been nearly drowned by creatures not much bigger than that and nearly killed by a tiny monkey.

"What sort of magic?"

"Mostly popping-up magic," Mallory said conversationally.

"Popping-up magic?"

"Yep. One minute nothing and the next minute *poof!* There it is. They can start out one place and pop up someplace else."

Duncan didn't like the sound of that. "Why aren't you afraid?"

"Because there's something both you and obviously the fellow who sold us this boat don't know about water demons that I do."

"I don't know anything that you didn't just tell me."

The shrieking had gotten louder so Duncan grabbed his sword and unsheathed it.

"Careful or you'll cut yourself. Besides like I told you, he can pop. Even a trained swordsman…"

"I'm trained," Duncan said loudly, hoping he might intimidate the demon.

"All right then, even a *good* swordsman wouldn't be able to strike him before he moved."

"How do we get rid of it?"

"We can burn the boat up. That's about the only way. See, he's permanently attached to the ship. He can't leave it and live. Once they attach themselves to something they're rather like a barnacle. They become part of the boat or dock and it becomes part of them. That's why they will tear up everything in a boat or on a dock but won't do anything to damage the boat or dock. In other words he has no problem tearing up stuff but he takes care of *his* stuff."

"Great. So the boat is worth nothing."

"Not unless we could find a couple of chumps as eager as we were to buy it from us. Then get rid of them before the demon becomes active at night. You see, water demons are completely nocturnal," Mallory said with a smile, and he didn't seem to be upset at all.

Till that moment Duncan would have thought that the one thing that might upset Mallory would be losing a bunch of money, but he still didn't seem upset at all.

"When's it going to show itself?" Duncan asked in a whisper.

"When it decides the shrieking isn't scaring us enough."

"Great. If I act really scared will it stay away?"

"I didn't know you were acting and probably not." Mallory shrugged.

"How will we know where he is going to appear?" Duncan asked, swinging his sword around and making Mallory duck to avoid being hit.

"Would you put that thing down before you hurt someone, namely me?"

Duncan admitted he was more likely to hit one of them than the creature, or even to scare it. He set his sword down on the deck but well within arm's reach. "How will we know where he is?" he asked again.

"We won't till he gets here, and then there will be a little popping sound, like pop corn sort of, only louder, and then there he'll be," Mallory said.

Duncan listened as hard as he could, but all he could hear was the strange shrieking that seemed to be coming from the boiler. "It's in there," Duncan whispered, pointing at the door to the engine room. "Maybe we should sneak up on it and…"

"What do you not understand about 'he pops'? You can't sneak up on it."

That certainly did nothing to put Duncan at ease. Just then he heard a loud pop-corn type noise, and then the creature was standing right in front of him. Duncan screamed, threw his hands over his face, and crawdad-crawled across the floor till his back hit a wall. He didn't even think to grab his sword and now it was all the way across the room from him. So even if he'd thought so before, he now knew that he was no warrior.

The creature laughed at him, and Duncan cringed.

It looked like a little red and orange devil. It was sixteen inches tall with horns like a bull atop its head that were nearly as big as it was, and a long tail like a lion which twitched in the air—not unlike Mallory's. It had little, beady red eyes, hardly any nose, and a mouth way too big for its face. Its huge mouth was filled with little pointed teeth.

"What are you doing on my boat?" it growled in a voice so small Duncan got the impression he'd ruined his voice with all his screaming.

Duncan looked at the water demon through a slit between his fingers. "Now look here, demon. This is our boat. We bought it. Show him the papers, Mal."

"You own nothing!" it thundered in a big, deep voice, very unlike the one he'd used only a moment before and more like what Duncan expected from a demon.

Mallory cleared his throat, reached out a clawed finger, and tapped on the tiny demon's shoulder. The demon turned and saw the dragon for the first time. Mallory snorted, blew a little puff of smoke in the demon's face and said a low throaty, *"Boo!"*

The tiny creature screamed in a shrill voice, then there was a loud pop and it was gone leaving a steaming pile of green yuk in its wake. Duncan looked at Mallory and the dragon smiled.

"Come on man. Think about it. Dragon trumps water demon every time. No sword can catch him, but dragon fire is another story. All I'd have to do is fire up the furnace and we'd have fried demon on the deck."

He should have known Mallory had something up his sleeve. "Would it have killed you to just tell me that?" he snarled at the dragon.

"No. But then I would have missed out on seeing you squirm and cry like a child."

"I didn't cry."

"If you say so," Mallory laughed, then yelled, "Foul beast! You get back here this minute and clean up your mess. Or the next time I see you I will cook you and feed you to this human."

With a pop the creature was back with a tiny mop and bucket, and it started cleaning up the mess with one watchful eye on the dragon.

"Why don't you just kill it and put it out of our misery?" Duncan asked in disbelief. The demon turned quickly, cut him a look, hissed, and Duncan cringed.

"It has as much right to live as you or I do."

"Hello, it's a demon."

"That's just a name. Probably one of your kind gave it."

"Because it looks like it came from hell."

"It's a creature just like you and me, whose ancestors were deposited on Overlap in the same way. Besides," Mallory turned his attention to the demon, "you aren't going to cause us any trouble are you? Terrorize us or tear up our stuff?"

"What stuff?"

The dragon glared at the demon and let a little puff of smoke curl out of his mouth. "Let me ask again. You aren't going to be any sort of problem are you, demon?"

The creature shook his head quickly. "I be good," it said in its tiny voice.

"I doubt it knows what that means," Duncan mumbled. The thing gave him the creeps. It had cleaned up the mess and popped away mop, bucket and all, and there was real quiet for the first time since it got dark. "Come on, Mal," Duncan said in a whisper, "isn't this carrying your non-violent thing a bit far?"

"He's more afraid of us…excuse me, me, than we're…excuse me… you're afraid of him." He looked troubled then. "It does, of course, mean we can't get a good price if ever we decide to sell the boat, because we'd have to sell it quick. Of course I'm in no hurry to sell the boat. What about you?"

"Now it has that thing on board, you bet I want to sell it…" And that's when it hit him. Mallory couldn't sell the boat as long as the creature was on board. At least not for any more than they'd paid for it. Mallory wouldn't want to sell the boat unless he could make a profit. It would go against the very fiber of Mallory's being.

In order to sell the boat he'd have to break his own non-violent rule and kill the demon thing. So if Mallory could control the demon this might actually work in Duncan's favor. "Can you really make it leave me alone? Not tear our stuff up?"

"Of course," Mallory said. "Most things can get along if they just open a channel of civil conversation."

Mumbling about the sort of financial genius who bought a boat with a demon on board, Duncan moved back to where he'd left his soup and started eating. He kept only half an eye and ear open for the little popping demon.

"If you think about it, this really is rather good fortune," Mallory said.

"How do you figure?" Duncan asked.

"Normally thugs and thieves come out at night, right?"

"Right."

"Who's going to steal this boat or mess about on it with the water demon on board?"

Duncan started to agree then glared at the dragon. "Yes, yes, I suppose next you'll be all about telling me how we should have paid much more money for such a nice boat with such a helpful demon on board."

"Precisely," Mallory said with a laugh.

Outside the wind started blowing harder, but while he could hear it, he couldn't feel it except in the gentle swaying of the boat. He knew it was cold outside, but he was warm. Then it started to rain and he wasn't getting wet. Duncan began to think that, all things considered, sharing their space with the demon was a small price to pay for such comfort.

Then there was a loud clap of thunder and the next thing he knew, the demon had popped up mere inches in front of him, and he quickly decided he'd rather be both cold and wet.

"Afraid of the storm?" Mallory asked the creepy thing, and it nodded. "Then sit down. Mind you, you'd best behave or I'll have to fry you."

It nodded again, and then said in its deep, terrifying voice, "I be good."

"Would you like some soup?" Mallory asked.

"Don't feed it!" Duncan shrieked.

"Why, because it will stay?" Mallory asked with a sarcastic grin. "I told you we can't get rid of it, so we might as well be civil. Who's to say they don't act the way they do because no other creature ever treats them with kindness." Mallory handed the demon what was left of his soup, and it sucked it up greedily.

"No, we just like to scare things," the demon said with a shrug.

"Because they're creepy," Duncan muttered, and Mallory ignored him.

"What's your name?" he asked the Demon.

The demon belched as loudly as any full-grown human, and then said in its small voice, "Fred."

"Fred!" Duncan said in disbelief. He laughed. "His name is Fred?"

"That is what he said," Mallory replied. "It's a perfectly good name."

"Fred is a good name for a demon?"

"Can you think of a better one?"

"Beelzebub, Lucifer, what about Brimstone?"

"That's your problem, Duncan. You always want to type-cast everyone," Mallory said to him. Then to the water demon, "Fred's a fine name."

"Thanks. I was named after my father." Again with the deep voice, and Duncan realized that the creature's voice changed with each sentence out of his mouth which was more than disconcerting.

"That's nice," Mallory said.

"Not really. He was a jerk," Fred said.

"My name is Mallory and my friend's name is Duncan."

Duncan grumbled, nodded in the demon's general direction, then stood up and grabbed his blanket from the pile where Mallory had dumped all his stuff. He picked a place close to the stove, spread his blanket on the floor, lay down and rolled himself up in it. He tried to get comfortable and realized that the only thing harder than the ground was a wooden floor.

He wanted to tell Mallory and his new "friend" to shut up so he could get some sleep. Since he was glad the demon wasn't screaming any more, he just slung his arms up to cover his ears and tried to get comfortable.

They had just started talking about the evils of prejudice and people's misguided preconceptions when Duncan was finally able to block their voices. He was warm and dry, and outside it was raining and cold. It wasn't too surprising that he fell asleep thinking more about the great boat he owned than the water demon he had to share it with.

Six

S adie and Bilgewater sat at a back table where they had been playing for peanuts with some of the locals for several days. They still hadn't made enough money to pay the bar tab and hotel bill they had racked up during their stay.

Bilgewater was wearing his black slacks, a white shirt with puffy sleeves, and a silver and black brocade vest. His sleeves were held up with black and red garters and the jacket that matched the vest was hanging on the back of the chair he sat in. Sadie was also dressed in her showy best, a brown and gold calico dress with long sleeves ending in tight cuffs, a high collar, tight waist, and pearl buttons that ended just below the waist. Around her neck she wore a beautiful pink and cream colored cameo that she told people her grandmother had given her on her deathbed. In point of fact, she'd won it in a card game. If things didn't get better soon Sadie had said she would have to part with grandma's cameo just to pay their bills.

Bilgewater admitted that if people knew them well it would have been their worst tell. The more desperate for cash they were the flashier they dressed in an effort to create an illusion of success.

Fortunately no one really knew Bilgewater or Sadie well.

They were in a bit of a pickle. They weren't making any money where they were and they couldn't afford to move on. It was nearly winter and they were looking at the very real prospect of finding themselves out in the cold. Or worse yet, having to find actual jobs.

They'd have to move on down the road even to do that. There was nothing for them where they were.

It was a farming community, and there weren't many jobs once winter came. Usually the town was a good mark this time of year. Harvest time was over. The locals' pockets were usually full. It was getting cold out and there was little to do, so the farmers were bored and inclined to gamble and drink. The more they drank, the more they were sure they were going to win a big pot, and the more they were sure they were about to clean up, the easier it was to win their money.

Bilgewater and his partner felt obliged to help the farmers part with their flexible income. But this year some blight had cut the farmers' profits in half and the inhabitants of this village had very little extra cash. They were, in fact, mostly playing cards with men who were risking what little they had for the chance of making enough coin to get them through the rest of the winter.

It took all of the fun out of it.

They had talked about sneaking away in the night without paying either their bar or lodging bill. But the tighter money, was the less likely business men were to let you get away without paying them.

Besides, it really went against… Well not so much his but Sadie's nature. Of course so did getting poor farmers to gamble away their last dollar, which was why they weren't doing so well.

The other thing was, when you lived the way they did. it was a bad idea to leave bridges burning in your wake. After all, you could never be sure where you might end up again.

He was about ready to fold for the night when the door opened and a short, orange, square-looking creature walked in grinning from… Well, arm to arm. Bilgewater had seen a lot of these beings in his time in the town. They seemed to match the plant life and animal species here, so he was pretty sure that they were the original inhabitants of this piece of Overlap.

Bilgewater still had no idea at all where they kept their ears.

There was something about the way he carried himself. Something about his very nature that let Bilgewater know the creature had just come into some serious coin.

He leaned over to catch Sadie's ear and said, "Let's get out of this game." He pointed with his head towards the stranger who had just walked in. Sadie nodded, so she must have seen the gleam in the man's eyes as well.

He and Sadie claimed the game had gotten too rich for them and folded. They moved to a table close to where the creature was perched and ordered a couple of drinks and a meal.

"I ain't seen you smile like this in years, Growler," the bartender, who was the same sort of creature as the man he spoke to, said.

"Ain't had me a reason to. Ever since that grifter stuck me with that haunted boat my life's been a living hell. That demon has tormented me every night on the boat or off it." He turned to Bilgewater as if he were an old friend and said, "Water demons are tied to a boat, but that doesn't keep them from popping up on the deck and screaming all night long. Worse than a cat in season. "

He turned back to the bartender. "That boat and that demon aren't my problem no more. I sold it to a couple of yokels for three times what I thought I'd get. I feel sorry for them, but let the buyer beware, right?"

"Cha-ching!" Sadie whispered in Bilgewater's ear.

"Cha-ching indeed." Bilgewater smiled back. He got up and moved to the bar to sit beside the "lucky" fellow. "My good man, it sounds like you have had quite a stroke of luck. I'd like to buy you a drink to celebrate your good fortune."

"Thank you kindly, sir, but I insist… Let me buy you a drink. After all, I have plenty of money," the talking rectangle said.

"You are a gentleman, there is no doubt. Let me introduce myself. The name's Bilgewater, and this is my friend, Sadie. And you are?"

"Growler, just Growler. Drink for the little lady, too, Bruster," he said, turning back to the bartender. Bilgewater noticed Sadie's lip twitch just a little at the "little lady" line, but she just grinned and bore it.

She was a pro. There was no doubt. Knowing Sadie, she'd take her vengeance at the card table. Of course it was up to Bilgewater to get Growler to the card table.

* * * *

Bilgewater didn't have to dust off many tricks. It really wasn't all that hard. A few drinks and Growler was easily talked into a friendly game of poker. It was even easier to talk two of the fellows they'd been playing with earlier into the game when Bilgewater informed them of Growler's good fortune.

It was possible—and often much smarter—to make sure that everyone but the real mark made some money at the table. Spread the wealth and people were less likely to run you out of town with pitchforks and torches or let others do so.

Growler wasn't in much worse a mood after he'd lost a couple of hands than he had been before and he turned out to be a super-chatty guy. "So how long you two been married?" he asked.

Sadie and Bilgewater exchanged a look that said they couldn't think of a much more disgusting prospect. Then they said with one voice, "We aren't married."

"I'm sorry. I just assumed. Same species, different sex…"

"We're just friends," Bilgewater said.

"Sometimes not even that," Sadie said with a sly smile.

Bilgewater laughed. "Yes, like when you take my money like you just did." Of course, he and Sadie were partners. At the end of the night they always split whatever they made. That wasn't something the other players needed to know.

Bilgewater suddenly wondered exactly why he and Sadie had never been more than friends. She was attractive enough for sure, long brown hair, bright green eyes, a rocking body and delicate features. She never failed to turn heads.

Then he knew why. Bilgewater was a ladies' man. He knew how to use his dark, brooding brown eyes, his curly black hair, the stubborn cut of his rugged jaw, his swarthy complexion. He was an elegant man—at least when it came to dress and his way with the ladies. Bilgewater knew how to charm women and they loved him, there was no doubt.

Unfortunately any time he'd had a romantic relationship with a woman it had ended badly. Usually with some woman he'd nearly loved screaming that she never wanted to see him again and wished he were dead. He'd never tried to get romantically involved with Sadie because he knew it would just be a matter of time till she was screaming that she hated him and wished he was dead.

Sadie was a good partner and his only true friend. She was the only person he trusted and he was pretty sure she was the only person with any sense that had ever trusted him—which might be more important.

Sadie, for her part, insisted they leave wherever they were any time any man started talking in terms of more than a day. Bilgewater had once thought he was going to lose his partner to love but instead she had come to him in the middle of the night and insisted they leave immediately.

"Why?" Bilgewater had asked. "I thought…"

"I have no desire to be anyone's wife or mother. I don't want to have to count on anyone else or have them count on me. Now let's go." Then she grinned and held up a pouch full of coins. "I took all his money and I'm sure he's going to be ticked when he wakes up."

"Why'd you rob him?"

"I didn't rob him. He said I could have all that was his."

"Sadie, you know that's not what he meant."

"Look at it this way, he offered me more than I took," Sadie said, but there was a tear in her eye, and he knew what she wasn't saying. She took money from him so that he wouldn't be heart broken, just mad.

Someone, sometime, had broken her heart. She'd told him as much but never said who, how or why. The details didn't matter. Such things made people who they were.

What life had made Bilgewater and Sadie into allowed them to be friends and partners, to enjoy a lifestyle few people understood.

Bilgewater wanted to change the subject so he did. "So just who were the geniuses you sold your demon-haunted boat to?"

"A couple of greenies from out of town. Way out, if you know what I mean."

"I'm not sure I do," Sadie said.

"A great blue dragon and a big dark-headed guy with a bad hair cut. Fellow looked like a Romancer by the way he dressed and the sword he carried. Mind you don't see many of them this far down river."

Sadie took in a breath but said nothing as she and Bilgewater exchanged a curious look. Growler went on. "Anyway, they were excited to have the boat. Had a pocketful of money and just handed it right over. I made them take off way before dark, so now they're out on the river somewhere listening to that awful thing screaming and tearing up their stuff. I have all their money and I'm finally rid of my curse." He laughed loudly and happily.

By morning Growler was out of money but he still didn't have a demon filled boat. So as Sadie took the last of the money Duncan and Mallory had paid him, he was still surprisingly cheerful. Bilgewater and Sadie both agreed that wouldn't likely be the case when the creature slept off his liquor.

The gamblers paid their debts, saddled up, and hit the road before the talking rectangle could wake from his booze-induced comma.

"Where to?" Sadie asked Bilgewater as they hit the end of the town and there was a fork in the road.

"For now, let's follow the river. Who knows? We may run into the dragon and his friend again. At the very least we'll find a better town to winter in."

Sadie nodded in agreement. "I can't believe Mallory let himself get grifted like that. I think you could sell that dim wit Duncan magic beans, but Mallory?"

"I don't know who grifted whom. Less than two hundred coins between what the other guys and we won, and we cleaned him out, I'm sure of it. So Duncan and Mallory bought themselves a steam-powered river boat for less than two-hundred coins. That's quite a deal."

"But there's a demon on board."

"Think about it my dear. If you're a seven-foot tall dragon and a huge guy with a sword are you going to be afraid of a small water demon?"

Sadie laughed, "No, I suppose not."

* * * *

Mallory stretched and woke up with a kink in his tail. He wondered briefly what they should do next. He noticed Duncan had already gotten the fire going and thought about what they might eat for breakfast.

The human walked into the kitchen—where they had both spent the night—carrying two fish already cleaned and ready to be cooked. Duncan stopped, looking at the stove, and Mallory could almost read his mind. "I'll figure out a way to cook them if I can have one."

"Wait a minute! I thought you were a vegetarian."

"I am, but I eat fish…"

"Fish isn't a vegetable," Duncan said in a taunting tone.

"True." Mallory thought about it for a minute. How did he justify eating fish? He smiled. "But when fish look at you, they don't know what you are. They don't look at you and think, 'Why are you doing this to me?'"

"You don't know that! Maybe that's exactly what they think when you pull them out of the water," the human said.

Mallory didn't like thinking about that at all. He'd rationalized in his own mind why it was all right to eat fish and he didn't want Duncan to ruin it for him. "You gonna share your fish or not?"

The human smiled and handed the fish to Mallory. "I'll share."

Mallory opened the oven door and stuck them on the rack inside. They cooked quickly if not so completely.

Duncan sat down on the floor to eat his fish. Mallory simply took the whole fish and put it in his mouth. Then he started chewing it up—bones and all. He delighted in the crunching sound the bones made and watched with mild amusement the look of disgust mixed with a thread of terror that crossed the human's face.

He swallowed then smiled at his friend and said, "Now aren't you glad I don't eat meat?"

"I should think so! Absolutely."

The rest of the day they floated down the river with Mallory steering as Duncan tried to figure out why the engine wasn't working. At one point Mallory heard pinging and then cussing. He didn't know whether that meant things were getting fixed or more broken. He wasn't worried. The river flowed at a good pace and the boat was easy to steer.

He again wondered why he didn't see any other boats. This far down river, the traffic should be pretty heavy. Also he hadn't seen a single town and that made even less sense. It was puzzling and a little disconcerting to him, though he couldn't say exactly why it made him so uncomfortable.

The boat hit a good current and started going pretty fast. Mallory felt really good about that until he realized that in order to slow the boat down you had to be able to put the paddle wheel in reverse. Which they couldn't do if the engine wasn't working.

Duncan came bounding up the stairs and took the wheel from Mallory. "We have to steer the boat out of the current, closer to shore," the human said, fighting with the wheel. The boat didn't want to turn, no doubt because it was enjoying the current so much. Mallory moved to help Duncan, taking hold of the wheel and putting all his shoulder in to it.

They succeeded in turning the boat. It lurched hard to starboard, followed by a crunching sound and a thump. They went flying into the back wall of the wheelhouse where they landed with a thud on their butts.

When they climbed to their feet Mallory still wasn't sure what had happened. He figured out pretty quickly that they'd run aground because land was looking awful close and personal. And they were sitting on about a thirty-five degree angle.

"Well that sucked pond scum," Duncan said.

"At least that," Mallory mumbled.

They climbed down the stairs and out onto the deck where they could see the front of the boat pushing against a small tree. The tree had bent almost double when the boat hit the shore.

"I guess we should see if there was any damage to the hull," Duncan suggested.

"How?" Mallory asked.

"I suppose we get in and swim around, looking and feeling around for a hole." The human shrugged as if to say, *I've never run a boat aground before, I'm just guessing. You got any better ideas?* Mallory didn't, so he shucked his vest as Duncan took off his tunic.

He looked at Duncan expectantly.

"You take that side and I'll take this side," Duncan said, and jumped into the water. Mallory knew the water was going to be cold, so he steeled himself and slid in.

He swam around his side, feeling around, diving under, and checking till he was sure he'd freeze to death. He and Duncan both got back on the boat at the same time. They ran to stand by the kitchen stove, learning in the process that they couldn't both get through the door at once.

Duncan looked at Mallory and chuckled through chattering teeth, "You must be cold. You're blue."

"Ha, ha. Did you find any damage?" Mallory asked.

"No, did you?"

"No."

"We were lucky," Duncan said, his lips nearly as blue as Mallory. "I say if we get the boat off dry land we head for someplace warmer. I don't think I've ever been in water that cold in my life."

Mallory nodded in agreement. "If we go far enough we might even hit a part of the world where it's still summer."

After they warmed up Duncan put on dry pants and shirt. Mallory didn't put his vest back on since he didn't want to destroy it. They climbed onto the land to try and push the boat off, but that was mostly a huge waste of time and energy.

"What now?" Mallory asked.

Duncan looked cold and more than a little defeated. "As luck would have it I had just finished the repair to the engine when we started going too fast and it dawned on me that without the engine we couldn't slow the boat down."

Mallory nodded. "We probably both came to that conclusion at the same time, not that it helps us now. What was wrong with the engine anyway?"

"The thingy was all gerfunkted and the mishtagog was out of line with…"

"You don't know, do you?" Mallory asked, remembering that his friend was a self-confessed tinkerer.

"Of course I do! I just don't know the names of the parts. There was this bar, and it had a bend in it, and it wasn't supposed to… I don't think. It was supposed to be attached to this other thing, but with it bent, it wouldn't reach, so I took it off and hit it with a hammer till it was straight again. Hey, you know, if the engine is fixed, I could try the paddle wheel in reverse and see if it can pull us off the shore."

"That's an idea. I'll tell you what. I'll stand here and push. It couldn't hurt, right?"

"Right." Duncan jumped back onto the boat and headed for the engine room. Mallory took a deep breath and looked up at the sky. "A little help here."

A few minutes later Mallory heard the engine start. He could see that the paddle wheel was engaged, so he put his shoulder to the bow of the boat and pushed as hard as he could. A few minutes later he was knee deep in mud, the paddle wheel stopped with a loud clang, and the boat was still stuck on land.

Duncan showed up with two pieces of something that was obviously supposed to be one piece.

"That doesn't look good," Mallory said, making a face.

"The thingy snapped right in two. We need a new one," Duncan said with a sigh. "Who knows how many times it has been straightened? It was weak; you can only bend metal just so many times before it breaks."

Mallory nodded as if he understood that. "Great," he said. Which it wasn't at all.

He reluctantly cleaned off in the cold water and then climbed up on the deck. They walked back into the kitchen to warm up, and as they did a plume of black smoke puffed out of the cook stove. "Beautiful." Mallory sighed. And again it really wasn't at all. He played with the damper on the pipe till the smoke stopped.

"As long as we can't fix the engine we might as well be stuck, since we can't actually run the boat without it. If only the shyster who sold us this piece of crap had actually spent even a second telling us how it really works."

"But we know why he didn't," Mallory said. A thought suddenly came to him, and he immediately felt like an idiot. "You know who probably knows more about this boat than anyone?" It was obvious from the look on the human's face that he didn't. "Fred! He's been attached to this boat most of his life."

"Who says he'd tell us if he knew?" Duncan asked.

"It's in his best interest for the boat to be kept up and running," Mallory said. "Plus, he and I have an understanding."

"As long as I don't have to deal with him," Duncan said.

* * * *

They had gone to the wheel house and from there they walked out on the upper deck. They spent the better part of an hour looking and listening, but they neither heard nor saw any sign of a town nearby or any other traffic on the river.

They were about to go back inside when first they heard and then saw a small boat. "Get inside and get down," Duncan ordered.

"Why?" Mallory asked.

"Why? Because you're a big blue dragon, and some folks find that a little off putting."

Mallory mumbled something about small-minded people's preconceived notions. He went inside and got out of sight anyway.

Duncan jumped up and down, flagging his arms around wildly, yelling, "Hey you there!" till he got their attention. The boat pulled up along side and he was relieved to see that it was humans—so maybe he was prejudiced, too.

"Run aground?" the one at the wheel of the small boat asked.

Well duh, sprang to mind as an answer to this rather stupid question, but since he needed their help, Duncan just explained with a tiny lie. "Our engine broke, we got caught in a quick current and we were forced to run aground." It sounded better than "We ran our boat aground because we don't know anything about it."

"Do you need a tow off land then?" he asked.

Duncan thought about that for a second. It wouldn't do them much good till they had a new part for their engine. They'd have to anchor and stay close enough to shore to put down their gangplank, but at least then they'd be level and ready to go if they could find or fix the part. "That would be great, thanks." He started to go back inside but then turned and asked, "You guys afraid of dragons?"

"The sacking-villages kind or the accountant type?" the captain of the boat asked.

"The second kind."

"Nope, one of them does my taxes."

* * * *

Duncan met the captain of the other boat on the deck and introduced him to Mallory. The captain's name was Anthony. A rather short roundish man, Anthony walked to the bow of the ship and looked down. "You aren't hung up bad. We ought to be able to break you free pretty easy."

"Thank you very much," Mallory said. "What about the engine part?" Duncan held it up so Anthony could see it.

Anthony clicked his tongue and said, "You need a new part. As old as this boat is you'll likely as not have to have it made. Bad place to break down. There isn't anything approaching a decent machinist around here for a hundred miles." He chuckled a little. "Yup, you couldn' ah picked a much worse place ta break down. This has gottah be the most backwards sector on all Overlap. Your only chance is to find someone with a forge and have 'em make you something that will work good enough to get you out of here."

"If I could find a forge I could fix it myself I think. Maybe I could even make a new part," Duncan said.

Anthony looked him over carefully. "You aren't…you aren't a tinkerer are ya?" Anthony asked a hint of agitation entering his voice.

"No, oh no," Mallory said quickly. "My friend is a licensed professional."

"Oh well, that's different then, isn't it?"

"Could you maybe take us up river or down to find a forge?"

Anthony laughed. "You fellows don't have any idea where you are, do ya?"

Duncan looked at Mallory and Mallory looked at Duncan. Duncan knew he didn't and from the short time he'd known him, he'd learned that Mallory had an even worse sense of direction than he did.

Duncan watched as a lie started to form on Mallory's lips but then he obviously realized that wasn't going to help them, so he swallowed his pride and said, "No, we've just been going down river. You know, just two adventurers going with the flow."

"Well the flow just landed you in Winterhurst, the coldest, and most backwards sector on all of Overlap. And we're about fifteen minutes from winter," Anthony said, laughing. "I'd love to help you boys out, but my boat is way too small to pull yours any distance. The truth is I shouldn't be out here now. Seems like you and I are the only ones crazy enough to be on the river in these parts this time of year. I'm just picking up a couple of more nets—hopefully full of fish—and then I'm heading back up river, away from the coming storm. I won't be back down this way till things warm up again.

"Fishing's good On the Sliding West, no doubt, but I don't come this way often and never in the real cold."

"We can just wait for another boat," Mallory said, shrugging.

"When's the last time you seen a boat, fella? Didn't ya hear what I said? Only a fool would be on the river today." Anthony shook his head and laughed. "Nope, you couldn't have landed in a much worse place, being a dragon with a broken boat and all. There's a big storm heading this way in the next couple of days. Everyone who runs the river knows that. Nope, there won't be another boat down this way till spring thaw."

"Are we at least in walking distance of a town?" Mallory asked.

"When's the last time you boys saw a town?"

"Not for a while," Duncan said, thoughtfully.

"Are you saying all the towns are inland?" Mallory asked.

"Several miles inland. Folks that live around these parts are so backwards they're afraid of the river because it slides," Anthony said, moving to tie a tow rope he was thrown by his crew to the back of their boat. Duncan helped him. He looked at Duncan, "You'll be damn lucky to find a decent forge, much less anything else. If I were you I'd just count on being here till spring. Then you'll be able to hitch a ride with someone going down stream and find someone heading back up through these parts."

"But there is always traffic on the Sliding. Always," Mallory said, confused.

"Didn't you hear what I said? Boy, you guys really don't have any idea where you are. This ain't exactly the Sliding." He pointed across the river. "That there is an island. It's smack in the middle of the river. The only slides on the other side. This here is the Sliding West, and it don't slide…"

"Wait a minute, wait just a minute. If this part of the river doesn't slide why are the locals afraid of it?" Mallory asked.

"I told you they was backwards. Hill folks. Real superstitious. Look, beyond that big block of land is the Sliding. You guys done wound up on the wrong side." He laughed again. He sure did think their predicament was funny. "Didn't you notice the river got smaller?"

"I just thought it did. I mean everything's always changing on Overlap, the plant life, the animals, the soil, the people," Mallory said.

"Yeah, well the river got smaller 'cause that island splits it in two." Anthony laughed again. "You all hang on now. Go ahead boys! Give her a good, hard pull." Duncan hung on and with one good pull their boat was free. Mallory went and dropped the anchor.

"Thank you very much," Duncan said. "Could we maybe get a ride with you guys back to civilization?"

"Sorry, boat's hardly big enough for the crew I've got and the fish I'll pick up. Less of course you could pay for the fish I can't haul."

Duncan sighed. "I'm afraid all we have to our names is five coins."

"Sorry, wish I could do more, but I gotta think about me an' my crew first. You understand I'm sure. Tell you what. If you're still here when I start running my spring nets I'll give you a lift up stream to a good machinist I know."

"Thanks," Duncan said and waved, watching helplessly as the other boat roared away.

Mallory joined him and Duncan snapped, "Could you not see that the river was splitting?"

Mallory looked at him like he'd gone right around the bend. "Don't get pissy with me. It didn't split on my watch. Even if it had I can't say I would have known which was the river and which was the side-thingy, and neither would you. I think it split somewhere above where we bought the boat. One of the times when we couldn't see the river."

"Oh, that makes sense," Duncan said, the wind taken out of his sails a bit. "So what now?"

"Do you think you can put that piece…what did you call it?"

"The thingy."

"Do you think you can put the thingy back together? Fix it?"

"Not without a forge. Even then I'm not sure a weld would hold. There is a lot of tension on that piece," Duncan said. He thought about it a minute and then added, "I'm sure I could build a new thingy. It's a simple enough piece. If I had the right piece of metal…but again I'd need a forge and an anvil."

"Could you hobble it together good enough that it will get us out of here?"

"You mean like stick it back together with sticks and rope and such?"

"Yes."

"No. It wouldn't get us three feet," Duncan snapped back. "There is a lot of tension on the thingy."

"Don't jump on me for being ignorant. I'm not the one who named a vital part of our boat the *thingy*," Mallory said calmly. "Now let's think for a moment. It's true we have no idea how we got where we are. However that doesn't mean our friend Anthony has told us the *truth* about *where* we are."

"Huh?"

Mallory talked slower. "Look, he and his crew, they just kept laughing. I realize our predicament would be funny if it wasn't happening to us, but how do we know that he didn't tell us all that stuff about where we are and how dire our circumstances are as some sort of sick joke?"

"Why would he?" Duncan asked.

"For fun? I don't know. I'm just saying…"

"Then where are all the towns? I haven't seen any. You haven't, either. It's been most of two days," Duncan said.

"Then he might be wrong about the river traffic, and someone might come by who can help us and…"

"Alright, Mal. You know what? You're right. Maybe someone might come by. Meanwhile, we don't have enough food to last a week, winter's coming, it's already cold, we have no way of knowing how long we'll be stuck here, and…"

"Geez! Could you whine any more than that? Buck up, little camper. Tell you what. I'll stay and watch for any sign of a town or a ship. I have better eyesight and better hearing than you do. You scout around close and see what, if anything, besides fish there is to eat and see if you see any sign that people have been around."

"What sort of sign, Mal?"

"I don't know. An old fire pit, a road, a little girl selling cookies…"

Duncan really wanted to be mad, but what Mallory said made sense. "Ah…all right then, let's do that!" He stomped to the gangplank and released it, letting it fall ashore with a loud plop, just because.

"Do you feel better?" Mallory asked.

"A little." Duncan walked down the gangplank and started walking around looking for anything that might be useful and any signs of man. He found several edible plants and a bunch of rabbit-type animals that weren't really rabbits but weren't much like anything else he'd seen, so he just called them rabbits. He was pretty sure they'd be yummy cooked—maybe with a nice sauce. He found bamboo and cattails and lots of deadfall wood, but after several hours of finding stuff and dragging it back to the boat, what he hadn't found was any sign of intelligent life.

He was about to give up looking and just collect food and wood when he saw something through the trees that looked promising—a small clearing. He walked towards it, almost running when he saw sections of log twelve inches around and about two feet in length which had clearly been saw cut. Someone had been here cutting wood, and maybe they'd come back for these.

But as he looked them over he could tell they weren't recently cut. In fact, when he rolled one around to see how hard it would be to move all the bark fell off, so the wood had been cut several seasons back. Still it meant civilization couldn't be too far away.

He hefted a couple of the sections onto his shoulders and hauled them back to the boat.

He walked in with them just in time to see Mallory trying to push his way through all the greenery and wood Duncan had collected through the day. The main room on the bottom deck was now completely full except for the area behind the bar.

"What on earth are you doing?" Mallory asked, spitting some bamboo leaves out of his mouth. It was only then that Duncan realized that he'd just been grabbing anything and everything that might be even the least bit useful.

"Preparing?" Duncan explained with a smile and a shrug. "I guess I freaked out a little."

"Maybe just a little," Mallory said as he pushed his way into the kitchen.

"Look, I brought us chairs," Duncan said, carrying in the two massive pieces of tree and setting them on the kitchen floor. Mallory looked at them and nodded approvingly.

"Some place to sit is always nice. The bedrooms have small closets. I checked them all and found quite a haul—three half-burned candles, a few empty tin cans, a couple of old rags, and a dead rat. I decided not to keep that—just stuck it in the boiler fire."

"That's probably best." Duncan laughed.

"I found a whole box of short rolls of wire." Mallory held up one of the small rolls and Duncan smiled.

"That's spent bailing wire." He nodded, thinking of lots of things he could do with that.

"And there was this." Mallory held up a small, rather rusty metal tackle box. Before Mallory could say more, Duncan grabbed it out of his hands and opened it. There wasn't much, but there were half a dozen rusty hooks and a bunch of line. The horrible panic Duncan had been feeling left him.

"There's a medicine chest and a closet in the bathroom, but there was nothing there as good as the dead rat. I didn't see or hear any hint of a boat, and no smoke from any town. Of course that doesn't mean there isn't one, just means we're in no position to see the smoke from its chimneys where we're at."

"It's all right. I've been in much worse spots," Duncan said, more to comfort himself than anything else. Which was why what Mallory said next was just all wrong, and not what he wanted to hear at all.

"Maybe," Mallory shrugged. "Truth is we don't really know what we're in for, do we?"

His statement annoyed Duncan more than a little. "That being the case, would it have killed you to just agree?"

Mallory laughed. "Killed no. Look, I'm not worried. We have a roof over our heads, a heater, all the fish we can catch, and half the forest here in the boat with us."

Duncan looked back at his haul for the day and had to admit he didn't really know what he intended to do with half of it.

It was starting to get dark, so he broke up some deadfall and threw it into the boiler. In a few minutes the kitchen was heating up.

"That's not all just for looks," Duncan said of the haul. "A lot of it's fire wood, some of it's stuff we can eat, and among other things I was planning to make us some beds."

"A bed would be great but we might as well put them in the kitchen for now."

"Why? We have plenty of rooms. I could have a room. You can have a room."

"Ah, but this is the only one with a heater of any kind," Mallory reminded.

"Yeah, right." Duncan was looking at the space and the materials he had, building in his head. He'd have to build smaller beds if they were going to fit in the kitchen.

Mallory put a pot on to boil, and Duncan saw the bag of oatmeal sitting out and ready. "In the upstairs hall there's an opening in the wall—to the chimney no doubt, but no wood stove. Unless you can make one out of bamboo and rocks and mud…"

"We'll just winter right here." Duncan went into the other room and started pulling out some of the larger saplings he'd cut. He started cutting them to length, swinging his sword around and using it like an axe.

He had just cut the last one when he realized all of his light was coming through the kitchen door. At precisely the same moment there was a loud popping noise and the demon appeared, standing in the middle of the bar. Duncan screamed and his sword went point down into the deck where it proceeded to bounce back and fourth for several seconds before just vibrating on a low hum.

"What the!…" was all Mallory got out. When Duncan turned, Mallory was standing in the door to the kitchen. "Is there some problem?"

"That…that…get that thing out of here!"

"Really, Duncan, you have got to stop jumping at shadows," Mallory said. "Come along, Fred. You can help me in the kitchen. I have a few questions for you about the boat."

Fred mumbled something in a gravely, mostly-incoherent voice at Duncan and then popped off to the kitchen to help Mallory. A few minutes later Duncan walked in with his sticks, following the light. He sat down on his stump and tried to ignore the demon, but it was hard because he was wearing a chef's hat perched between his horns and carrying a little wire whisk.

"Where does he keep getting stuff from?" Duncan asked, making a face.

"He lives here. I'm sure he's carved himself out a dwelling somewhere on board. Most probably in the walls."

He didn't want to think about that creepy thing slinking around in the walls so he just focused on his project. He started lashing the sticks together with the baling wire.

"I'd feel a whole lot better if we had some more supplies, more blankets. If I had a cloak that fit me," Duncan said.

"Did it fit you before you started cutting little pieces off it to do everything from mend your britches to starting fire?" the dragon asked with a smile.

"Not really." Duncan laughed. "But it has gotten increasingly smaller."

"I wish there was some way of knowing if there was any place close that could fix the thingy, so we could get down river before the real cold.

It would suck to sit here all winter and then find out there was a black-smith shop just a few miles from here."

"Maybe we…"

"What?" Mallory asked.

"Maybe we should leave the boat, pack up, and just start walking down stream."

"Did you see a road today?"

"No."

"Who knows where the next town is? Anthony said all the towns here were inland and low tech. He made it sound like we are in the middle of nowhere. No, worse than that, a cold nowhere. Maybe the next town is far enough away that a dragon and a human would freeze or starve to death before they ever reached it."

Duncan nodded and said, "At least maybe we can stay warm and eat here."

"Maybe." Mallory looked thoughtful as he stirred the oatmeal he was no doubt over cooking because he always did. "We need more supplies than we're going to be able to dig out of the woods. You know that, right?"

Duncan didn't want to hear that. He knew it; he just didn't want to hear it.

"I think we need to explore the surrounding area. Put a real effort into trying to find a town."

"But you heard Anthony. People around these parts would be scared silly of you."

"I could stay here, watch for boats, get more wood and all. You could go."

"How? I didn't find any sign of life out there… Except wait…" He jumped up and pointed down at the chunk of wood he'd been sitting on. "I almost forgot I found these and clearly…"

"They were cut with a saw," Mallory said, annoyed with himself that he hadn't noticed before, but more annoyed with the human. "Seriously, Duncan, you'd forget your head if it wasn't attached. No one cuts firewood far from where they need it. That means someone is close."

"I don't know, Mal, the wood's been there a long time."

"It's big. It would have to be split. They may have decided it wasn't worth going back for. Tomorrow you go to where you found the wood and walk till midday straight out from it. Then if you don't find something, you turn and come back. Then the next day you go in another direction. No sense walking along the river because we know all the towns are inland. I'll just bet civilization isn't very far away."

Duncan frowned and sat down again. "I'm going to go stomping around in the cold woods all day while you lay around next to the stove watching for boats?"

"It's a sacrifice I'm willing to make for both of our sakes. I'm a giver. It's what I do."

"So you keep saying," Duncan mumbled and kept working on his bed. "All right. I'll go first thing in the morning. See if I can find anything that looks like it might be linked to a village."

"And I'll sit here by the fire and watch for boats."

Duncan heard the demon laugh and he pointed his knife at him. "That's enough out ah you."

"It's not his fault the people around these parts are so backwards," Mallory said, clicking his tongue in a disapproving way. "You have anger issues, Dunc, real anger issues."

* * * *

Mallory actually helped Duncan put the bed frame together, but of course there was no time to weave the platform, so he and Mallory wound up stacking some leaves Duncan had brought in earlier up in the corner to make a bed.

When Duncan woke up in the morning the only cover he had was his poor, abused cloak. The dragon had taken his blanket. He jerked his blanket off Mallory, who didn't so much as stir. He stood up and wrapped the blanket around him.

He looked at the bed frame in the light of day. It was sort of lopsided and one leg was shorter than the others. Duncan supposed that's what he got for trying to build anything by the light of the oil lamp.

He went to the boiler room, opened the furnace, stirred the coals and added some wood. It was cold, and he didn't imagine the day was likely to get much warmer. He wasn't looking forward to spending the day outside, walking around looking for a village that may or may not exist. Still, the sooner he got dressed and got going the sooner he could come back home. And who knew? He just might get lucky and find a town with a forge today.

* * * *

Mallory was more worried than he was letting on. The truth was he'd never once in his whole life wintered anywhere it got cold enough to make ice and never outside a city.

It was true that he could handle more cold than a human but not a lot more.

Roughing it wasn't really Mallory's cup of tea. He preferred a life of luxury. Warm water, soft beds, and meals more like feasts.

Still, if he was going to be a world-traveling dragon of adventure he supposed his mettle would be tested from time to time. Especially since he wasn't willing to do anything as drastic as getting a job.

The mere thought made him shudder, and memories of sitting in his family's office building in his little cubicle made his skin crawl. He'd take roughing it over being stuck at a desk any day.

Besides, it was just a matter of time till he made his fortune.

He threw some more wood into the boiler then went back into the kitchen and sat down on his stump. He carefully listened for any sign of a boat. He looked at the bed frame and frowned.

Duncan had unselfishly offered him the first bed, telling him that he deserved it. Mallory had almost instantly started to have this strange feeling that he soon figured out was something like guilt.

Before he took off, Duncan had said he doubted the five coins they had would buy much in the way of supplies, much less a new part for the boat. He'd said maybe there was no sense trying to find a town. Mallory knew he had to give Duncan some of the money he'd been hording in his cheek pouch.

"Oh…didn't I tell you? I found fifteen coins while I was cleaning the ship," Mallory had said.

"Cleaning the ship?" Duncan asked, making a face as if that was the most startling part of Mallory's announcement.

"Picking up yucky stuff and burning it in the stove is cleaning," Mallory defended.

Duncan nodded as if that made perfect sense and then he seemed to hear the rest of what Mallory had said. "You found fifteen coins and it just slipped your mind?"

There was an accusatory tone to his voice Mallory didn't like. It was as if the human didn't believe the perfectly good lie he'd just told him. "You were so excited about the tackle it just slipped my mind."

So Mallory had slipped away to "get the coins" which he did—out of his cheek pouch. The human had left with twenty coins, which should be more than enough to get them some supplies and get the part fixed.

Of course that was only if Duncan was lucky enough to find a town.

Mallory still had ten coins, but that wasn't just his insurance, it was Duncan's as well. At least that was how he rationalized keeping it secret for now.

Mallory had promised to catch some fish for dinner. Now, most dragons were fantastic fisherman. In warm water they would jump into the river, swim around after fish, catch them and eat them whole, hardly coming up for air.

That had been a bit too primitive for Mallory's liking. He preferred his fish in stick form, breaded, fried, and resembling a fish in no way at all, when he could get it that way.

Still, he'd seen all manners of creatures fish, so he knew there were many ways to accomplish the task, and he was pretty resourceful when he had to be. He found a good strong piece of bamboo, stripped the limbs off of it, and tied a piece of fishing line to it. Then tied on a hook. He took his pole and grabbed the can of worms he'd dug up earlier. He started to go out on the front deck, thinking about how cold it was going to be. Dragons, Mallory decided, were meant for a warmer climate—not the coldest part of the planet.

He had just convinced himself there was no alternative to standing on the cold deck with a pole when his eyes were drawn to the staircase and he had an idea. Taking his pole and the worms he made his way up the stairs and into the bathroom. He flipped the lid up on the "toilet" and looked down into the water below.

Deciding it was worth a try, he left his fishing gear and went downstairs again, grabbed Duncan's blanket with one hand and one of the stumps in the other. He carried them to the bathroom, sat down, threw the cover around his shoulders, and got comfortable.

He started to put a worm on the hook and stopped remembering what Duncan had said about fish. He wondered if worms had feelings, too. He looked closely at the worm, but he couldn't even find its face, so he stuck it on the hook.

His rule was he couldn't, wouldn't, eat anything that could smile at him. The worm couldn't smile, and he'd yet to see a fish smile, so he was morally good to go.

He took one last look down the rusty chute that led to the water and then he started fishing in the toilet. Mallory shrugged, knowing it might look weird, but after all no one was looking.

It wasn't like there was anything foul down there. The chute, like the rest of the ship, hadn't been used in years. Even if it had been it hadn't been used *here*. There was just the water and hopefully some fish at the bottom of the hole.

He hadn't been fishing long when he got a bite. He nearly lost the fish in his excitement. After falling all over himself and the bathroom he managed to pull the fish out of the hole. And then he just sort of looked at it, wondering what to do next. Then he took the fish in one hand, grabbed the hook with the other, and pulled the hook out.

He turned the fish to look at him. Mallory stared at the fish for awhile. He smiled to see if the fish would smile back. He told the fish his best joke. Nothing. If it didn't want to be eaten it had plenty of time to crack a smile.

Mallory then wondered just what he was supposed to do with the fish next. He supposed he had to kill it, but he couldn't bring himself to do it. He carried the fish down to the kitchen and stuck it in the sink. He stuffed a rag into the drain hole. Mallory steeled himself, walked out into the cold, dipped both pans into the river, brought them in, and poured them on the fish.

By the time Duncan got home just at dusk Mallory had caught half a dozen fairly decent-sized fish and dug up a bunch of cattail roots for dinner. He was preparing the tubers to cook when Duncan walked in.

Duncan slung his pack off with disgust, which more or less let Mallory know right away that he hadn't found anything of value.

"There was nothing, nada." The human was obviously hungry because he immediately pulled the fish from the sink. He cut their heads off and started to gut and scale them over a dish pan Mallory had found. "I almost got lost, even marking the trail the way you told me to." He walked over and washed his hands in the not-so-clean water in the sink.

"How could you get lost?" Mallory asked. He had told Duncan to make a notch in a tree with his sword every few feet so that he could use the marks to be sure he came back the same way. Also, if he didn't return, Mallory could go looking for him.

"Obviously I didn't get lost. I said I *almost* got lost. At one point on the way back I got turned around and didn't know if I was following the marks coming back or going all the way to the end in the other direction again."

Mallory tried to figure out what that meant for only about a minute then said, "Maybe you should cut arrows onto the trees."

"Which way should they point?"

"Towards the boat." Mallory sighed. "Nothing, huh? You saw no sign of civilization at all?"

"None, not so much as a stray dog or a wisp of smoke. At one point I even tried screaming for help… Of course that was when I thought I was lost. Still, no one heard me."

"And you walked straight out from the place where you found the stumps."

"Well see, that was another problem, because I wasn't really sure which way straight out was and…"

"You know I listened and looked all day. I'm pretty sure Anthony was telling us the truth. A boat's not coming by till after winter. I'll go with you in the morning. I have superior hearing and sight. Two heads are better than one and all that good rot. If we find a sign of civilization I'll hang back and keep low while you go check it out."

Duncan looked relieved. He handed the clean fish to Mallory who took them, stuck a wire through all of them at the tail, then opened the oven, hung them in it and closed the door. Duncan looked at him, surprised, and Mallory said, "I'm not just another pretty face you know."

He then proceeded to tell Duncan how he'd caught the fish, and Duncan nodded appreciatively. He took the bowl of heads and guts away saying he was going to bait the fishing hole. Whatever that meant.

Mallory was not looking forward to their hike in the woods, but he knew he could do a better job finding civilization than the human could. After all, Duncan was just a human. When Duncan came back he was making a face.

"Another run in with Fred?" Mallory asked.

"Not yet. Did you notice how the shower works?"

"I wasn't aware it does," Mallory said, surprised.

"Well it does. There's a pump and it goes into a small tank just above the shower."

"That may be nice in warm weather," Mallory said, not understanding the disgust in Duncan's voice.

"Mal, think about where the shower is in relation to the hole."

"Oh yes...but we aren't using the hole."

"But they did."

"Yep that's pretty disgusting any way you cut it," Mallory agreed. Actually it sort of put him right off the thought of eating even as the aroma of cooking fish started to fill the kitchen.

"I don't know, Mallory. I don't know if we should waste our time looking for a village. We might ought to spend our time bringing in wood and whatever food we can find."

He had a point, but Mallory wasn't sure how much they could rely on catching fish. There was little else to eat that he'd found. Of course he hadn't put in a lot of effort either. "Let's try at least once more."

* * * *

The next day he led Mallory to where he'd found the sections of wood he'd brought back to the boat. It took them several minutes to find his old path leading them to both say at the same time, "We aren't trackers."

They laughed and finally found his trail from the day before.

"All right, let's think about this for a minute," Mallory said. He looked around him as if he knew what he was looking at, which Duncan was pretty sure he didn't. "I wish we had questioned Anthony a bit more about the towns around here." Duncan could tell Mallory was cold because he kept jumping from one foot to the other trying to get warm.

He had no idea how warm Mallory's scales kept him, but the only clothing he had was the vest. Duncan assumed the dragon was at least as cold as he was, and Duncan was so cold he was also jumping from one foot to the other to stay warm.

"If we think about it too long we're going to freeze and…" something suddenly dawned on Duncan and he asked in an accusing tone, "Wait a minute! You can breathe fire. How can you be cold?"

"Do you think there is fire in me?" Mallory asked with an air of disbelief.

Duncan shrugged. Of course he did.

"Well I don't. Let's go northwest." Mallory pointed into a section of the woods Duncan was pretty sure at random.

"That's not northwest," he said.

"Then what direction is it?"

"I don't know."

"Then how do you know it's not northwest?"

"How do *you* know it is?"

"I don't, but since we don't know for sure it's not, let's call it northwest," Mallory said. He started walking, so Duncan shrugged and followed him.

Every once in a while Duncan stopped to cut an arrow on a tree with his knife to mark their trail. Once he made the arrow point in the wrong direction and had to cut it out and start again, so he got a bit behind Mallory.

He ran to make up the distance and as he caught up—out of breath— he asked, "Mallory, just how do you make fire if it isn't in your belly?"

"Well as we both know, you constantly have gas blowing out one end or the other."

"What's that have to do with anything?" Duncan said, taking offense.

"The point is that we all make gas as we digest food. Dragon's don't pass gas…"

"Yeah right." Duncan rolled his eyes.

"Did you ever hear me rip one?"

"No but…"

"Tozactly. We have a chamber just over our stomach that collects those gasses. We have control of our gas. We can burp whenever we like—or not if we're in polite company. For the record, you, human, are not polite company. We can release it—all or none of it, a little or a lot. Lighting the gas…" Mallory laughed. "…well, it's a bit of a parlor trick really. I—like most of my kind—wear a flint ring on my bottom back-most tooth and a steel ring on the top one. It's as simple as burping and clicking my teeth together then opening my mouth and blowing the flame out."

"That is pretty cool," Duncan said. "I knew a guy who could light his farts."

"How uncouth," Mallory said, making a face.

"I don't really see the difference," he mumbled.

"I wouldn't expect you would."

They walked till midday and stopped to eat a quick lunch of what was left of the fish from the night before. They were getting ready to call it a day and head back to the ship when Duncan saw Mallory's ears perk up. The dragon's head turned towards some sound, something that a dragon could hear that a human obviously couldn't.

"What is it, boy?" Duncan asked with a laugh.

Mallory back handed him, nearly knocking him down. "Quiet. I hear whistling." The dragon started walking with a quiet precision Duncan couldn't match, though he did try, and he still didn't hear any whistling.

Mallory stopped in his tracks and whispered, "No, no! Don't quit whistling." The dragon listened very closely, glaring at Duncan, implying that he was making too much noise.

Duncan held his breath till he almost passed out in an effort to be quiet.

Mallory started moving again. "It's close. I can hear a squeaking wheel. Come on." The dragon started running and he followed.

* * * *

Mallory was afraid he was going to lose track of where the sound was again. He ran blindly through the woods dodging trees and rocks. Before he'd even realized he was close, he'd run onto a road.

The human pushing a wheelbarrow full of turnips jumped, dumping his load. He took one look at what had startled him, turned white as a sheet, and screamed, "Dragon!"

He and took off running in the direction he'd been pushing the wheelbarrow, leaving it and its contents behind without a second thought.

"Nice," Mallory said, shaking his head.

Fighting for his breath in the cold air the human ran up beside him and stopped. "The idea was for you to hang back. Not scare the living hell out of the locals." Duncan looked down the road at the back of the departing man, took a couple of moments to catch his breath, and then took off after the man calling out, "Wait a minute, wait!"

The man screamed in terror and doubled his pace. This forced Duncan to give up his chase and come back to where Mallory stood next to the over-turned wheelbarrow and the turnips.

Before Duncan could make another disparaging comment, Mallory explained himself. "I didn't have any idea how close to the road we were. Town, or whatever, must be that way because that's the way he was and is going. Come on." Mallory started walking.

"Mal, we don't know what's that way, or how far, and it's going to take us the rest of the day just to get back to the boat. We aren't prepared to spend the night in the woods in this cold."

"You're right. How annoying." Mallory thought for a moment. "Let's make a big arrow on the ground here out of sticks so when we find it we'll know which way to go."

Which they did. Then Mallory started loading all of the turnips back into the wheelbarrow.

"What are you doing?"

"Loading the turnips."

"Let him pick them up when he gets back," Duncan said. "We need to get home before it gets dark."

"Because of course there is something in the woods scarier than either me or what's on the ship waiting for us," Mallory teased. "I was getting the turnips for us."

"You can't just take the man's turnips and his wheelbarrow."

"And why not?"

"Because it would be wrong."

"You know what I think would be wrong Duncan? Us starving to death when fate has been kind enough to drop this lovely bunch of turnips right here at our feet."

Duncan seemed to think about that, weighing his moral outrage against the prospects of starving to death. "All right, but you can't just take the poor guy's wheelbarrow."

"Yes, I most definitely can," Mallory said, flicking a piece of turnip out from under one of his claws.

"Come on, Mal! You don't know that it's not the only thing he has for hauling stuff around," the human said, giving him a stern look—which didn't affect Mallory in the slightest.

"I know *we* don't have anything else to haul stuff in."

"We can put the turnips in my cloak and carry them between us."

"Tell me you're kidding. This has a wheel. Think how much easier it would make life back at the boat for us. Besides, I've already filled it half way up."

"We're already taking the guy's turnips."

Mallory didn't really want to stand in the cold arguing with the human over something he thought was stupid. "How about we take the wheelbarrow and the turnips and when fate smiles on us more favorably—than with a bunch of turnips—we'll bring his wheelbarrow back with a couple of coins in it for his trouble."

"That's a good idea," Duncan said. "We'll leave the wheelbarrow, take all the turnips, and put a couple of coins in the wheelbarrow to pay him for them."

"That's not what I said at all, Duncan. That's insane…"

"It's what we're doing." Duncan took off what was left of his cloak and spread it on the ground.

"Come on, Dunc, this is seriously stupid."

The human was silent as he dumped the turnips from the wheelbarrow onto the cloak. Then he said, "Believe me, Mal, you have no idea just how vindictive farmers can be."

The human put the wheelbarrow back on the road and stuck a couple of coins in it. Then he went to pick up the rest of the turnips and throw them on his cloak. He looked up at Mallory expectantly. "Aren't you going to help me?"

Mallory started slinging the turnips into the cloak. "I don't really see why I should have to help at all," he muttered. "If Mr. Goodie Two Shoes wants to do a good deed he ought to have to pick up the damn turnips himself and haul them back to the boat." He glared daggers at the human, knowing their trip back to the boat was going to be no picnic.

"What's that you said, dragon?"

"You heard me well enough."

"It's the right thing to do," the human insisted.

"The right thing to do for who?" Mallory asked. "Not for us. Now we have to haul these things all the way home and we're two coins lighter than we were when we left the boat. I swear, Duncan, if we're stuck here all winter for lack of those two coins I'm going to kill you myself."

"Wouldn't you feel bad just taking the guy's stuff?"

"Honestly? No, not at all."

"Come on, he only dropped his stuff and left it at all because you scared him near to death."

"Am I supposed to feel bad because he judged me without getting to know me first? Because he decided I was going to burn his town and eat his children?" Mallory spit back. "Come on, let's just go before I take the money, the wheelbarrow, all the turnips, and leave you behind as payment."

* * * *

Duncan didn't talk to him most of the way home, but it wasn't just because he was mad.

No, it was because the dragon was right. Carrying those turnips in that cloak was just as difficult as he had said it would be. When they'd started out, the cloak full of turnips between them, Duncan had thought, *this isn't so bad, and I feel really good about not taking the guy's wheelbarrow and paying him for his turnips.*

By the time they had walked less than thirty minutes his arms and legs were screaming, and all he kept thinking was that Mallory had been right. It would have made life a whole lot easier to just take the wheelbarrow. How stupid was he going to feel when and if they found town he was two coins short of getting just what they needed?

Then he convinced himself that right was still right, and even living the way he and Mallory did they had to have some lines they didn't cross.

When they got to the boat they carried the turnips into the big room and dropped them unceremoniously on the floor behind the bar. Duncan dragged his cloak out from under the pile with an effort.

His arms and legs felt like they'd been stuck with a thousand needles, and the boat was painfully cold.

"Stove's cold," Mallory said, and headed for the boiler room. Duncan followed him and watched as Mallory filled the furnace with kindling then blew a plume of fire into it. It started with a loud crackle. "With our luck forty ships went this way today."

Duncan laughed and started to feed a couple of bigger pieces of wood into the fire. One thing about Mallory. It never took them long to get a good fire going.

"I doubt it. And we're close to people. I just know it. I'll just follow the arrows till I get to the road, and then I go up the road till I find…well, whatever is there. Who knows but that fame and fortune is waiting just beyond where we left the turnip farmer's wheelbarrow?"

"Turnip farmer. Turnip farmer? Have you written a whole story about him? How do you know he wasn't a turnip thief? Just a man who goes around with a wheelbarrow stealing other people's turnips taking them to town selling them as magic beans. You gave our money to some grifter who goes around taking the food out of widows' and orphans' mouths. Selling them stolen vegetables and telling them they will do everything from heal the pox to getting rid of acne," Mallory said.

"You wrote a better story about him than I did," Duncan said with a smile.

"Yes, well all I can say is thank the gods we got hold of these turnips before he could use them to turn out the pockets of starving villagers. If only we'd taken that wheelbarrow we might have saved hundreds more…"

"Are you quite finished now?" Duncan asked with a laugh.

"Are you sorry you doubted my superior wisdom?"

"My arms feel like they're about to fall off. Is that the same thing?"

"Close enough," Mallory smiled and nodded. "So I guess we're having turnips for dinner. I'm thinking boil them up and mash them? I'm cold. I'd rather eat something warm. How about you?"

Duncan nodded and Mallory went inside. If the dragon was still sore over the money or toting the turnips, it didn't show.

Once he had fully loaded the furnace he started to go inside, and that was when he noticed something. There was a smaller pipe off the main steam pipe that ran the engine. It had a valve in it and it ran into the wall.

Curious, he went into the kitchen, tracing the pipe which went through the kitchen into the big room and disappeared into the upstairs floor. He went back to the kitchen, grabbed a candle and lit it off the one Mallory already had going.

Mallory was busy cutting up turnips and gave him only the slightest raise of an eyebrow as Duncan took off again. Like maybe as long as he wasn't yelling that they were going to die, it wasn't anything for Mallory to worry about.

Upon further investigation Duncan found that the pipe went through every room in the boat including the wheel house.

He ran back downstairs and answered Mallory's unanswered question. "This boat has steam heat. Very primitive, but steam heat nonetheless." He walked back out to the boiler room, reached up and turned the valve on.

There were some odd screaming-type noises all around the boat that weren't much different than the demon made.

When he walked back in the kitchen the pipes were still banging and clanging and whistling.

"What in hell have you done?" Mallory demanded.

"It's just the steam going through the pipes. It will quit as soon as it works all the air out of the system. I think."

"I'm beginning to see why folks hate tinkerers," the dragon mumbled.

"The worst that will happen is that the heating system won't work and then I'll just shut the valve back off. Nothing ventured; nothing gained."

"As long as you're sure nothing's going to blow up. I have to tell you I'm going to be extremely put out if you blow us all up."

There was a popping sound that had nothing to do with the pipes, and this time Duncan didn't even jump when he saw the demon. He guessed it was true you could get used to almost anything.

"Pipe leak in bathroom," it said, and then it handed Duncan an adjustable wrench.

Duncan took the wrench and the candle and ran upstairs to find the leak. He put the wrench on the fitting, tightened it, and the steam quit hissing out of the joint. A few seconds later the pipes stopped screaming and thumping. When he touched it the pipe was warm.

Duncan smiled, took the wrench and went back downstairs. "I think it works."

"If it does that means we won't be confined to the kitchen for the winter," Mallory said.

"Of course if I find a town, and if we can fix the part, we may get out of here tomorrow."

"That's a lot of ifs." No doubt noticing Duncan's attachment to the tool, the Dragon said, "Now give the demon his wrench back."

Duncan turned so that his back was to the demon and looked at the wrench in his hand. "But we need it."

"It's not yours. It belongs to Fred."

"Ah come on, Mal," he whispered. "It's just that demon."

"Oh I see. You gave two coins and a wheelbarrow to a turnip thief, because, 'It's the right thing to do,' but you're just going to take Fred's wrench because you need it. What a hypocrite."

"That thing lives on our boat and eats our food," he defended. "It's hardly the same thing."

"Why? Because that thing looked like you and Fred doesn't?"

Of course that was exactly why but Duncan knew that wouldn't really go over well with his big, blue friend. "What does he need the wrench for?"

"Look, dim wit," Mallory said, so maybe he was still a little sore over hauling the turnips. "How much useful stuff do you think he has squirreled away? Do you really think he will be this helpful again if you take his wrench? Now give it back and say thanks."

"Thanks? Again I feel I must point out that he is a parasite that lives on our boat and eats our food."

"Exactly. He lives on our boat, so I think it's better for all of us if you make friends with him. Remember his name is Fred."

Duncan walked over to where the demon was sitting on the heating pipe, apparently warming his butt. Duncan reluctantly handed the wrench back. "Thanks, Fred," he said.

"You're welcome," Fred said in his booming, straight-from-hell voice, then popped off apparently to put the wrench away.

"Was that so hard?"

"That thing is creepy, Mal," Duncan said.

"I don't know. He sort of grows on you after a while."

"Yeah, like a wart."

* * * *

The next day Mallory and Duncan took off walking the same trail they had before. When they got to the road the wheelbarrow was gone but their arrow was still there.

"All right. You go on and see if there is a town. If there is, find a blacksmith and see if they can fix the part," Mallory said. Duncan nodded his understanding. "That's the top priority—get the boat fixed so we can get out of Winterhurst. If there is no way of getting the part fixed, for whatever reason, get us all the supplies you can get.

"Meanwhile, I'll get far enough off the road I can't be seen, but stay on our trail. I'll make us a camp, get a fire going and keep it going. If the town is so far away you can't make it back before nightfall, you stay there, and I'll wait here for you. If you can make it back today we'll camp here tonight because there is no way we can make it back to the boat at night."

"I'm not an imbecile…"

"If you say so," Mallory said with a crooked smile.

"Ha, ha, my point is that's the fifteenth time this morning you've told me the same thing. I'd like to just get going."

"Oh really? Then why are you wasting time arguing about me wasting your time telling you what you already know?"

"Argh!" Duncan took off at a near run, as much to get away from his infuriating partner as to find something approaching civilization.

He hadn't gone far when he saw a small wooden farmhouse with a wood shake roof and in front of it a sign saying something he couldn't read. He saw a man splitting wood and called out to him, "Sir, how far to town?"

The guy slipped, almost hitting his leg, so it was little wonder that he turned and glared at Duncan. He probably would have gotten really angry with him if he hadn't seen the stranger's size and the sword on his back.

"About a mile that way." He pointed with his head.

"Thanks!" Duncan nodded back and started running again.

The town wasn't much to look at, maybe sixty buildings in all. Most of those wood-planked, single-storied homes with wood shingle roofs and stone chimneys. There were more outbuildings than homes, and on the main street—if you could call it that—there was a livery stable, a small general store, and a bar. The store and bar were, in fact, the only two-storied buildings he saw. Each had a covered wood-planked porch across the front.

He was about to stop and ask a guy coming out of the store if they had a blacksmith when he smelled the familiar smell of sulfur. He walked down the main street towards the smell, and at the very end of the street there sat the town smithy.

It wasn't much, just four posts and a roof with two wood walls. There was a huge pile of coal, an anvil, a make-shift bellows, and brick forge. Not the best smithy he'd ever seen for sure. It made the one back home in Spurna look like it was state of the art, and he knew from what he'd seen in the city that it wasn't.

Still in that moment it was the most beautiful thing he'd ever seen.

The town blacksmith held a piece of metal in his heavily-leather-gloved left hand, and in his right a big hammer. He pounded the metal lying on the anvil with the hammer, making a sound that Duncan knew well.

The smith was a big man. Though not as big as Duncan, he had huge arms and strong wrists just like the smith in Spurna. He wore a grey flannel shirt that was probably once a lighter color, nearly-blue pants, and a leather apron that went from just under his chin to down past his knees. He was covered in soot from head to toe.

Duncan found he had a bit of a lump in his throat. The only place he'd ever felt the least bit comfortable back home had been at the smithy's forge. If he said the village smithy had been like a second father to him that would be true. Mostly of course because he also treated Duncan like dog sweat and constantly told him what a worthless screw up he was.

Ah, memories.

The blacksmith saw Duncan standing there and abruptly stopped hammering the metal he was working. "We don't get many strangers around here and none this close to winter," was what he said by way of a greeting.

"My boat broke down many miles from here. I left my wife and two kids at the shore, and I've been walking for days." It was the story Mallory had spun for him to tell. The dragon said it might get him sympathy, and he also thought it couldn't hurt to keep their exact location a secret.

Mallory had trust issues. In fact, as far as Duncan could see Mallory didn't really trust anyone.

He held up the two pieces of the part and held them together the way they were supposed to be. "I'd like to have a new one made if that would be possible."

The guy walked over, took the pieces, rolled them around, looked them over, then handed them back to Duncan and said, "Sixty coins."

"Sixty!" Duncan nearly swallowed his tongue. "Sixty?" He had noticed that while everyone basically used the same size silver coin that some places put a higher value on them than others. Mallory had told him that Austin had more or less robbed him in Tarslick, charging him two coins a week to sleep with the horses. This seemed like a ridiculous price. "How much would it be if you just put the pieces back together?"

"Eighty coins."

"Wait a minute. That's even more."

"It's harder to put the pieces back together than to make a new piece," the smith said. Duncan knew enough to know that this was probably true.

"How much would you charge me to rent your forge for a few hours? You give me the metal to work and then I do the work myself."

"Let's see some tinkerer..."

"Ah, I'm a licensed professional," Duncan said quickly.

"Whatever. Let's see. Some stranger in here using my tools, under my feet for the better part of a day." He seemed to think about it for a minute and then said, "A hundred coins."

"Now see here, smith, that's just not right."

"I've got no shortage of work to do. It's all about supply and demand, boy. Lots of people need me; I only need a few of them. Either you have my price or you don't. It's no sweat off my neck," the smith said.

"I don't have that kind of money. All I have to my name is eighteen coins."

"Son, I don't pick up my tongs for less than twenty."

Duncan's guts turned, remembering the two coins he'd insisted they leave for the turnip thief.

"Seriously, could we maybe come to some agreement? Perhaps I could work off the price?"

"Got half the town working of their debts now." He laughed. It wasn't a pleasant sound. "I'm not a charity, boy. Now if you don't mind—and even if you do—you've wasted enough of my time." With that and not another word the smith walked over and put his metal back on the fire.

Duncan thought for a minute about pulling his sword and demanding the guy fix the part. Then he got an image of him tripping over his own sword, his head landing with a thump on the anvil, and the smith beating him to death with his own broken thingy.

"I hope a red-hot ember falls in the front of your pants," he mumbled as he walked away.

He didn't know whether he should even bother to go to the store. If the man's prices were any indication of what his coins were worth here, he might have enough money for a peanut.

He wasn't good at talking people into stuff. That was what Mallory was good at. Duncan was out of his league.

He went back to the general store he'd seen, walked in, and was happy to see that it was fully stocked. As he closed the door the place was abuzz with people chatting and shopping, but when they saw him the silence fell so hard and so fast not even a bug chirped.

The talking started back up as quickly as it had stopped, but the tone had changed. They were all watching—if not talking about him—which wasn't necessarily the most comfortable position to be in.

He went right to the wall where the dried beans and flour were and reluctantly looked at the price tags. Then he started really looking at all the price tags, making sure he was seeing what he thought he was seeing.

The prices he was looking at were as low as the smith's prices were high. It didn't make any sense.

He walked up to the thin man with the handlebar mustache behind the counter and asked, "Is there another smith anywhere around close? Your smith is a little steep."

"A little steep." The storekeeper laughed. "He's a crook. Earl is the biggest thief in all of Winterhurst. What did he try to get you for?"

Duncan held up the pieces and told him what he'd said.

"He must have liked your face. He charged me forty coins just to weld my plow," an old man playing checkers by the window said.

The storekeeper held out his hand to Duncan, "Name's Sam. Those two old geezers sitting in the window are Mort and Felix."

"I'm Duncan." He shook the storekeeper's hand and smiled and nodded at the two old men. There were three or four people shopping, but Sam didn't introduce him to them, so he wondered why he'd introduced him to the two old men.

Sam most have read the expression on his face because he leaned in and whispered, "Mort and Felix used to own the store till they decided to retire and sold it to me. They come in every day. They're waiting when I open up in the morning and they're the last ones out when I close in the evening. Can't say as I know why, but they're sort of a fixture around here."

Duncan nodded like it made sense. "Is there another blacksmith?" he asked again.

"There's not another blacksmith around here for a hundred miles," Mort said.

"Ain't no one likes the fool enough to pay those prices if they had any sort of option," Felix added.

"You have a broken plow, you pay the forty coins he charges or you starve come winter. Horses have to be shoed, tools fixed," Mort said with a shrug. "He's got us by our jugs if you know what I mean."

"Nearly everyone in town owes him money. I don't think anyone makes a dime in this town that they don't give part of it to Earl—willingly or not," Sam said, frowning. "No one likes it, but what you gonna do? He makes sure no one in town who might like to be a blacksmith ever gets enough money together to get the equipment they'd need to start their own shop."

"Couldn't you all get together…?"

"And do what?" Mort asked. "He's not just the blacksmith, he's also the mayor and the constable."

"Wait a minute. If no one likes the guy how did he get to be your mayor and your constable?" Duncan didn't understand at all.

"He's got three sons your size or better. Everyone in town owes him money, so he buys their votes," Sam said.

"No one dares to cross him because of those idiot boys of his," Felix said. "I tell you if I was younger…"

"Who are you kidding?" Mort said. "When you were younger you still weren't any bigger. You would have done nothing. Nothing I tell you would you have done."

"And I suppose you would have done something, Mr. Big Shot," Felix said.

"No, but I never said that I would," Mort said with a shrug.

The old men got into an argument.

"All day it's like this," Sam said with a sigh, pointing towards the two. "So is there anything I can do for you?"

Duncan didn't really know what to do. He would have liked to been able to ask Mallory, but he couldn't. He found himself in the uncomfortable position of having to make a decision—which would have been easier if what he chose to do didn't affect anyone but him.

They couldn't pay the blacksmith's fee. That being the case, they were going to have to winter right where they were. The only thing he could do was buy as many supplies as he could with the eighteen coins he had.

The only good news was with the prices being as low as they were he was going to be able to get everything on their list and then some.

So when it came right down to it, he really didn't have to make much of a decision because he really didn't have a choice. Surprisingly, this made him feel much better.

"I guess I'd better get as many supplies as I can," he told Sam.

"Well if you can't find what you're looking for just ask me," Sam said.

The old men quit arguing.

As he shopped Duncan listened closely to the conversation his questions about the blacksmith had started.

The people hated the mayor but hated him more because in this community the fact that he was the blacksmith gave him more power than being the mayor did. Sam had apparently tried to undermine the smith by buying some inexpensive tools from a traveling salesman and passing the savings on to his patrons. Earl had retaliated by building a hog pen next to Sam's house.

According to Mort and Felix—who seemed never to quite agree on the details of a story, so that the telling took a while because one was constantly interrupting the other to contradict him on such important points as what color shirt someone was wearing—the traveling salesman never came back through. The town gossip ranged from Earl had paid him well not to do business with Sam to—what Mort and Felix did agree on—that Earl's sons had followed the traveling salesman out of town and killed him.

They believed this because the next day Earl's youngest son was wearing the same shirt that the traveling salesman had been wearing. The color of which was either red or green depending on whether Mort was color blind or not as Felix screamed at him that he was.

Seemed like everyone had tried to stop the man but had all wound up paying one heavy price or other.

Duncan bought oil and candles, some more fish hooks, a couple of bolts of fabric, some needles and thread, and a thick wool blanket. He spent the rest of the money on food, spices, salt, dried beans, rice, flour, corn meal and baking powder. When he was down to their last coin he stopped shopping. He held on to one coin because he didn't want them to be broke, even though he knew one coin wouldn't do much.

The storekeeper seemed thrilled with his purchases. Almost too happy. Like maybe he didn't sell that much stuff in a week. Duncan filled his pack then stuck the rest in his cloak and tied it closed. He went to pick up the bundle, thinking it would be no problem.

It was all he could do to lift it. It was extremely heavy. In fact, he could get it picked up off the floor, but he couldn't really move with it. That was good. It meant they had lots of supplies. But it wasn't good at all because he had no idea how he was going to get it back to where Mallory was.

He was about to ask if he could come back for half of it the next day when Sam said, "Wait a minute there, big fellow."

The storekeeper walked out from behind the counter and grabbed a well-used wheelbarrow from where it was leaning against a wall. "Take this, no charge. Leroy borrowed this from me some two months ago to bring his purchases home and I hadn't seen it since. I asked him about it several times, but he had always just forgotten it and was going to bring it in the next time he came. You know how that sort of thing goes. Well today, as luck would have it, he comes in telling some crazy story. Said some huge, blue dragon jumped out of the woods yesterday and chased him down the road. Leroy said he just ran off and left the turnips—wheelbarrow and all—to that varmint. Said he felt bad about leaving my wheelbarrow so he went back."

"Yeah right," Felix scoffed. "Leroy and his turnip wine. He's always drunk."

"Well there's enough truth in that statement I guess." Sam laughed. "Leroy said when he came back the wheelbarrow was still there. All the turnips were gone but there were two coins in the wheelbarrow. Since that was about three times what the turnips were worth he said he was sure it was an omen that he needed to bring the wheelbarrow back."

"Poppy cock!" Felix snorted.

"Drunk as a skunk no doubt," Mort added.

Sam seemed to ignore them. "Anyway, it's one of the ones I let the patrons use anyway, so take it."

"It could take me longer to get it back to you than it took him. I'm a long ways off," Duncan said.

"Look, I've gone without it all this time, so I must not really need it. You've put a lot of money in my till. Go ahead and take it."

"You believe all that nonsense about a dragon?" Mort asked the shop keep.

"Not for a minute. You know Leroy. He's always got some story to tell. Course this is the first time he brought something back he borrowed, and the first time he showed me money at the end of it."

"Bet he just sold his turnips to someone hungry enough to pay that price," Mort said, waving his hand in the air. "That turnip wine is going to kill him dead one day I tell ya."

"Ya ever taste it?" Felix asked Sam. "Nastiest stuff I've ever had in my mouth, and afterwards I had the worst gas."

"For days," Mort said with a chuckle. "Dead of winter we had all the windows and the door open."

They all had a good laugh as Duncan loaded all his stuff in the wheelbarrow.

"Thank you very much. I'll try to get it back to you as soon as I can," Duncan said, and started for the door.

"That'll probably be spring. My wife's mother's wart says there's a big storm heading this way in a couple of days."

Duncan thanked the man again, then wheeled his load out the front door and down the front steps.

At the bottom he looked back towards the blacksmith shop, wondering how they were going to get around Earl to fix their thingy.

He started pushing the wheelbarrow down the road. He thought about how much fun it was going to be to tell Mallory that he'd been right about the wheelbarrow thing. He frowned thinking that would mean that he'd have to tell him that the smith wouldn't even consider the repair because he was two coins short. Of course he could always leave that part out. After all, the guy still would have wanted more than they'd had.

He cut his intended gloating short when he noticed the shadows were getting long. He had to get back to camp before it got dark. But even in the wheelbarrow that load was heavy, and he'd already had quite a hike that day.

When he had tried to run and push the wheelbarrow he'd almost dumped it and after that…well, he just didn't even have the energy to walk really fast. By the time he got back to where he'd left Mallory it was dark enough he probably wouldn't have found the camp if he hadn't seen the light from the fire.

He barely had the energy left to get the wheelbarrow across the roadside ditch and through the woods.

"Wow! That's quite a haul," Mallory said, getting up from where he'd been sitting on a log to help Duncan the last few feet—for which Duncan was glad. "What about the part?"

"Let me," Duncan huffed, "catch my breath."

Mallory nodded.

As Duncan plopped down on the log Mallory had been sitting on the dragon handed him a pan of hot tea he'd made from some bark he'd scraped off a tree. He'd done this before. Duncan didn't know what the tree was, but the tea was good and it was warm, so he drank it.

Mallory opened the cloak bundle, immediately extracted the wool blanket Duncan had bought, and threw it around himself.

"This ought to get us through winter." He dug around a bit more. He held up the two pieces of the broken part looking a bit defeated. "I guess this means it will have to. No blacksmith?"

"No, it was worse than that. There is a blacksmith, but he's a crook." Duncan explained what had happened to him at the blacksmith's shop between labored breaths and sips of tea.

Mallory stroked his cheek frills. "Sounds like he's got a racket going."

"You sound almost like you respect what he's doing," Duncan said, glaring across the fire at the dragon.

"Not at all. I hate a bully. But now we know what he is, we might be able to use that against him."

"How so?"

"Well I don't know off the top of my head. Mind you, if he's hated by everyone in town it shouldn't be too hard to find a way to get our part fixed."

"I don't see how one thing helps the other." Duncan rubbed his hands together close to the fire. He didn't know if his fingers were numb from the cold or from hanging onto the handles of the wheelbarrow so tight for so long. Either way it sucked.

"Think about it. When I was home there was no one in town that respected me, and I'm guessing it was the same for you?"

"Respect? They didn't even *like* me," Duncan said. Mallory's words brought back some bad feelings, but he still had no idea what the dragon was getting at.

"If you got into trouble at home, if you needed anyone, was there ever anyone you could turn to?"

"No, no not at all," Duncan said, nodding his head and feeling like a bit of a dunce because now it seemed clear to him what Mallory was getting at.

"And that was just because we weren't respected or liked. Because we were seen as rejects. But this guy has worked hard to make everyone in town indebted to him. He has abused his power and because of this they all hate him—and rightfully so. Who do you think will come help him if he's in trouble? How easy would it be to get the town's people to help us make trouble for him if they think we can stop his reign of tyranny?"

Duncan laughed. "I like the way you think, Mal."

"I swear, it's getting colder by the minute," Mallory said, and then pointed Duncan towards what was left of a pot of rice with wild onions. Duncan devoured the food, realizing he hadn't eaten since that morning. It wasn't nearly enough, but it would have to do.

"We better head out first light," Mallory said. "Sooner we get back to the boat the better."

But Mallory could have saved his breath. By morning they were huddled together wrapped in all the blankets, both bolts of cloth, and his cloak, and they were still so cold that they were all but lying in the fire pit. They didn't even stir the coals and make breakfast. They just bundled up as best they could, loaded the wheelbarrow up, and headed off back down the trail they'd marked.

They took turns pushing the load. Even pushing a fully-loaded wheelbarrow through the woods they got back to the boat in record time. No doubt spurred on by the extreme cold. When they could see the boat they sighed in relief and then Duncan, who was pushing the wheelbarrow, moved double time. Mallory ran ahead of him and opened the door for him. He pushed the wheelbarrow through the open door into the main room and left it there.

He and Mallory proceeded to get right in each other's way trying to get to the boiler room to make a fire. Duncan loaded the furnace and Mallory started it going. They worked at getting a big, hot, fire roaring, and then they ran back into the kitchen to soak up the warmth.

"I have to tell you that I'm not looking forward to winter here. The people I spoke to in town all made it sound pretty rough. Maybe we could just float again and run aground someplace warmer?" Duncan said.

"As much fun as that sounds like it would be, I think we got lucky, Dunc. We could have just as easily split the boat in two—or three for that matter," Mallory said.

Duncan nodded his head in agreement. Then he remembered something. "The shop keep said his wife's mother's wart said there was a bad storm coming in a couple of days and… Well, one of those days is gone already. It did get a lot colder last night."

Mallory smiled. "Does her wart actually talk to her and give her weather reports, or is it one of those it-tingles-so-it-must-be-going-to-rain things?"

"I don't know," Duncan said. "I didn't think to ask. Anyway it is colder, and if it's just going to get worse...."

"We better get a whole lot more wood," Mallory finished. He looked really worried. "Normally people have most of the summer to get enough wood for winter."

"Then we better quit talking about it and get to work."

The wheelbarrow made the job a whole lot easier. They had put the cloak full of supplies into the kitchen and then they got right to work gathering wood. They ran around the woods till it was too dark to work anymore, picking up deadfall, breaking up what they could, sticking it in the wheelbarrow, and dumping load after load on the boat. They carried in bigger pieces that would have to be cut and dealt with later. As the last lights of the day faded to nothing they struggled to get their last load of wood across the gangplank.

Just as they crossed onto the deck and Mallory opened the door for Duncan to bring the last wheelbarrow in, it started to snow.

Duncan came from a part of the world where it didn't snow, so he had no idea what it was when giant white flakes started to fall on him.

He screamed and ran through the door, pushing the load of wood and nearly knocking Mallory into the river. "The sky is falling! The sky is falling!" He started rubbing at his arms where the snow had hit him. "It's melting my flesh, it's...."

"Snow," Mallory said with an air of disgust as he closed the door. "It's frozen rain, you imbecile, not some attack from above. It's really cold and makes things slick, but other than that it's harmless. Haven't you ever seen snow before?"

"No," Duncan said, straightening himself. He looked around the room which was now nearly bulging with wood, bamboo, and leaves.

Mallory looked out the window at the snow now coming down in flakes the size of coins, so quick that the ground was already covered. "I guess that old woman's wart was right."

Seven

By morning there was about four inches of snow on the ground, and the river had a thin sheet of ice on it. It was bitter cold. They had slept in the kitchen because even with the steam heat the other rooms weren't comfortable enough to stay in for long, much less sleep in.

Mallory let Duncan sleep. The last couple of days he'd worn himself out, and he was after all only a human. Mallory stoked the furnace and got the fire blazing again. Then he wrapped a blanket around his shoulders and went up to the bathroom to see if he could catch some fish for breakfast.

As luck would have it the fish were biting, and he caught a couple right off. He started to head downstairs with them when he saw the pump that went to the shower tank. He remembered the ice covering the river and had an idea. He pumped till the tank was full then grabbed the fish and went downstairs. The rest of the boat was cold enough he was happy to be back in the nice, warm kitchen, but at least he hadn't had to chop a hole in the ice to fish.

Mallory tried the faucet on the kitchen sink and after a couple of bangs and clangs water ran out. At first it was rusty, but then it ran clear. Well, as clear as river water ever was. He filled a pot and put it on to boil.

The human was right. The boat was full of surprises. They really hadn't had a chance to check it out in any detail. They'd been way too consumed with such minor things as trying to survive.

The information Fred had given him was sketchy at best. The demon didn't know much since he'd spent most of his time when the boat was actually running scaring all hell out of whatever creatures were trying to use it.

Mallory sighed. He was sure they'd have learn all there was to know about the boat in the coming months. He stuffed a rag in the drain hole, filled the sink part way, and set the fish in it the water.

He wasn't looking forward to a long, cold winter confined to the boat but couldn't think of any way around it.

On the blanket on the pile of leaves in the corner Duncan started to stir. He made a face and groaned as if he'd awakened to find every muscle in his body knotted up.

Mallory just shrugged, mostly unconcerned with the human's comfort. He grabbed one of the rags he'd found and started to clean the cabinets using the water in the sink with the fish in it.

The cabinets were pretty dirty but the fish didn't seem to notice when he put the rag in to clean it off and then wrung it out again.

Duncan got up, stretched, and started to go outside to relieve himself. He came back to the kitchen and said in a voice full of surprise, "The ground is white."

"That's the snow."

Duncan nodded then put on his boots and his cloak before going outside. As he opened the door Mallory screamed after him, "Be careful! The deck might be...." There was a load crashing sound followed by Duncan cussing a blue streak. "...slick."

Mallory walked out of the boat to see Duncan trying to stand up. He put down a hand and helped him to his feet.

"Just walk very carefully," the dragon cautioned.

By the time Duncan got back from his trip he looked like some snow creature. He apparently took offense at the smirk on Mallory's face and said, holding up his hand with his forefinger and thumb barely apart. "I'm this close to using the bathroom upstairs."

He shook himself off like a dog, sending chunks of snow everywhere. He walked quickly to the stove to warm himself.

"That would make using the water pretty gross, and look." Mallory turned on the facet and let the fish have some more clean water. "The tank over the shower feeds the kitchen sink, too."

Duncan nodded his head in appreciation. One of the fish jumped a little and splashed water everywhere. Duncan walked over and looked down.

"You already went fishing." He made a face as he realized what Mallory was doing, "You're cleaning the cabinets from the water in the sink with the fish."

"Yeah so? It's river water so I'd be using fish water in any case. I don't see any difference."

"Point taken." Without another word Duncan took the fish and went with them to the boiler room, Mallory guessed to kill and clean them. Mallory changed the water in the sink and finished washing out the rest of the cabinets.

As he waited for them to dry he rummaged through the wheelbarrow till he found a bag of coffee. He carefully measured it out and then put it into the water that was boiling in the pan on the stove.

Duncan came in and took a deep, appreciative breath. "I have missed the smell of coffee."

"Me, too, not to mention the joy of drinking a hot cup," Mallory said. Duncan sat the cleaned fish on the counter.

"The water has frozen all around the boat," Duncan said curiously.

"Yes, I'd noticed." There was clearly something more on Duncan's mind. Mallory could almost see the wheels turning in the human's tiny little head.

"I'm going to take the head and guts up to the bathroom. I'll pump the water tank full again then dump the guts in the toilet. The fish should have them all eaten before we need to fill the water tank again." In the door Duncan stopped and Mallory was sure he was going to say whatever was on his mind, but then he just started walking again.

Mallory shrugged, strung the fish on the wire and hung them in the oven. Then he started putting all the food supplies away in the cabinets, glad to see that they were nearly full when he'd finished.

Duncan came back in and walked over to the stove to warm himself and said, "All the steam heat does is make the rest of the boat bearable, not really warm."

"That's what I thought. But in a warmer climate it would probably be enough to make the other rooms comfortable. Between you and me, I've been to a lot of places and at all times of the year. Now I admit I purposely try to winter someplace warm, but I have never been anywhere that got even as cold as it already is here."

Duncan nodded but there was still something un-weather-related on his mind.

"So what is it?" Mallory asked, checking the oven to see if the fish were done yet, which they weren't.

"Huh?" Duncan asked.

"What's churning around in your insignificantly small human brain?"

"Ah, nothing." Duncan shrugged. Then his head jerked up as if he'd just heard what Mallory said. "Hey!"

Mallory looked at Duncan and tapped his claws on the floor expectantly.

Duncan looked some embarrassed but then just spit it out. "You're a boy, right?"

"I'm a male of course," Mallory said, taking immediate offense.

"Don't get mad. That's what I thought. But…where's your…?" He continued in a whisper and winced as he spoke, "Was there a terrible accident?"

Mallory laughed so hard a little fire came out his nose. For several seconds he was so amused he couldn't even think to answer. Finally he calmed down enough to say, "It's retractable and quite sound, thank you."

"Oh! Oh, good," Duncan said, ducking his suddenly red face.

Mallory laughed more. "So how long have you wanted to ask that question?"

* * * *

Bilgewater and Sadie had made it to the big city of Jerk Water proper just before winter hit. They had found a decent, reasonably-priced stable for their mounts and inexpensive quarters for themselves. They planned to hole up there through the worst of the weather.

And Jerk Water was certainly not low on places to find a game or a party. If they played their cards right—both literally and figuratively—they should be able to winter in comfort and even in style.

A particularly ripe night at one of the town's many casinos had left them feeling flush, and they found the need to spend a lot of coin. They had gone to one of the better restaurants in town and ordered the surf and turf meal and a not-inexpensive bottle of red wine. In fact their meals had just arrived when Sadie started pointing none too delicately to someone behind Bilgewater.

"Look who that is," she said in an excited whisper. Realizing that she was on the verge of making a spectacle of herself she quit pointing and pretended to be swatting a bug out of the air.

Bilgewater turned only slightly and glanced fleetingly over his shoulder. When he saw who it was he cringed.

"Should we maybe slip out the back way?" Sadie asked.

Bilgewater looked at the delectable dinner he hadn't yet been able to taste and shook his head. "I don't think we should let that moron ruin our meal. Ignore him. Chances are he won't even recognize us."

"I think… Yes, he's waiting tables," Sadie said, and started cutting her steak up—all of it at once—into square pieces that, as far as Bilgewater could tell, were all the exact same size.

"Why do you do that?" Bilgewater asked around the not-too-delicate piece of meat he was chewing on.

"What?" Sadie asked in confusion. "I think he just saw us."

"Look, just ignore him and enjoy your meal. If he is still angry we'll blame everything on Duncan and Mallory. After all, they aren't here to defend themselves, and they took the bulk of his purse, not us."

Sadie nodded. "Works for me."

They had eaten their dinner and had just been served dessert. "Looks like we're in the clear. Our friend seems to have forgotten us."

"Think again. He's headed this way," Sadie said.

"No problem. Follow my lead. Dig into your dessert and pretend not to notice him till he gets here."

Sadie just nodded and focused on her slice of cheesecake, cutting the entire thing into neat, perfect squares.

Bilgewater just shook his head and smiled.

"Hey, I know you two," the man said in a deep, angry whisper. The fact that he was whispering told Bilgewater that the man didn't want to make a scene. No doubt he couldn't afford to lose his crappy job waiting tables, which meant the fellow had fallen on hard times.

Bilgewater stood up, suddenly towering over the much larger man who'd been bent over to catch his ear. He stuck out his hand. "Humphrey isn't it? So nice to see you again. Sadie and I were going to go look for a game later. Care to join us?"

Humphrey straightened up. "Join you! You two and your fancy lizard friend took me for every penny I had. You even stripped the clothes from my back, then you two skipped town."

"We did not skip town, did we, Sadie?"

"No, I don't even think we jogged a little," Sadie said, still making uniform squares of her cheese cake.

"Come on. I know you two were cahoots with that that dragon and his Romancer pal."

"Why, sir! How dare you slander me and my lady friend? It was a friendly card game, a fair and just one as I recall. As for us being in cahoots with those two scoundrels, I can assure you that could not be farther from the truth," Bilgewater said noticing that Sadie had started eating her little squares of dessert, acting as if this entire exchange had nothing to do with her.

This was of course why Sadie was so good with cards. She was capable of just disengaging from what was going on around her and focusing only on what she wanted to focus on. As if to prove his point she said, "You should have ordered the cheese cake. It is divine."

"Perhaps next time, Sadie," Bilgewater said, and sat back down.

"You have any idea where that dragon and his friend are?" Humphrey asked.

"None at all," Bilgewater said, then added just to give credence to his words, "but if I did don't think I'd give him to you first. That dragon has more of our coin than he has of yours."

"I suppose you know nothing about those two beating me up and leaving me for dead, then," Humphrey said, looking at Bilgewater with distrust and more than a little malice.

The maître d' strolled over to their table, no doubt having seen Humphrey's posture. "Is their some problem here?" he asked, glaring at Humphrey.

Sadie smiled her most brilliant smile and said, "None at all. We've had a delightful meal and were just catching up with our old friend, Humphrey."

"Well I'm afraid I will have to steal Humphrey from you. There seems to be a problem at one of his tables." The maître d' pointed towards a thin, blue creature with a tail who was holding up an empty glass and twirling it around his head. He clutched at his throat with his empty hand and coughed dramatically.

Humphrey nodded to the maître d' then glared at Bilgewater and went off to take care of his table.

"Do you believe Duncan and Mallory beat that man up?" Sadie asked thoughtfully.

"It doesn't really seem their style, does it?" Bilgewater shrugged. "I doubt they would do it at all unless they were provoked or threatened. I can see that moron doing both those things. A dragon is always a dragon no matter how civilized he may be."

"You don't poke a bear with a stick."

"Precisely, my dear."

"He's still alive. If the dragon wanted him dead, he'd be dead. I think those two would rather run than fight," Sadie said. "For a minute there I was sure you were going to tell him where Duncan and Mallory most probably are."

"Why would I do that? Those two might just mean a big payday for us someday. At the very least they amuse me, and I certainly have no fondness at all for Humphrey," Bilgewater said.

* * * *

Bilgewater and Sadie had happened to be in a little boat bar trying to decide where they should winter when a fishing crew had come in, smelling of fish and eager to celebrate the end of their season by getting quite drunk.

They'd been playing cards with some of the crew when they started laughing over some poor fool and his dragon who'd gotten their boat stuck.

Their captain walked over and it was clear he didn't share their amusement.

"We pulled them lose easy enough," he told Bilgewater, "but their motor is broken and they're stranded there. I felt bad leaving them like that, but there was nothing I could do. I have to take care of me and mine first, right?"

"Of course. I'm sure they'll be fine."

"I don't know. It's a backwards place and the winters are foul. Not a good place to be a dragon and a foreigner."

"Where were they stuck?" Bilgewater asked.

"On the Sliding West, right in the middle of Winterhurst, with a snow storm on its way. I hope they are a lot smarter then they seemed, or no one will find them alive come spring."

* * * *

Bilgewater looked into the last of his glass of wine. "I think, Sadie, that Duncan and Mallory have enough to worry about right now without siccing Humphrey on them."

Eight

"**B**ecause dragons don't wear pants! It's degrading, like putting pants on a duck," Mallory said indignantly. "Tell me, would you put pants on a duck?"

"If it was cold I'd at least put a shirt on him. Who are you trying to impress, anyway? There's no one out here to see you except me, and I think you're incredibly ugly anyway."

"Talk about the pot calling the kettle black," Mal muttered. He looked at the old pants Duncan was offering him skeptically.

"Look, I made myself a new pair so you can modify these however you have to. You know you'll be warmer."

Mallory took the offered pants, tore a hole in the seat, stuck his tail through, and pulled them on.

"See? That's not so bad, is it?"

"They're warm. Sometimes one must forget about fashion for the sake of comfort," Mallory said.

"Fashion? Seriously, dragon, what sort of fashion statement does being naked make exactly?"

"Well, for one thing, it screams out that my race is much more advanced than one with skin they have to cover to keep from sustaining injury. That we aren't so ugly that we have to cover ourselves...."

"Do you have an answer for everything, dragon?"

"Well I wouldn't be very clever if I didn't, would I?"

Duncan smiled and shook his head.

Over the last two weeks the weather had gotten progressively worse. It seemed it snowed nearly every day, and the more it snowed the colder it got.

Duncan had made another bed frame for himself. They had spent a couple of days splitting bamboo and weaving it into mats that they attached to the bed frames.

They'd measured out the right amount of cloth and then Mallory had sewed his own mattress as Duncan had sewed his. They'd made what looked like big pillow slips then stuffed them with the leaves and grass they'd hauled into the boat before the snow fell. Then they'd stitched the ends closed. They made themselves some pillows in the same way.

Duncan wouldn't have believed it before, but you really couldn't just sleep all the time. He would have said he was an expert at killing time, too, but the truth was they were more or less stuck on the ship, and there wasn't all that much to do.

Whenever it wasn't actively snowing and the wind wasn't blowing they'd venture out to gather more wood. But they couldn't stay outside long before they had to worry about frostbite.

Duncan used his sword to cut down small trees and chop wood. Oddly it seemed to him that his aim was truer when he was chopping wood than it ever had been in sword practice. Of course it was easier to hit something if it wasn't moving around trying not to be hit.

Only two weeks had passed, and they'd already made beds and cut and stacked all the wood they brought into the boat. It made it a lot easier to walk from the kitchen upstairs to the bathroom when they needed to fish or pump water but made him wonder just what they were going to do for the rest of the winter.

He had sharpened his sword more in the last two weeks than in the entire time he'd owned it. Since he'd been given the sword when he was twelve that in itself spoke volumes.

He looked out the window. The snow was falling again and there was already at least a foot and a half on the ground. The ice on the river was now thick enough he could have walked on it if he wasn't afraid of slipping and falling.

Mallory had suggested that Duncan make some snow shoes from woven bamboo. Duncan did so, and while they worked pretty well they were hard to walk in. They had cleared the ice on the gangplank and the deck where they had to walk by dumping the ashes from the stove on it every day.

Duncan hoped they had enough wood because he was pretty sure it would be impossible to get any after this next snowfall.

It was too hard to walk in the snow, and it was too cold to be outside long enough to relieve themselves. They had, in fact, started going in a bucket they kept in the boiler room, and once a day they argued over whose turn it was to dump it. Whoever lost had to hold his nose with one hand, and carry the bucket to a pit they'd dug on shore—the whole while praying that he didn't slip on some ice, falling flat on his rear in the freezing snow, watching in horror as that bucket of waste flew up in the air to land…where ever it may.

Outside the wind was really blowing. In fact, the windows on the starboard side of the ship were coating over with snow so fast that soon you wouldn't be able to see out of them. Yet the boat barely moved at all, no doubt because of the thick ice all around it.

At his shoulder, Mallory, no doubt seeing what he was looking at said, "Another bad storm."

"You know at first I thought the snow was pretty," Duncan said. "Now it just looks cold."

"No doubt about it, we're wintering right here," Mallory said with a laugh.

"I guess by spring we will have thought of every way there is to eat turnips and fish," Duncan added with a sigh.

They'd already had fish and turnip stew, fish cakes, turnip cakes, turnip bread, fried turnips, baked turnips, mashed turnips, etcetera, etcetera.

"Variety is the spice of life." The dragon laughed.

"What are we going to do all day, every day?" Duncan asked.

"What we've been doing. Working on getting this boat ship shape and ready to sail. Keeping the fire fed, eating, sleeping....."

"It's pretty monotonous, isn't it? I swear, Mal, if we have one more conversation about how cold or white it is, I'm going to scream."

Mallory chuckled a little. "I hear ya. Snow-covered landscape is only pretty when it's a novelty. When it's all you see out the window all day every day, well, the bloom is off the rose as they say."

"I wish we could have managed to get that part fixed and steamed out of here before the cold hit. That jerk blacksmith."

"That man will rue the day he messed with us, that's for sure. I'm cooking up a plan that blacksmith won't soon forget. Don't you worry about that. I've got plenty of time, and by spring thaw I'll know just how to get him to fix the part. Maybe even be able to get him to pay us for the privilege."

"Just what do you have in mind?"

"That's the thing about a really good plan, Dunc. It doesn't come to you all at once. The minute it has fully gelled, all will be revealed."

* * * *

In the next two weeks the arguments about whose turn it was to dump the bucket became more heated as the snow got deeper and the wind colder. And in spite of their best efforts they had way too many conversations about how cold and white it was.

They took turns fishing and cooking without fighting at all. They kept themselves reasonably clean heating the water on the stove and taking washcloth baths in the sink. They washed their clothes in the same sink and hung them on some ropes they had strung near the ceiling in the kitchen to dry.

They made a broom from some dried grass they'd pulled before the snow got too deep. They tied it to a stick with some wire and used the broom to sweep every room on the boat. Twice actually.

They'd washed and scrubbed everything they could find to wash and scrub.

After having done all that, they basically had nothing at all to do most days. Just fish, cook, do minor cleaning, eat, sleep and stoke the furnace. Of course there was always talking about how cold and white it was outside.

In fact for the last three or four days everything had just been complete routine to the point that Duncan had started to look forward to seeing the demon at night. At least it was different from what was going on during the day.

Fred had come up with several very useful items that he was happy to let them use. Among other things a tea strainer, several sections of rope, and some tin can lids. When he'd first showed up with the tin can lids Duncan had thought they were useless. Then one day he noticed that they fit over knot and rat holes very nicely. He'd nailed them over holes all over the ship and was sad when he ran out.

They had just settled down on their respective beds and were starting to eat their dinner. As the last lights of dawn faded the demon popped in wearing a red-checked napkin tied around his neck. It had a bowl in one hand and a fork in the other.

"You're late," Mallory said.

"I was washing my hair," he said with his big demon voice.

Fred maybe had three hairs on his entire head. He walked over to the counter where Mallory had left him some food in the pot. He carefully spooned it into his bowl then flopped down on the counter to eat.

"My gods I'm so incredibly, unbelievably bored!" Mallory said.

"Me too," Duncan said, sighing almost with relief.

"Me too," the demon said with his small voice. When they both glared at him, he shrugged and said in his big voice, "Me used to raise hell every night. Scare all hell out of rectangle guy. Now am like pet rat."

"Really ugly pet rat," Duncan mumbled. Then he said to Mallory, "Don't get me wrong. I'm glad we have plenty of food and are warm. I'm happy we have a nice place to live and comfortable beds and all that. But having everything we need, well…there just isn't much to do, is there?"

"Tozactly!" Mallory said. "It's that whole 'beware of what wishing for can get you' thing." He looked confused by his own words then shook his head. "That isn't exactly what the saying is, but it means about the same."

"When I was back in Spurna all I ever used to do was lie around and hide from the war. I could happily sleep away most of the day. I didn't care if I ever did anything at all. Maybe I'd tinker with something…."

"Tinker!" Fred hissed in his big voice. "Me know there something about you I not like." Then in his small one added, "Tinkerer. I shouldah know."

"Oh yes. You're one to judge anyone. A walking fungus that lives to scare things and tear stuff up," Duncan snapped. "My point is that since I left home, good, bad, or indifferent, I sort of got used to always being one step from trouble."

"Yeah," Mallory said, as if he knew exactly what the human was talking about. "It's nice not to have to worry about where we're going to sleep or if we're going to be able to eat. But because we don't have a problem—at least not one we can do anything about right now—there is just nothing to do. Sit and wait the weather out."

Duncan sighed. "I keep thinking I would have been a few coins ahead if I'd bought fewer supplies and bought a set of checkers or a deck of cards. You don't happen to have anything like that do you, Fred?"

"Oh, Fred see how this is. You need something you call me Fred. You don't, I am walking fungus," Fred said all devil-voiced again.

"Do you have something like that or not?" Duncan asked.

"No…I have harmonica. Play real good. I go get." And with a pop he was gone. He came back a few minutes later with a harmonica and he started playing. He wouldn't have been bad at all if he didn't play the notes loud and then low and then loud and then low.

Duncan realized right then why the creature talked so funny. It was a matter of wind. He breathed funny, so he spoke funny.

Mallory suddenly reached inside his vest and started feeling around. At first slowly and then more franticly. About ten minutes later he pulled out a deck of cards. "Five card stud! Aces are wild!" he called out.

"Mallory, the only card games I know how to play are Go Fish and Spoons," Duncan said.

"Then I'll teach you. Since you have the learning curve of a turnip, that should consume most of the winter."

* * * *

The human was indeed a slow learner. It took forever to teach him the bare minimum needed to attempt a game.

Fred, on the other hand, was actually quite a good poker player, which was good because two hands in, Mallory realized he was already getting rusty.

No matter how many hands they played the human never seemed to improve. The truth was Duncan had no talent for cards. A sick three-legged cat could have read his tells. He was easily excited and whether excited or distracted it was easy to get him to bet far more beans than he should have.

The more bored Duncan got, the stranger the things he did to amuse himself. He ran up and down the stairs several times a day. He said to keep in shape.

"What shape?" Mallory asked in confusion.

"Hah?"

"What shape are you going for exactly? Won't having huge legs just make your head look even smaller?"

"My head's not small, lizard."

"If you say so." Mallory shrugged.

"Still you could be right about my legs." He then dropped to the floor and started doing pushups. It all seemed too much like work for Mallory's liking. He assumed the human was now willingly doing things he'd worked his whole life to avoid doing. He didn't say so because as long as Duncan was busy Mallory could have a little peace and quiet.

"Well at least some peace," Mallory mumbled as the thudding sounds of Duncan's size fourteen feet slapping against the stairs echoed around the boat.

Mallory put his mind on how best to deal with the crooked black-smith and get the part fixed. The plan would start to form, he'd get pieces of it floating in on different thoughts, it would be almost complete, and then he'd become all too aware of some missing element—the one thing that eluded him. The glue that held his plan together just wasn't there.

Duncan ran in the room and Mallory had to work at not screaming at him. He had been close this time, so close. Duncan dove under his bed, dug around and drug something out.

Taking a deep breath and swallowing his anger Mallory forced the calm words, "What on Overlap are you doing now?" through clenched teeth.

"I was thinking I'd clean my armor." Duncan held his charred chain mail up in front of him.

As Mallory looked at him, suddenly that last piece of the puzzle was in place. He jumped off his stump, walked over and ripped the shirt out of the human's hands. "Don't you dare clean this!" He held the shirt up and looked at it. "I know exactly how to take care of the blacksmith, get our part fixed, and put some coin in our pockets to boot."

"Honest?" Duncan asked excitedly.

Mallory smiled. "Oh, most definitely not." He laid out his plan.

"But do you think it will really work?"

"You cut me to the quick! Of course it will work. It's my idea after all."

"How do you know they'll be afraid of you?"

"That guy with the wheelbarrow was plenty afraid of me."

The human nodded, but then said, "Yeah but you ran up on him and apparently he's a bit of a drunk."

"You were afraid of me," Mallory reminded.

"Yeah, but I'm afraid of caterpillars."

"True, but take my word for it. Those village folks ain't ever seen the likes of me. You remember what our friend Anthony said? These people are backwards."

"Let's do it," Duncan said excitedly.

"I think we better wait for this ice and snow to melt first."

Nine

The winter seemed to drag on and ever on and yet Duncan never got any better at playing cards. It did pass the time, but they were both sleeping a lot. While Mallory spent more and more of his waking time working out the intricate details of his plan, the human was mostly delving ever deeper into cabin fever.

The human was now working out four or five times a day. He had built a woman from bamboo, dried grass, and baling wire, and Mallory didn't want to know what they did when they were upstairs alone.

The absolute extent of Duncan's ailment came to light when he argued with Mallory that it was his turn to dump the slop bucket. Mallory was trying to get out of it even though he knew it was his turn when he realized the human was saying it was *his* turn.

"Knock yourself out," Mallory said, letting Duncan *win*.

Mallory thought his big dragon brain was better equipped to deal with boredom and confinement. He had been wondering about fish-eating ever since Duncan had pointed out that they weren't a vegetable. They'd been baiting their "fishing hole" with fish guts and food scraps all winter and… Well the fish were easier to catch every day. They never seemed to wise up, so they must be pretty dim, and so Mallory came to the conclusion that they really were plants.

At one point he'd been sure that after this winter he'd never want to see another turnip as long as he lived. Then as the pile got low and the ground outside was still covered with snow he started to worry about not having enough turnips. After that he started savoring every bite of turnip he got.

The proof that they had been stuck inside way too long with too little variety in their diet was punctuated when Duncan made what he called chili beans. Under-cooked beans with some spice slung in it with chunks of fish and they both ate it and talked about what a nice change of pace it was.

Mallory had swallowed his pride and was now not only wearing Duncan's old pants but one of his old tunics as well. He knew what he must look like; he just didn't care.

He didn't really start to worry about how the cabin fever was affecting Duncan's sanity till the human nearly begged Fred to work at scaring him. In fact, his exact words were, "Do your evil best, demon!"

"Oh it's on, monkey boy," the demon hissed back in his tiny voice.

The very next day they ate the last of the turnips and started to talk about whether they had enough wood to last the rest of the winter.

They had been rationing how much they burned which was one of the reasons Mallory had given in and started wearing clothes. After all, they'd only had three days to gather wood before the snow fell.

While they'd gone out when they could, with the snow as deep as it was it was hard to find deadfall. It was harder still to chop down trees and cut them up with the sword. They still had coal, but they were trying to save it for when they got the part fixed. While Mallory admitted his fire could help occasionally he couldn't just sit around belching and lighting it all day to heat their space.

"Eventually I run out of gas," he'd explained to Duncan, "even with our bean and turnip-heavy diet."

* * * *

They were down to one emaciated stack of wood and were talking about burning the coal and then maybe their stump chairs when the sun came out—bright. Soon after that the wind stopped blowing and the snow started to melt. Water ran across the landscape, digging holes through the snow, till by day three the whole place looked like a giant spider web.

They ran out and gathered more wood, sloshing through the water, snow and mud. Mallory kicked his foot in the air, dislodging a clump of mud before walking onto the ship. He dumped his load of wood on the deck.

"Soon now," Duncan said, following Mallory in and dumping his wood in the same pile. "Soon we'll be able to put 'Operation Take All the Blacksmith's Money and Fix Our Boat' into full swing, and then we can get out of here."

"Way before next winter," Mallory added, his face knotted up in thought. "We have got to have a better name for our operation. A superb plan deserves an excellent handle."

"It was the first thing I came up with. So sue me," Duncan grumbled.

They both thought on it while they broke up deadwood into furnace-size pieces. They were making a huge mess, having brought snow and mud and everything else in on the logs. All Mallory could think was that cleaning up their mess would give them something to do.

"What about 'Operation Get Outta Here'?" Duncan asked.

"Too pedestrian," Mallory said.

"What does *that* mean?" Duncan asked, a bit put out.

"It means idiots can understand it."

The look on the human's face said he didn't know whether he should feel insulted or not. Then he said, "What about 'Operation Fix Thingy'?"

"We need something that sounds clever and a little heroic." Mallory thought about it then smiled. "I've got it. 'Operation Blacksmith Down'."

"How come everything you come up with is always so much better than anything I come up with?"

"I don't know, Dunc, why is that?"

"Jerk," Duncan mumbled.

"'Operation Blacksmith Down' it is then."

"It's a stupid name."

* * * *

As the last of the snow melted Duncan put on the new tunic and pants he'd made himself. They of course mostly looked just like his old clothes. After all he liked red and tan, so he'd bought red and tan cloth. Since the only pattern he had to work with was taken from his old clothes, he was wearing a red tunic and tan britches.

He loaded his pack and started for town with his one coin in his pocket. It wouldn't buy much and they were low on everything. But his main reason for going was not to buy supplies.

He tried to act surprised, but he really wasn't when the dragon appeared just as he was about to leave with two coins and a story. "I found these while we were cleaning."

Duncan glared at him. "And it didn't cross your mind to say anything till now." The dragon just smiled and shrugged.

"Just how much more money do you have squirreled away?"

"Why, Dunc! I can't possibly tell you how hurt I am. Mostly because you need to get going." Mallory shoved him down the gangplank. "Have a good day casing the town."

Duncan started walking. After a moment he turned and the dragon smiled and waved. Duncan glared at him then added the two coins to his pouch and started walking double time.

I wonder just how much money Mallory actually does have, and just where he's hiding it. Because of course during the long winter when he'd had nothing better to do Duncan had searched every inch of that boat—including Mallory's vest. He'd never found any money.

Duncan started pushing the empty wheelbarrow along. *Surely Mallory doesn't have enough to pay the crooked blacksmith his price, or he wouldn't have let us winter here. Maybe this is the last two coins he has. If we'd run out of supplies he sure would have felt funny holding them back.*

He had only a little trouble finding his old marks, and then the trail was easy to follow, no doubt because he'd been down it twice already. He walked as fast as he could and reached the road before midday.

He had hoped to make really good time on the road, but it was nothing but deep ruts and heavy clay that clung to his boots and the wheel of the wheelbarrow. He wound up walking most of the way in the woods just to the side of the road. The ground was soft there, but a thick leaf cover kept him from sinking past his knees in the mud.

The town was just as he remembered it except for the red mud that seemed to be everywhere. By the time he reached the store his boots and the wheel of the wheelbarrow were caked with several inches of red clay. He stopped on the front porch and started scraping the mud from his boots on the bottom step. He left the dirty wheelbarrow on the front porch and walked in.

The floor inside the store was covered in the red gunk. He wondered why he'd bothered to scrape his shoes off at all.

Sam recognized him right away. "I see you survived our winter."

Duncan nodded and said, "I've brought your wheelbarrow back, though I'm afraid it's a bit muddy."

The shop keep laughed. "Son, this time of year Hellsbut ain't never nothing but mud. Freeze-thaw makes the ground turn to mush. Don't worry about it. Always takes us a couple of weeks after the last thaw for things to dry out."

"Is it worth my time to even talk to the blacksmith about his prices? Has the winter softened him at all, do you think?"

The same two old men who'd been playing checkers in the window the last time he was there were there again. Duncan guessed Sam was right about them practically living there.

Felix looked up at him and said, "Are you kidding me? Boy, winter only drives his prices up. He doesn't work most of the winter. He tries to make up for it by charging even more while everyone is trying to get their seed in. He knows no one can afford to have their equipment be down at planting time. The man's a pig I tell ya."

"Why if I was a younger man I'd show him what for," Mort said.

"Listen to you," Felix said. "When you were a younger man a good stiff breeze still would have blown you away. You wouldn't have done nothing. Nothing I tell you would you have done."

Felix and Mort started arguing, so Duncan turned his attention back to Sam.

"Don't know what I'm going to do about the part then," Duncan said. "I can't go anywhere without it. I'm down to my last three coins and I need more supplies than I can afford. Is there no one in this town who can build another forge?"

"Folks have tried, but an unfortunate accident always befalls them or their forge. Have I mentioned Earl has three huge worth-nothing sons?"

"Nothing but bully boys if you ask me," Felix chimed in.

"Someone ought to show Earl and his three idgits what for," Mort said.

"Yeah, yeah," Felix said shaking his head.

"Do you have anything of worth you could trade him?" Sam asked Duncan.

Duncan almost smiled. This was the question he'd been waiting for. The one he'd put the bait out for. "My boat. But without that…. Well I don't need him, do I? There is my armor and my sword but without them I'll not be able to make a living if I do get out of here."

"Just what is it you do for a living, son?" Sam asked curiously. "Are you a mercenary?"

"I'll pay you today to get rid of Earl and his boys," Mort said.

"No sir, I'm no mercenary. You may think it sounds silly, because from what you've said, I'm guessing you don't have a problem with them in your sector, but I'm a dragon hunter. Dragons still cause trouble here and there from time to time, and I travel the river helping towns in need. Up till now I've made a fine living, but last year very few people had any real dragon problems. It seems more and more dragons are going into accounting and less and less are into terrorizing and sacking villages. Which is good, I suppose, for everyone except me. Well, I'd best get what I can and head back. I don't really know what to tell my family. At least the fishing has been good."

He worked at looking as low as any man could look. He got some more spices, beans, cornmeal and coffee he added, "I better get home. I can't believe such a mean-spirited old bugger could run a whole town and make so many people miserable. Is there no stopping him? Does he just own everything except this store?"

As easy as that, they were all telling him just what Earl owned and where it was.

"You have to remember I'm a stranger around here. I don't have any idea where you're talking about."

"Let me make you a map," Felix said. And just like that the old man hunted up a piece of paper and a pencil. Naturally Duncan happened to take that map with him when he left.

He nearly skipped home, feeling very full of himself. Step one of 'Operation Blacksmith Down' had been a complete success.

* * * *

Mallory rubbed his hands together in anticipation. He gave the map one more good look then handed it back to Duncan.

"You got it?" Duncan asked him for the tenth time.

"I've got it, Dunc, I've got it. For the eleventh time, I've got it. Sheesh!"

"I just don't want you sacking the wrong thing. These people have enough trouble from that blacksmith without you torching their stuff."

"I know what I'm doing, Dunc, just don't get caught sneaking around."

"I won't." Duncan put up the hood on the new cloak he'd made himself. The hood had been Mallory's idea, because as he put it, it did more than keep Duncan's tiny head warm.

The human would wait a few minutes before sneaking into town because Mallory figured no one was likely to notice Duncan sulking around while Mallory was doing his thing.

The road was still rutted but mostly dry. Mallory looked around to make sure Duncan was out of sight and then he ran for the edge of town.

A fellow came towards him with a hoe slung over his shoulder, whistling, and obviously not watching where he was going. Mallory slowed his pace to match the man's till the man saw Mallory's feet.

The man stopped, took in the feet, then looked up and up and up Mallory's body. Before his eyes reached Mallory's head, the man started shaking uncontrollably, apparently unable to speak or move. Mallory bared his teeth, showing their full length—something he saved for special occasions. Then he blew a small flame out of his mouth and let the smoke pour out his nostrils. He followed that with a small roar.

The man dropped his hoe, turned in one step, and took off running and yelling at the top of his lungs, "Dragon! Dragon!"

Mallory made a big show of chasing after him, roaring and occasionally spitting some fire at the man's heels. When they hit the edge of town the guy headed off one way and Mallory headed in the other direction towards his first intended target.

* * * *

Earl had been working at his forge and thinking of what else his money could buy when Thomas came running up looking white and screaming something. More irritated than anything else, Earl quit pounding the metal he was working and set his hammer and work aside. He walked up to the front of his shed.

"See here, Thomas, I'm trying to work. What on earth are you going on about?"

"Dragon! Huge! Big! Fire breathing! Claws and teeth of death and…. Dragon!"

"Clam down. Whatever are you going on about? There hasn't been a dragon in these parts for fifty years, maybe longer. You want the whole town to take to the streets in a panic?" Earl said, agitated. "Did you actually see something or did you get into Leroy's turnip wine?"

"Huge dragon…big teeth…breathing fire. Big! Big! Big!" Thomas got out and then without further explanation he just took off running again.

Earl was about to blow off the whole incident and go back to work when he heard a distant roar followed by screams of terror. Then, over to his right he saw flames and could hear pigs squealing. Before he had time to run towards the commotion, Thomas came running back past him in the opposite direction. He was screaming, "Dragon! Heading this way!"

Earl left his shop and was almost run over by a couple of big hogs. Right behind them was a huge, blue dragon. It ran towards him breathing fire and baring its razor-sharp teeth dripping with spit.

Earl froze right where he was, unable to move, and the dragon was soon only feet from him. If he hadn't had his leather apron on the fireball that hit him in his chest would have no doubt fried him. Instead it just knocked him on his back and seared his eyebrows.

The thing was gone as quickly as it had come.

The blacksmith jumped up and ran towards the fire, right into a stampede of frightened hogs. He was thrown one way and another till he lost his footing all together and landed with a thud and splash in a mud puddle. The pigs proceeded to take a course right over his body, as if not wanting to get their feet wet.

As he struggled up, spitting mud and worse from his mouth, he realized the fire had to be his own pigsty. The one he had so cleverly built next to the grocer's house. With any luck the grocer's house would go up as well. As he got closer it was clear that the grocer's house was untouched while Earl's fence had been completely destroyed. Not one of his pigs was in what was left of the pen. The pig house was already nearly burned to the ground.

To make matters worse, every person in town was standing around watching the building burn and the pigs run off. No one was making any effort to round up his pigs or start a bucket brigade.

"See here people, get some water. Put that fire out. The rest of you go after those pigs," he ordered.

No one moved.

"There's no building left to save. It would be better to let it burn," someone in the crowd said. Earl didn't know who it was, but he did have a point.

"We got bigger things to worry about, mayor," Sam said with no effort at all to hide his contempt. "That dragon could have just as easily killed us all and burned down our homes instead of your pig sty. You're the mayor. What are you going to do to protect this town from that dragon?"

"What about that young fellow with the broken boat?" Felix asked. "He said he's a dragon killer."

"Anyone know how to find him?" Mort asked.

"Well we know he's along the river somewhere," Sam said.

"Hold on here just a minute, fellows. Ain't no reason to go looking for no dragon-huntin' stranger. Man like that's going to want to be paid and paid plenty."

"It's the sort of thing we pay taxes for, mayor," Sam said. "I say we spend that money and get rid of this dragon."

"Don't be so hasty. There's no reason to believe the dragon will come back," Earl insisted.

"There's no reason to believe he won't," the widow Boil said. "What's all that money for if not to protect the town?" From the way the crowd mumbled they were all thinking pretty much the same thing.

"Look, if that dragon comes back we'll be ready for him. I'll put my sons on lookout around the clock for the next few days. If there's any trouble, we can all band together, take up weapons, and take care of the matter without any outside help."

"We don't have any weapons because some conniving blacksmith makes sure we spend all our money fixing our farm equipment." Earl looked around but couldn't see who had said it. What he could see was that the crowd was turning ugly. He started to sweat just a bit.

"This guy is a professional dragon killer. It's what he does. And because you wouldn't fix his part for less than an arm and two legs he's still around here somewhere. All we have to do is find him," Sam said. "I say we track him down and pay him whatever he wants to kill this dragon."

Duncan worked hard at not snickering over how his last comment had riled the crowd. This was every bit as easy as Mallory had said it would be.

"Now see here, people, where is your civic pride? I'm sure if we all stand against him, pitchforks in hand, that dragon will go running for the hills," the blacksmith said.

Duncan moved a little further into the shadows, cupped his mouth in an attempt to throw his voice and said, "Who is he kidding? Did you see the size of that thing? All those teeth, that armor-scaled hide? I'll bet that thing makes mincemeat of anyone who tries to stand against him."

This caused another big anti-Earl uproar from the crowd.

"Fork up the money and hire the dragon slayer!" someone yelled.

"What is wrong with you? Calm down I say, just calm down," Earl ordered. It got only a little more quiet than it had been before. "So far no one is hurt, and the only one who's lost anything of worth is me. My own sons will keep watch night and day at all the roads into and out of Hellsbut. We don't know this dragon has any intention of coming back. He's likely as not settled down feasting on one of my hogs right now. If he does come back, my boys will make quick work of him."

Duncan waited till he was sure that they had decided to stay the mayor's course, and then he snuck out of town to find Mallory.

"Well?" Mallory asked, warming his hands by the small fire he had made. Duncan filled him in on everything that he'd seen and heard.

"His sons are supposed to be big guys," Duncan said, somewhat worried.

"Where did he say he was going to have them keep watch?" Mallory asked thoughtfully.

"At all the roads into town," Duncan answered.

Mallory smiled and rubbed his hands together in anticipation. "So he needs a little more convincing. Well I can do that. There's no rule that says I have to enter town by any road."

Duncan chuckled. "For a pacifist, I think you're enjoying this a bit too much."

"I'm not going to hurt anyone. Of course they don't know that. There's nothing quite as invigorating as beating a bastard at his own game."

* * * *

Earl's sons had been none too happy about guarding the roads against marauding dragons big enough to slaughter and eat a whole hog. When they'd rounded up all their father's hogs as they'd been ordered to, they never found the biggest boar. Earl's oldest son Joe Bob had even been openly defiant.

"I say if there's a dragon slayer out there somewhere, you find him and hire him. Let some stranger get eaten instead of one of us. Besides, watching the roads in and out of town—isn't that a little lame? I mean seriously, Dad. Do you think this dragon plays by some rule book that says he has to come into town on the road? And it's colder than a well digger's butt at night and…."

Earl slammed a spear into each of his son's hands. "You boys are nothing but a bunch of lay-abouts. You let me support you as you get fatter by the day. Well, it's time you earned your keep. You go out there, and you watch for that thing. If you see it, you kill it. Now did you hear what I just told you?"

"Yes, Dad," they said, but he could hear them mumbling between themselves as they walked to the road. As they split off to go to their different posts each of them turned around and gave him a go-to-hell-look that, just for a minute, made his blood run cold.

Then Earl walked into his house, threw some wood on his fire, crawled into his warm bed and went to sleep.

Earl reluctantly crawled out of his warm bed extra early the next morning and ventured out to check on his sons. He found each of them asleep, leaning against their spear shafts. After he shouted them awake each one announced they had seen neither hide nor hair of any dragon.

Of course, this might have been due entirely to the fact that apparently none of them had their eyes open all night. After screaming at them each in turn about how sorry they were, he left them at their posts and started for his forge.

He got things fired up for the day, glad that he didn't have to sit in the cold and watch out for the dragon.

Earl wasn't really expecting any trouble, so he went back to doing what he did best—low quality work for three times what it would be worth if he did it right. He hadn't been working long when he heard a commotion from the west side of town, then the east, and finally the south. He ran to the center of town and was almost run over by his three sons.

"Dragon!" they screamed, basically bouncing into him and each other in their flight past him.

"Get out there and fight! There are three of you and only one of him," Earl ordered.

"Fight it yourself," Joe Bob said. He pushed the spear into his father's hands and then took off at a dead run. His brothers followed him, and Earl stood there alone with three spears in his hands.

The town's people ran around in a panic, mostly knocking each other down. In fact, they were doing nothing but making themselves easy prey for the dragon.

Then the dragon came into sight. Just as Earl decided to charge the dragon himself, it threw a fireball that hit the wooden shafts of the spears. They immediately caught fire, scorching his hand before he could let them go. Then, as if out of sheer spite, the dragon turned and hit the big window of the town saloon with its tail.

Of course the saloon was owned by Earl.

Enraged, he picked one of the charred spears up off the ground and slung it towards the creature. The dragon grabbed the shortened spear out of the air and slung it back to land with a thud at Earl's feet. Then it went running down the road past him and out of town.

No sooner had he seen the last of the creature and checked himself for serious injury than here came his sons on their mounts. They were riding hard *away* from the dragon.

Joe Bob shouted over his shoulder, "Dragon's all yours, Dad!"

"Wait a minute! You get your cowardly hides back here right now!" Earl screamed after them.

They didn't even turn around, much less slow their horses.

As he watched the fruit of his loins disappear down the road, the town's people gathered around him like vultures around a carcass. They glared at him for a second and then they all started screeching at once, demanding he do something.

"All right, all right!" Earl held up his hands as he faced the crowd. "Get a group together as soon as possible. Go find this dragon slayer you keep talking about, and we'll pay him whatever he wants."

* * * *

"Step three?" Duncan asked as Mallory came into view.

"Step three," Mallory said, smiling.

Duncan put on his leggings—one charred and dented from being used over a fire—and his chain mail—the big burned spot clear and visible from a distance. Then he strapped on his sword.

"Did you leave it dinged and a little dingy like I told you?" Mallory asked.

"You know me. If it saves me some work I'm all over it," Duncan said with a smile. He grabbed the broken thingy and stuck it in his pack then slung the pack on his back. "Wish me luck."

"Remember what I said. Be careful not to over sell it."

"Gotcha." He left camp, walked to the road and headed for town.

As he hit the edge of town he could clearly see that most of the town had gathered in front of the store. He tried to hide his smile, looking at the ground as he walked. After all, he was supposed to be a man at the end of his tether. No joy left in his soul. He was forced to make a horrible sacrifice for the sake of his family.

"There he is!" Sam yelled out excitedly. The next thing Duncan knew most of the town had come to greet him. He looked up and did his best to look confused.

"What's going on?" Duncan asked, working on an air of cluelessness that normally came easily to him.

"Are we glad to see you!" Sam said. "What brings you to town?"

Duncan could hear pieces of the muttered conversation all around him.

"Look at him. He's a monster."

One said, "Look at his armor. It's charred with dragon fire."

Still another said, "He must be the greatest dragon slayer on the whole of Overlap."

It was hard not to let his head swell and strut like a peacock. He had to really work on looking beaten and humbled.

He cut a glare at Earl to help him get back into character. "I have come to trade my sword and my armor—all that I have of worth, besides my boat—to get my boat piece fixed. I must move my family to a place where there is work for me." He pulled his pack off his back and rummaged through it. He held up the mangled pieces from his boat. "The two must be made one. There is no other way."

The whole town turned as a group to glare at Earl, who swallowed hard, stepped forward and said, "Perhaps a trade can be made, Dragon Slayer. I'll make you a new part if you take care of our tiny little insignificant dragon problem."

Duncan's eyes narrowed to slits. "Dragon problem? You have a dragon problem?"

"A small one, yes," Earl said. "With the emphasis on *small*."

"There is no such thing as a *small* dragon problem, Mr. Blacksmith," Duncan said. "Now let's see. When all I needed was a fair day's work for a fair price, you tried to crook me. Now that *you* need *my* services, you look to take advantage of me yet again. In what place on this world do you think building a boat part is worth risking one's life to slay a dragon?"

"The town has a lot of tax money!" one of the people shouted out.

"Why should we use any of the town's money? So far the monster hasn't torn up anything but the mayor's stuff. Earl is the richest man in town—not even counting our tax revenues which he keeps and doesn't use to fix any of the town's problems," Sam said. "He owns the town saloon and overcharges us for our drinks. He has cheated us all at his smithy at one time or other."

"Now see here, Sam, I'll not have you befouling my good name...."

"Befouling your good name?" Felix said. He started laughing so hard Duncan was afraid it might kill the old man. "If he gave you the middle name 'Sewage,' the people of this town couldn't think less of you than they already do."

Several people laughed, including Duncan. He looked at Earl and said, "Because of you, my family and I had to live through the harshest winter of our lives with far too few supplies. It seems only fair to me that *you* should pay my fee since apparently *you* are the only one who has suffered a loss of property at the talons of this beast."

Earl looked around him, and realized he was outnumbered, without his bully boys to protect him. So he sighed and said, "What's your fee, dragon slayer?"

"First you fix my part and remember that I'll know if you do a poor job. Then I'll want two hundred coins."

"Two hundred! That's usurious!"

"Of course I *could* let the dragon sack your whole town," Duncan said, pulling his blade and looking down the length of it, showing off its well-used appearance.

All around him the town's people started hollering at Earl, demanding he do whatever it took to get rid of the dragon.

"Fine," Earl said as if the word was dragged from him. "But for two hundred coins I shall want to see you kill the dragon."

Duncan cleared his throat. "Let's see. Some *tinkerer* following me around all day, getting in my way, that will cost you three-hundred coins."

Earl glared at Duncan as he ate his own words. "Fine, two hundred it is then."

Duncan handed the broken part to Earl. "I'll expect that part finished by tonight and accept it as an advance on my fee, if you please."

Earl obviously wasn't pleased, but he took the part and walked away with it.

* * * *

The bartender was sweeping up the glass from the window that Mallory had smashed. Duncan had been rushed along on a sea of mankind to the saloon where they bought him a tall, almost-cold beer and slammed it into his hand.

"Old skin flint paid a fortune for that window. Damn hard to move a piece of glass that big over all these dirt roads and get it here whole. Must be just crushing his evil old soul to see it smashed in a million pieces," Sam said.

Duncan realized the dragon had probably broken it for that very reason. The best way to get to a greedy man was always through his wallet.

"You see those thugs of Earl's grab their horses and run for the hills?" the bartender said, laughing. "Never thought I'd see the day those cocky boys were running scared. Made my whole year, I tell you."

"So how many dragons have you killed?" Felix asked Duncan.

Duncan thought about it. What was a good number? What made him look good without going into the unbelievable category?

"How many dragons have you killed?" Felix asked again, and Duncan realized the whole bar was silent, waiting for the answer.

"I'm counting," Duncan said. He thought quickly and then said, "Nine. I've killed nine dragons."

This seemed to impress the crowd without getting any of them to call him a liar, so he felt good about his choice.

"How do you fight a dragon?" someone he couldn't see asked.

"Well first you have to find out where the dragon's lair is," Duncan said, watching as everyone moved even closer to him. "See, a dragon finds some cave or overhang he likes, and he decides to live here. Problem is, dragons are sort of solitary creatures. If there are people close to where he wants to live he tries to get rid of them. Usually by killing them or eating them—sometimes both. Oh, dragon attacks start out pretty simple—tear up a few stock pens maybe eat a few animals…" Duncan motioned to where the bartender was still cleaning up broken glass. "… break a few windows. But if that doesn't do it, if all the people don't turn tail and run, well then the dragon he gets real testy. It's never long after that he starts with the killing and maiming and eating of people.

"It's all about finding where they've toed in, then—every dragon's a little different. Some you have to just fight, some you can trap. Depends on what kind of dragon it is, really, and whether they're in it for food or just playing a game. Any of you know if there is a cave around close?"

"There is a haunted cave up west of town not too far, called the Devil's Hole," Mort said.

"Haunted?" he asked.

"Yep, sure enough. A witch used to carry on the black craft up there. Sacrifice children and such. She died a hundred years ago, but her spirit's still there," Felix said.

"How do you know?" Sam asked skeptically.

"I seen me a wooden stick figure by the entrance one time," Mort said.

"There was a stack of rocks, too. It was scary," Felix added.

"Is there another cave around?" Duncan asked, since he didn't much care for the sound of a haunted cave.

"Nope," Felix said, and everyone else in the bar agreed. "'Sides, you don't really think some dead witch is going to scare off a dragon, do ya?"

Duncan took in a deep breath, let it out, and knowing Mallory said, "No. Probably not. Guess I'd better have a map to this cave. That's most likely where this dragon will be holed up."

He watched as several men at once started drawing a map out on a dirty tablecloth covering one of the tables. They were having trouble agreeing on exactly where the cave was. After several false starts they drew what looked to Duncan like a fairly straight-forward map, till Felix told him he was looking at it upside down.

* * * *

"All I'm saying is you were laying it on a little thick," Mallory told Duncan as he held the torch and lead the way. "You sure we're going west?"

"What exactly do you mean?" Duncan said, more than a little put out.

Mallory worked at imitating Duncan, "Because of you my family had to live through one of the harshest winters of our lives, yadda, yadda, yadda…. The mighty talons of the beast as they rip through flesh. Whatever! And then there was all that talk in the bar about how my kind eat people and such…."

"I thought that was pretty good story telling," Duncan defended. "Do you really think it was such a good idea for you to hang around in town just so you could listen to me talk?"

"Please, I'm a creature of stealth. I can easily hide undetected in the shadows. Besides, I had on your cloak," Mallory explained.

"Hello! You're a seven-foot tall, blue *dragon*."

"Did you see me?"

"No, but…."

"Then I rest my case." Mallory looked around with the torch. "Now once again, are you sure we are heading west?"

Duncan shrugged. "This is the direction the guy with the green shirt pointed."

"Maybe we shouldn't have tried to find this place in the dark," Mallory said, stopping to look around—which wasn't much help.

"Maybe we shouldn't try to find it all. It's supposed to be haunted…."

"Haunted, my old aunt's well padded posterior."

"Bring the light over here," Duncan ordered. Mallory held the torch out and Duncan unfolded the map again. He pulled a face. "It isn't much help. Bent tree, hollow tree, big rock. Let's face it, in the dark all the rocks and trees look more or less the same. Still, we came straight this way…."

"We think."

"It wasn't supposed to be that far from town. We've got to be getting close. Keep walking that way," Duncan ordered, pointing.

Mallory nodded and kept walking, though he was sure at this point they were getting more and ever more lost in the woods. He stepped on something and reached down to pick it up. He looked at what he held in his hand and then turned towards Duncan, lighting the thing. "Look, a stick figure."

Duncan screamed like a child then said "Oh no!" and disappeared. There was another shrill squeal that was followed shortly after that by a huge thud. It sounded like a two-hundred-fifty-plus pound human in full armor falling into a largish hole, probably in the mouth of a small cave.

Mallory once again marveled at his own fantastic hearing. Holding the torch high he moved carefully towards where Duncan had been when he last saw him.

He held out his torch and looked down at Duncan lying spread-eagle in the bottom of a small hole about six feet below him. Mallory held the torch high and confirmed that they were in the cave. "Look, we found the cave. What good luck!" Suddenly curious, he raised the torch higher. "Well what do you know? Apparently we found the cave some time ago and have been walking in it. No wonder there were no stars."

"Shut up and help me out of this hole!" Duncan thundered, as he stumbled trying to get on his feet.

"Well I don't know why you're mad at me. It's not my fault you fell into the hole."

"You have the light," the human hissed, as he finished getting to his feet.

"Well obviously you weren't walking where I'm walking, or you wouldn't have fallen into the hole. After all I didn't fall into the hole."

"Just help me out of this pit, Mallory."

Mallory stuck the torch between two rocks then lay down on his belly and stuck his arm down. Duncan was just out of reach so Mallory picked up the stick figure from where he'd dropped it and held it down for the human to grab. Duncan backed away.

"What on earth is wrong with you? Just grab on, and I'll pull you out."

"I'm not touching that evil thing." The human proceeded to tell him some story t he humans at the bar had told him about some witch.

"Are you kidding me? Just grab the scary stick figure. We don't have time for this nonsense."

"I swear, Mallory, if some evil witch ghost comes and eats our souls...."

"I'll take full responsibility. I have to tell you, all the witches I've ever known have been very nice."

The human finally took hold of the stick figure, and Mallory pulled him out of the hole. Duncan looked surprised at the ease with which he did it, and Mallory grinned. "Yes, I'm quite strong."

Duncan dusted himself off a bit and pulled the pack off his back. Mallory grabbed the torch and held it up high again. "Seriously, what's so scary about a stinking stick figure? Look, here's about a bazillion of them just hanging everywhere. They should make a great fire." He looked around at the cave roof and walls and finally found the cave mouth. They weren't very far in, for which he was glad. The only thing worse than being lost in the woods would have been to be lost in a cave in the woods.

He started pulling the stick figures down and stacking them near the entrance to make a fire. Hopefully he had picked a spot far enough from the mouth that it couldn't be seen but close enough that he didn't smoke them out of the cave when he lit it.

"That's it?" Duncan grumbled as he started gathering wood himself. "You aren't even going to ask me if I'm all right?"

"Are you all right?"

"No. Now that you ask, I'm not. I've hurt my knee and I think I sprained my right pinky finger," Duncan whined.

"Good."

"What!"

"That way you can limp into town tomorrow, announce that you've found me, explain that we've already scuffled, and that I'm going to be a challenge," Mallory said.

"Yes, that's great," Duncan scoffed. "Too bad I'm not bleeding from a head wound. That would make me look even more convincing. Do you ever hear the things that come out of your mouth, Mal?"

"I'm sorry you hurt your pinky finger," Mallory said. But it was obvious from the tone of his voice that he really wasn't.

"You don't think those things are creepy?" the human asked of the stick figures.

"Not really."

"How do you suppose they got there?"

"Don't know and I don't care. Going to make great fire wood."

"I'm not sure we should burn those things." As the words left Duncan's mouth Mallory started the stack on fire.

"You know, I'm not so sure we should be sleeping in this cave tonight."

"Why? Do you think the villagers have followed you?" Mallory asked, looking around quickly.

"No, they'd never come up here. I told you they think the cave is haunted by a witch. That's why I don't think we should stay here." He lowered his voice. "What if it *is* haunted?"

"Please! Everyone knows there is no such thing as ghosts. Sheesh!" Mallory threw some more flame into the wood.

* * * *

Duncan saw a spook dancing against the cave wall and jumped, landing in Mallory's arms with his arms locked around Mallory's neck.

"What on earth is wrong with you now?" Mallory asked.

Duncan pointed at the strange shapes on the wall, and Mallory laughed and dumped him. "That's just our shadows, stupid. See?" Mallory turned sideways and opened his mouth real wide, making what looked like a huge dragon fifty times his size.

He started dancing around watching his giant shadow as it looked like the worst monster Duncan could imagine.

Suddenly Mallory stopped dancing around, turned to Duncan and smiled.

"Duncan my boy, you're a genius."

"Huh? You just said I was stupid."

Mallory told him just what he had in mind and Duncan laughed. "Wow, I *am* a genius."

Earl was already having second thoughts even before he'd finished making the new part for the "dragon slayer's" boat. By the time he had given the part to the stranger that night Earl's second thoughts were becoming serious doubts. Then, after he'd had a night to sleep on it—or not sleep as the case may be—he'd decided that two hundred coins was a lot of money any way you sliced it. Way too much to part with, considering what he'd already lost.

He still hadn't caught all his pigs, his sons had left him high and dry, and the beast had broken an eighty-five coin window out of his bar. Not to mention that he'd spent a good piece of iron and the better part of a day building that new part. Earl could see no reason why he should bear the burden of paying the dragon slayer.

He saw the tax money as his, too, since he normally got to spend it on whatever he wanted.

He'd been up most of the night trying to figure out how to get the stranger to kill the dragon without paying him. When the town's menfolk woke him at the crack of dawn, he was already mad. Grumbling at them about the early hour he dressed as quickly as he could.

Now he was marching up the side of the mountain after the dragon slayer and almost every man in town big enough to carry a hoe, rake, shovel or pitch fork. He took the one spear that hadn't been completely ruined by the dragon's fire and walked in the rear.

"I don't see why we have to come if we're paying him good money to kill the thing," Earl mumbled. The town's men all shushed him at once, making more noise than he had. It was that very moment that it started to sink in. He wasn't in charge anymore.

Soon the cave was in sight. The stranger threw up his arm as he stopped, successfully stopping the human tide. He turned around and in a whisper told them, "You need go no further. The job of killing this dragon is mine and mine alone. The only reason you are here at all is that if he should kill me, you will be the only hope for your town and your families. If he gets past me you must attack him with your full force. May the gods make my sword strike true, and may they have mercy upon all our souls."

Earl was about to tell him out right that he was a big, boasting moron when he suddenly saw the shadow of the creature in the mouth of cave. It looked huge—much bigger than it had in town—and it had looked pretty darn big then.

The dragon let out a roar that seemed to shake the very ground they stood on, and they could see in the shadow its long, sharp teeth and claws as they raked the air searching for prey.

All the men moved back as a group, clutching their hoes, rakes and pitch forks to them. Earl found himself moving ever further away from the group and the cave entrance with his spear clutched to his chest.

No one was volunteering to go with the stranger, when the big guy took a big breath, turned around, and started marching towards the cave. His armor rattled with every step he took. It was clear to see from his stance that there was no fear in him at all.

Obviously the man was an idiot! He was all arms and legs and that dragon was going to eat his lunch. And when he'd finished off the huge stranger, the beast was going to turn on them—a bunch of farmers with no fighting skills and no real weapons.

Earl didn't like their odds. He started to sneak away from the group as their attention was focused on the "dragon slayer." When the dragon let out a roar that sounded like thunder if the strike was at his feet, Earl turned tail and ran for town as fast as he could go.

He tried to calm himself down. *I'm being silly. Of course the stranger will vanquish the dragon. If he doesn't then there is no way it can get past all the town's men, they'll make short work of him. After all, the stranger would have got a couple of licks in. If that idiot with the bad hair cut does get his fool-self killed then I don't have to pay him. If a chunk of the town's men get killed that means more of everything for me. I hope that dragon eats Sam in one bite. It would serve that busybody right.* He slowed his pace.

But wait. What if that dragon kills that big idiot and all the town's men, and doesn't have so much as a scratch? That couldn't happen, could it? It could; it might. I'm not sure that dragon slayer is what he says he is, and the town's men couldn't stand up to me and my boys. That dragon is going to make mincemeat of the lot of them.

Earl picked up his pace again, running faster and faster till he got to his smithy. He ran to a chest in the back where he stored old tack, opened it, dumped the contents on the ground, crawled inside and slammed the lid shut behind him.

I'll just stay right here till I know what's going on. After all, I'm the most important person in town. These people can't go on without me. So by protecting myself from certain death I am in fact saving the whole town.

He congratulated himself on being such a selfless, caring, and giving leader and decided to take a little nap.

* * * *

Duncan pulled his sword, almost tripped over it, and as he recaptured his balance turned back to the group of men watching him and whispered, "A trick to throw the dragon off." He winked, and Sam nodded and gave him a thumbs up.

Duncan raised his sword high above his head and strode with great purpose into the mouth of the cave where he could now clearly see the fire burning behind a pile of rocks.

Mallory looked at him from where he stood in the light of the fire, casting spooky images visible to the men waiting to kill him if Duncan failed. Of course the pose Mallory was striking to get the image he wanted looked sillier than menacing, standing as he was on one leg with his talons stretched out in front of him. His mouth was open as wide as he could get it and his tongue was hanging out to one side.

Duncan giggled a little and whispered, "You look like a sick fish."

In answer Mallory roared again, and as the sound echoed off the cave walls even Duncan found he was a little scared. Of course it had more to do with the ghost he was sure lived in the cave. He looked at the fire and realized Mallory had thrown all of the stick men onto it.

"I really don't think you should have done that, Mal," he said, indicating the fire.

"Would you quit! You've been weird ever since you woke up and found that stack of rocks by your head. Seriously, you humans are scared by the silliest things."

"How'd the rocks get there?"

"They were probably there when you bedded down and you didn't notice. Now could you focus? We have work to do."

Duncan nodded. "Foul beast! You will no longer terrorize the good people of this village!" Duncan swung at the air in front of Mallory as they had practiced the night before, and Mallory jumped smartly out of the way, both for the show and because—as he had said last night—he didn't trust Duncan's aim.

Mallory let out a wounded sound then roared again and clawed at the air. Of course the shadow made it look like he had smacked Duncan upside the head. Duncan threw himself on the floor of the cave and immediately picked up a handful of mud and started rubbing it on his coat of mail and his face.

Mallory slung a flame over the top of him just for show, and Duncan could hear the men outside gasp. He jumped to his feet and ran at Mallory, going past him in a way that made him look like he actually sliced into the dragon.

Again Mallory cried out in a pained way.

"Now who's way over the top?" Duncan whispered. Mallory smiled back and spit another fire ball over Duncan's head. "Hey, dragon!" he yelped, then added in a whisper. "That was a little close. I can smell singed hair."

"Sorry." Mallory grinned back.

"Die, foul beast!" Duncan bellowed. He lunged forward, driving his sword into the log they had put there for the purpose. Mallory started crying out as if he were dying and stumbled around clutching at his chest. He did this for several minutes and Duncan whispered, "Really, Mallory. Quit hamming it up and die already."

Mallory frowned at him then hopped in the air and fell with a thud to the ground. Duncan moved, lifted his sword high in the air and brought it down on the same log he'd stabbed earlier. Mallory let out one long, lingering death cry as Duncan grabbed a dead fish and ran it through with his sword. He slung some more dirt on his body and smeared some fish guts on his head. Then he limped out of the cave mouth.

He didn't have to work on the limp because his knee still hurt from falling into the hole the night before.

As he stumbled from the mouth of the cave—not really for show, because he'd tripped over another little pile of rocks—he noticed the villagers weren't as close as they had been. They also were roughly half as many as they had been before he went into the cave. He noticed, too, that Earl was one of those missing.

As he closed the distance he made a big deal out of cleaning his bloody, gut-encrusted blade on his shirt tail.

The small group of men applauded, but Duncan held up his hand. "Please, do not cheer me, for it pains me to kill such a noble beast," Duncan said. He had to bite his tongue to keep from laughing. "I did what I had to do, but I take no joy in my work."

"Is he dead?" Sam asked.

"Quite! Would you like to see?"

The remaining town's men moved with caution to the area he led them to—a view they'd chosen that blocked them from seeing the true size of the fire they'd built and revealed only the parts of Mallory he wanted them to see. A rock was between the group and Mallory, blocking their view of the dragon's neck, so that they could see only his head and his body. The best thing about this was that the villagers were convinced that they could see everything. It helped that Mallory was doing a good job of looking dead, his eyes just staring and blank, his tongue lolling out of his mouth. The men started to get closer, gaining courage after seeing that the dragon was dead. Duncan quickly put out an arm to stop them.

"I must warn you! Don't go any closer. See his eyes? Though the dragon is dead, the eyes are still seeing, and if he sees you in his dying eyes then his family will come to avenge him for a hundred years. It's why I must always keep moving. Too many dragons have seen me with their dying eyes."

They nodded and backed away.

"We should leave quickly now. In another hour even his carcass will be gone," Duncan said.

"How?" Sam asked skeptically.

"No one knows. That is why we must go. It is said that when the dragon disappears it will take all those who witness his departure with him to the great beyond. I do not know if this is true, but I have never met anyone who has seen a dragon's body disappear, and I have never been willing to wait around and see," Duncan said. This had them all walking back to town as fast as they could go. Duncan winked at Mallory and followed the men.

Mallory had been right. The villagers were so superstitious they would believe whatever he told them.

He knew as he was walking back to the village that Mallory was doing his disappearing act: heading back to their boat with the new part to wait for Duncan.

As they got closer to the village, he could see that every person in town was gathered around the front of the general store, all quietly wait-ing to hear news—good or bad. When they saw him and the other men they started to cheer, chanting his name over and over.

Duncan waved his hand in the air. "No, no, I don't deserve that...." His words were drowned out by their cheers, so he just smiled, bowed, and said a lot of thank yous.

"Where's Earl?" Sam demanded to know, looking around at the crowd.

"First time that monster roared I saw him running back to town," Felix said. "Probably gone to change his britches."

"Go find him. Make sure he isn't taking off with the town's money," Sam said, and the men all ran in opposite directions.

"Tell us how you did it," one of the women said to Duncan. So he told his story, lingering on the parts where he looked especially brave.

Poor folks, they really were gullible. Duncan felt almost bad about fooling them. But the truth was the villagers' real trouble wasn't Mallory, it was Earl. If Mallory was right, the two of them had destroyed Earl's hold on the town. If the town let him hornswoggle them again, then they deserved whatever they got.

A moment later, Earl was marched up to the porch of the store between two big guys. "We found him hiding in a trunk."

Calls of "coward" and "crook" and even "traitor" came from the crowd.

"The dragon is no more, thanks to Duncan. It's high time we end Earl's little reign of terror. I say we throw him out of all his offices right here and now and take back all of our tax money," Sam declared.

"You…you can't do that!" Earl said.

But a bunch of the men marched Earl up to his house to get the money, anyway. A few minutes later they came back handling Earl roughly, and the barkeep explained, "Tax money is all gone. Earl says his sons must have taken it."

Sam glared at Earl. "So…the money you have been collecting for years, that you said you were using to improve the town…."

"And I have," Earl defended.

"How?" Sam demanded. From the murmurs of the crowd, they wanted to know, too.

"I bought things for the town," Earl said, pulling away from the two men who held him. He straightened himself out and stood as tall as he could, trying to restore some of his dignity.

"Things?" Sam asked.

"And stuff," Earl added.

"Things and stuff?" Sam said in disbelief.

"Yes, there is a lot of things and stuff you need for a town like ours and…."

"Crook!" everyone said at once.

"There was lots of money left over from buying stuff and things. The boys must have taken the rest of the tax money when they rode out of here. You should round up a posse and go after them," Earl suggested.

"Sam, open the store right now," Felix said.

"Why?" Sam asked.

"Cause I need to buy some rope for a neck tie for Earl." And it was clear the rest of the town agreed with Felix.

Duncan cleared his throat. "Before you hang this man I'd like to have the two hundred coins he owes me."

"I don't have it on me," Earl said.

"Then go get it," Sam ordered. Earl seemed only too glad to do so. Sam added, "Sean and Christopher, go with him and make sure he doesn't lose his way." The two men who'd hauled Earl in followed him.

The whole time they were gone not one word was said about the dragon. No, the whole time they were all just wondering what to do about Earl. And it looked like most of them wanted him hung.

"He's our only blacksmith," Sam reminded, being the voice of reason. "I say he has to work off the tax money.... No, I've got a better idea. We'll let him off the hook for the tax money, but he tears up all his IOUs. From now on he'll charge a fair amount for his work, or we'll string him up and go find ourselves another blacksmith."

There was a moment when looking around him at this nice town filled with nice people that Duncan almost told them he'd be their blacksmith. That they could go ahead and hang Earl and that he would just stay right there. But then two things jumped to mind.

First, how was he going to cover all the lies he'd already told? Where was his family? Why didn't he have to keep moving to keep the dragons from exacting their revenge on him?

The second reason was a little more puzzling to Duncan because a few months ago he would have thought he'd be happy to settle down and be a smith. Now the real reason he didn't want to stay was that he liked the life he lived with Mallory. He liked living by his...well, most of the time Mallory's, wits. He'd had the same old thing day in and day out all winter, and he was ready to...well do the sort of thing he and Mallory did.

Earl was red but silent when the men returned with him.

Duncan held out his hand, and reluctantly Earl handed him two heavy cotton bags.

"We counted and made sure it was all there," Sean said. "But except for fifty extra coins that was all the money we could find. Seems his boys didn't just take all the town's money, they took most of his, too."

Sam glared at Earl. "We've decided not to string you up, Earl, but you'll be tearing up all your IOUs, and there will be no more price gouging."

"You can't do this, Sam, it isn't...."

"Fair?" Sam laughed then, not a particularly pleasant sound, and said, "It is way past time for you to reap what you have sown."

"Now see here..." Earl started.

"Let me at him, I'll tear him limb from limb!" Mort hollered. Felix held the little man in place.

"Why you wizened-up old fart...."

"You better watch it, Earl," Felix hissed, "or I'll let him go."

Duncan suppressed a laugh. Earl was silent. Maybe he realized that the town would help the old man beat him up.

"Well thank you kindly," Duncan said to the town's people holding up the money. "As much as I would like to stay I think it's best I go away before the dragons come to find me. Winter's over and soon they'll be on the move. I've been here way too long as it is."

Sam stepped forward, took his hand and shook it. "Our town will forever be in your debt. We will make a statue of you and put it in the town square."

"A statue," Duncan said in a far away voice. A statue—and he wasn't even dead. *Take that, Dad.*

"I will name my new son Duncan!" a pregnant woman screamed out.

"We will all name our sons Duncan!" another woman hollered.

Duncan once again had the urge to stay. His head was growing bigger by the minute. He could definitely get into this worshiping him thing. He waved, said his good byes, and started up the road at a quick pace, leaving the happy villagers behind him with only a small thought to what they were going to do to Earl.

It was certainly a completely different experience than leaving Spurna had been.

He felt like a hero. They had conned the whole town. They'd also put on a good show, and no one was the wiser. The only person who got hurt was Earl—who'd been abusing the whole town for years, so he had it coming.

Yes, Duncan felt ten feet tall and bullet proof. Of course considering that it had all been a big show, the town probably shouldn't be considering making a statue of him or naming their babies after him. He started to feel a little bad again, but then he felt the weight of the two hundred coins at the end of his arm and felt instantly better.

* * * *

Mallory was bored and way tired of waiting for Duncan to return— hopefully with their two hundred coins. If he admitted it, he was more worried than bored. A lot of things could still go wrong with their con, especially since it hinged on the human's performance.

He stood in the boiler room looking from the part in his hand to where it went and wondering if he could put it on himself. It seemed simple enough, put it in place and screw the bolts that held it back in place. He wasn't quite sure which end went where. They looked the same but there was a very slight difference, and he was pretty sure that they were different for a reason.

He finally put the part down, deciding it could wait till Duncan got back. They'd been here for months. Another day wasn't going to make that big a difference.

He decided to pass the time by catching some fish for dinner. He supposed he could go out and fish off the deck, but he was supposed to be dead. On the off chance that someone from the town happened to come their way he didn't want to get caught on deck, obviously not dead at all. Besides, he was all set up in the bathroom, and the fish were still biting like crazy there.

Silly plants.

He had just put the fish he'd caught into the sink when he looked out the window and saw it was starting to get dark.

Mallory was now more than a little worried about his partner and the money. He started to wonder if the human might take the money and run. He quickly dismissed that idea, though. He might do something like that but not Duncan.

He filled and lit one of the running lights so that the human could more easily find the boat. He didn't like any of the scenarios that were suddenly running rampant through his head. They all started the same way. Duncan said something stupid, and the villagers figured them out.

It was almost dark when Duncan came stomping across the gang-plank.

"What took you so long?" Mallory demanded, worry immediately becoming anger.

"Excuse me. I had to kill a dragon," Duncan said.

"I know. I was the dragon," Mallory answered.

Duncan laughed. "Wow! Guess I really did get into character. There were a lot of villagers wanting to show their deep admiration for me. It was hard to walk away from that."

Mallory was already tired of this exchange. "Did you get the money?"

"Yes."

"Show me the money," Mallory demanded.

Duncan handed Mallory both bags of coins. They wound up sitting at the bar in the front room, one on either side, counting the money and making little stacks then counting it again and making new stacks.

"That was the easiest two-hundred coins I've ever made in my life," Mallory laughed out.

"Lots easier than fighting a monkey, I'll tell you that right now," Duncan said. "And you know what? I feel like we did that town a lot of good...."

"Yeah, yeah. We're regular priests, taking from the rich, giving to the poor, and all that. Look, this is too good a con. I say we go down the Sliding West just far enough to get away from Hellsbut's hearing and then do it again."

"What do you mean?"

"I go in all dreaded-dragon-like and make a mess, scare the bejesus out of people. Then you go in and save the day and get paid," Mallory said. "It's just too easy."

"I don't know, Mallory. I don't know that it would work again. This town already had a bully and…."

"Don't get soft on me now, Dunc. I'm telling you this is a great con. Here's what we do next time…" And Mallory told him his plan to make their con work in any town that was afraid of dragons.

Ten

Winter was over and it was time for Bilgewater and Sadie to move to happier hunting grounds. You could gamble and win just so long in a town before people started to catch on and you made more enemies than friends.

They'd managed to steer clear of Humphrey. If he'd come looking for them he either hadn't found them or he'd been a lot stealthier than Bilgewater gave him credit for.

They had come to a little town just on the border of Winterhurst. In a rustic bar they were dealt into a poker game with several big, rather stupid young men who seemed to think they were quite good at poker. Talking to them, it was clear that they had, at least temporarily, taken up residence in the bar.

Things had been tight the last few weeks, and Bilgewater and his partner were happy to take some of the money these boys were spreading around.

Even when the locals lost a huge pot to him or his partner they didn't play any smarter or get irritated. Bilgewater knew they were playing with money they hadn't worked for way before the youngest of the three, named Little Earl, said, "Daddy must be crappin' bricks about now." The other two laughed.

"So you three are brothers, then," Sadie said, using all the feminine wiles she could dredge up. The idea was to make sure they paid more attention to her than they did to the cards.

She looked briefly at Bilgewater, who nodded. He'd come to the same conclusion. People who had worked hard for their money weren't in any hurry to push a big pile of it to the middle of the table on the chance a pair of twos would win a hand.

"Yes ma'am," Little Earl said.

The middle one, Seth, seemed down in the mouth, and the oldest brother, Joe Bob, hit him in the shoulder hard enough to rock him in his seat and said, "Now don't you go feeling bad. Ain't like most of it were his money in the first place."

"He was always using us to do some dirty deed or other," Little Earl added. "We weren't sons—we were servants. It's about time we got paid for what we done for him."

The way they were talking it was clear they were too dumb to hide that they were playing with stolen money. Of course, Bilgewater could not care less where they "found" the money as long as they hadn't stolen it from him.

"Then he's got us propped up on spears out in the cold. Expecting us ta protect the town from a dragon. He risked our lives jus' ta save him a couple a hundred coins. That's how much he cared—he gave us pointy sticks and told us ta go kill a dragon. How crazy is that?" Joe Bob reminded Seth, who nodded and they all went back to playing cards.

None of them noticed at all how Sadie and Bilgewater's ears perked up at the mention of the dragon.

"So you fought a dragon?" Bilgewater asked.

"Are you crazy?! Cause we ain't. That thing came after us and we turned tail and ran. Ain't no glory in being dead. We may be big, but we aren't stupid, no matter what the old man might think," Joe Bob said. "The thing was massive and it had a million teeth."

"And it breathed fire," Seth added.

"What color was this dragon?" Sadie asked, a smile curling her lips. Bilgewater kicked her under the table. As she yelped he gave her a look like he couldn't imagine why she would cry out like that.

"Why does that matter?" Little Earl asked curiously.

"Oh some dragons are much worse than others. A lot depends on what color they are," Bilgewater supplied.

"This one was blue," Seth said.

"Those are the worst kind," Bilgewater said, as if he had all the knowledge in the world about dragons. "So…did you kill it?"

"I told you, we ran. I don't know what happened after we left. The town wanted to hire some stranger, a dragon slayer, to kill the beast, but our old man, he didn't want to cough up the coins," Joe Bob said. Bilgewater realized that Joe Bob was a bit in his cups. "That's what we were worth to our father, brothers. Two hundred coins. That's all we were worth."

"Do you know the name of this dragon slayer?" Bilgewater asked.

"No," Joe Bob said. "Why is that important?"

"No reason, really. Just curious. We've run into a few dragon slayers in our travels. Just wanted to know if it was anyone we knew."

"I didn't hear his name," Joe Bob said with a shrug.

"It started with a B," Seth said.

"No, no, it didn't," Little Earl said. "His name started with a D. It was Du something."

"Duncan?" Bilgewater supplied.

"Yeah, that's it," Little Earl said. "Big guy, bigger than any of us. Had a burned circle right in the middle of his chain mail. Said he killed a hundred dragons."

"You know him?" Seth asked.

"Sure do, he's a…" Bilgewater didn't know what Sadie was about to say but he kicked her under the table again and shot her another look. Sadie glared at him and said, "He's the bravest dragon fighter I've ever known."

The conversation wound down as they returned to their cards. By the end of the night the three brothers were so drunk they could hardly see, and Sadie and Bilgewater had most of their money.

As they left the bar and headed for their hotel Sadie asked, "Just what are you up to now, Bilgewater?"

"Sounds like our friends Duncan and Mallory have found themselves a sweet little con. Too sweet for them to just do it once," Bilgewater said.

Sadie nodded. "Oh, now I get it. And there are only so many places they could run that particular con. Most of Overlap knows dragons don't normally run around sacking villages, so they have to be around here close."

"We know they wintered near the water around Hellsbut, in Winterhurst sector," Bilgewater said thoughtfully. "I suggest we start looking for them. We can make a substantial amount of money off those fellows. If we do it right they won't even know we're there. We had best leave bright and early. I don't want to be in town when those three bully boys wake up hung over and find that we've cleaned their plow."

* * * *

Mallory was holding the lantern while Duncan worked on putting the piece back into place. He didn't want to tell Mallory, but he wasn't really sure which end went where. He was about to just do his usual *see if it fits this way* thing when Fred popped onto a beam not six inches from Duncan's face and screamed in a voice so loud and shrill that it sounded like someone had loosed all the demons in hell.

"Stack of rocks! Stack of rocks!"

Duncan shrieked and jumped back into Mallory stepping on his foot. Mallory almost dropped the lantern, and Duncan hit himself right between the eyes with the part.

"Why you little…." He swung the part, Fred popped away, and Mallory grabbed Duncan's arm.

"You'll break the part." Mallory leaned against the wall, picked up his foot and looked at it. He held the lantern so he could better see. "You chipped one of my claws."

"Me? That thing…."

"How smart was it to tell a demon to do his evil best?" Mallory reminded.

"*You* told him to do that. How else would he know about the rock thing?"

"You were late. I was bored." The dragon shrugged and laughed.

"I don't care what you say, that pile of rocks was not there when I went to sleep, and what about all those stick men?"

The demon popped up on the steam pipe and said in his tiny voice. "Scary stick people… Oooh. Piles of rock." He started laughing so hard he was almost hysterical.

"Great," Duncan spit out and rubbed at his head. "I was a hero in that little town."

"A hero," the demon boomed. He was still laughing so hard what he said next was barely audible. "Afraid of a pile of rocks."

The dragon started laughing, too, and Duncan was starting to regret not staying in Hellsbut.

"Come on, Dunc, where's your sense of humor?"

"Clearly, I left it back in town with my pride," Duncan mumbled. Then to the still-laughing demon. "Don't scare me again."

"No promises," it growled out and left.

"You tell it to stop, Mallory. You told him to start it up again, now tell him to stop."

"Chill out, will ya?"

"I was a hero, dragon. They are going to build a statue of me in the town hall. A statue and I'm not even dead. Women are going to name their babies after me."

"And what about me?"

"Huh?"

"I had to play the villain. I was forced to let a town full of people think that I'm a mindless beast, that a scrawny human such as you could kill me. There can't be a hero without a villain. No one is going to build a statue of me or name their babies after me."

The dragon had a point. "Oh," Duncan said. Then he looked at the part in his hand and where it went. He finally went ahead and tried it the way he was holding it. It wouldn't fit that way which meant it would only fit one way so he turned it over and it easily slid into place. He started to put the nuts back on and Fred popped up with a wrench.

Duncan took the offered wrench. "Me sorry," Fred said in his big demon voice.

"It's all right." After all, now that he wasn't in the haunted cave it did seem absurd to be afraid of stick people and piles of rock.

The demon nodded and Duncan used the wrench to secure the nuts.

"For a jerk, Earl does pretty good work. This fits like a glove."

"What's wrong, Dunc?"

"I just want to get out of here long before anyone has a chance of figuring out what we did. You know I didn't save them from anything, that you aren't really a blood-thirsty, mindless beast. Those were nice people. I like being their hero even if I didn't save them from anything."

"You did save them from something, Dunc. You saved them from Earl."

"Yeah, I guess. I'd still rather get out of here while they still like me."

* * * *

As soon as the weather had warmed enough for the steam heat to keep the upstairs rooms comfortable, they had moved their beds to separate rooms. Duncan woke up the next morning and the first thing he saw was the bamboo and straw woman he'd made. He nearly screamed thinking it was a giant stick man. Which it wasn't. It was a giant stick *woman*.

"That's not funny," he hissed. He jumped out of bed, grabbed her up and headed for the boiler room.

"No woman of mine's going to make a fool of me," Duncan swore. He broke her up and stuffed her pieces into the furnace mumbling, "I'm tired of being the butt of everyone's jokes." He started the fire going, having no guilt at all. She shouldn't have scared him if she wanted to live.

By the time the first rays of the sun were peeking through the trees, Duncan had pulled the gangplank up, cast off, and had the boat rolling down the river.

It was near midday before Mallory appeared carrying a tin can full of coffee which he handed to Duncan. The can was too hot for Duncan's hand, so he set it down and motioned for Mallory to take the wheel.

He had noticed a long time ago that the dragon's perceptions of hot and cold were different than his own. The dragon didn't seem to even notice heat that would burn Duncan's skin, and he seemed not to get as cold as quick. Mallory hated to get cold, though, and it seemed to take him longer to get warm again.

"We never did get a map," Mallory said.

"Forgot all about it. We're still on the Sliding West, though, because I've been watching for the two rivers to become one again."

Mallory nodded thoughtfully. "When that happens, or just before it does, I'm thinking there will be a port on the river, and I'm guessing a good-sized one."

"Why?" Duncan didn't understand. After all, the locals were afraid of the river.

"Because the Sliding West doesn't slide, remember?"

"So?" Duncan shrugged not getting it.

"So if it doesn't slide that means the end of it would be a great place for a harbor and a town. It's expensive to build docks along the Sliding because it moves. Mostly you have little floating docks you can relocate after a slide. Someplace like the Sliding West that connects to the Sliding but never moves would be the perfect place for a major port. We could dock the boat there, get a map, and then try all the villages within hiking distance in the interior of Winterhurst. You know, places that might need to be saved from a murderous, rampaging dragon."

"What if there isn't a harbor?"

Mallory shrugged. "Then it would still be a good place to dock the boat, and we can still walk inland to look for villages."

"Without a map?"

"There's going to be a harbor there," Mallory assured him. "What's this thingy?" he asked, pointing at a gauge on a panel just right of the wheel.

"I think it says how fast we're going."

"How fast does it say were going?"

"I said I think that's what it is. I don't know for sure, and I sure don't know how to read it."

"You know, eventually we're going to have to learn more about sailing this boat," Mallory said.

"I keep hoping we'll come across an owner's manual, but if we do it will probably be in some language neither of us can read." Duncan picked up the can of coffee, which was now cool enough to hold, and took a sip. "Hey Mal, what are we going to do with all our money?"

Mallory laughed. "Why spend it, of course. We're going to live like kings. This is just the beginning, my friend! It's our destiny to be rich."

"I was thinking maybe we should buy some things we need for the boat. Maybe paint it inside and out, get some real cups, stuff like that."

"Of course, that goes without saying. Two such wealthy gentlemen as we can't be living in a dump like this."

* * * *

The harbor at the end of the Sliding West was huge. A city built on the river, home to a mixture of different creatures and conflicting technology. The buildings were mostly made of brick or stone, but the roofs were made of leaves from the palm trees that grew all throughout the town and the wooded area behind it. The leaves were thick, so Duncan got the feeling that instead of changing leaves every year they just added another layer.

The dock was wooden boardwalks sitting on rock and concrete peers. For two coins a month they rented a slip for their boat at the marina.

Noslide—not a very imaginative name in Duncan's opinion—was a hopping little city. It was full of shops that sold a multitude of items, and for every shop there was a casino or night club.

Mallory increased their stash of coins by gambling in the clubs at night. Duncan split his time between watching Mallory's back, chasing women, and drinking more beer than he probably should.

During the day they shopped for the things they needed for the boat and painted it inside and out. They christened it Demon Home. Mallory said that painting such a name on the hull—which Mallory did using his tail because he had more reach that way—would avoid future lawsuits.

"You know, in case people come on board uninvited and are scared to death by the demon," Mallory said as he finished the last stroke.

"But I don't understand," Duncan said. He took the brush from the dragon's tail. "They shouldn't be on our boat unless we invite them. And if I did invite someone I'd tell them about the demon. If someone comes on the boat and they aren't supposed to be on it and he scares them to death, as far as I'm concerned it's their own fault."

"Yes, but depending on where you are, the law may not see it that way. There are places where if a person gets hurt while robbing you or your home, *you* can be sued for their personal injury."

"What's *sued* mean?"

"They can take your money."

"Let me get this straight. Someone breaks onto our boat to rob us. He gets scared by the demon that we certainly didn't invite to attach itself to our boat, and ends up hurt or dead. Then they can get money from us because they were hurt?"

"That's right."

"That's the stupidest thing I've ever heard."

"Then you just haven't lived long enough, Duncan." Mallory laughed.

Duncan nodded with appreciation looking at the sign on their boat. "Good job," he said. "Sort of makes it seem more like home in a way." He looked at the dragon. "Do you ever miss them, Mal?"

"Who?" Mallory asked. He walked back into the main room with the paint can as Duncan followed with the brush.

"Your family, your people."

Mallory smiled and put the lid back on the paint. "I don't have people."

"You know what I mean!"

Mallory made a noise that was as close to a raspberry as a dragon could make. He shrugged his shoulders, took the brush from Duncan and went to the kitchen to clean it in the sink.

"Do you?" Duncan prompted, following him.

"Truthfully?" Mallory did seem to think about the question then. "I sometimes miss what I think it ought to have been. Family ought to be those who know you and understand you and love you no matter what. I never fit in, so they always made a point of telling me that I was different and by *different* they meant *wrong*. Maybe I would miss home if I'd ever felt like I had a home."

"Me too," Duncan said. "This boat feels more like home to me than my 'home' ever did. You feel more like family to me than my old man. You know what I mean?"

Mallory looked away quickly then and whispered so low Duncan almost couldn't hear him, "Yeah, I know what you mean." Then he quickly laughed. "What a bunch of sappy crap! Let's go out and get some dinner. I've got my mouth all set for a nice fresh salad—maybe with some beets. I love beets."

"Little too much like a turnip if you ask me, and I've eaten enough turnips to last me a lifetime."

Duncan followed Mallory off the boat and down the dock towards town. "So the boat's all painted, and we've spent about as much money as we can afford to spend on outfitting and stocking her. We've learned enough about towns all across Winterhurst, so I think it's time we lock our boat up and head inland to seek our fortune."

Duncan scoffed at the notion that they'd spent most of their money. He knew that was a lie. Nearly every day Mallory played cards, and every time he played, he won more money. The dragon was hiding money from him and he knew it. Duncan kept looking for his secret stash, but he never found it. "We still have at least one hundred coins in the safe,"

Duncan said in a whisper to Mallory without telling him that he knew he had more somewhere else.

The safe was a plank in the floor under the bar they fixed to come up, so that they could hide stuff under it. Duncan got the feeling that the dragon had a need to hoard. While it was annoying to never know how much money they had it was also reassuring to know that there was always more money than he thought they had.

"You have seen, my friend, how fast we can blow through a hundred coins," Mallory said, waving one of his claws through the air. "Look, we've been flush and we've been broke. Which is more comfortable?"

"To be flush," Duncan admitted.

"So there is no sense in waiting around till we're broke again to get more work, is there?"

"Get more work." Duncan laughed. "I like the way you call it *work*."

"If it's how we make money, then it's work," Mallory said with a chuckle. "And admit it, being a hero can be tiring work. I know running around looking hungry and crazy is." He changed the subject. "Where is that clothing shop where you bought those new boots and the short pants?"

"Down this way." Duncan started leading him.

"I need a cloak."

"A cloak in this weather! Soon it will be like a furnace."

"Why wait till the cold weather to buy a cloak? Besides, I think you'll find the cloak I have in mind can be used for more than just staying warm in the cold weather."

Eleven

Bilgewater slid out of his saddle and looked up one road and then down the other. He rubbed his chin as Sadie rode up beside him and got off her horse, rubbing her backside.

"Seriously, Bilge, let's cut our losses and head for the harbor. We aren't going to find them, and I'm tired of looking. Let's just go to a nice city for awhile, play same good games, and eat some real food."

"We missed them in that last little town by hours."

"Maybe they've quit that con and moved on."

"Would you? They've pulled this con twice now and made a bunch of coin each time. They aren't going to stop now, and you know it." Bilgewater looked at the road signs on the post ahead of them. The arrow pointing left said Buck Snort. The one pointing right said Wart Haven. Neither sounded like a very pleasant, much less prosperous, place.

He was about to suggest they head to Buck Snort since it was slightly closer when down the road to Wart Haven something caught his eye.

He started towards it. "There is something tacked to that tree." He pointed and Sadie sighed but started to follow him. Bilgewater laughed as he pulled the paper from the tree and tossed it towards Sadie.

She looked at the crude picture on it and read the words out loud.

"Wanted. Preferably dead. Small—but way too big for us—dragon. Fifty coin reward." Sadie looked thoughtful. "Fifty coins? I doubt Duncan and Mallory would go to the trouble of causing trouble for a mere fifty coins."

"They wouldn't bother to get out of bed. Oh this isn't Duncan's price, Sadie. Don't you see? They don't want to pay what Duncan is asking. They're shopping around, trying to find someone who works cheaper."

"You think anyone will?" Sadie asked. "Do you think we should volunteer? We know he's not going to kill us. He doesn't even eat meat, and fifty coins isn't bad…."

"I'm thinking there is a much better way to make money in Wart Haven with those two in town. And if someone else shows up, well that just might play right into our hands." Bilgewater laughed and jumped back into his saddle.

Sadie gave him a dirty look and then climbed into hers. "Bilgewater, I hope you at least have an inkling of a clue what you're doing."

"My dear girl, you can bet on it." Bilgewater turned his horse in the direction of the town. "Let's go to Wart Haven. It sounds like a lovely place."

* * * *

Mallory looked at the poster hanging on the tree, frowned, and turned to Duncan. "Seriously, this picture is insulting. I've seen better heads on a pimple. I should level the whole town on principle. There is nothing terrifying in that face! It's just blue and rather silly."

"We've got bigger problems than a messed up the picture on your wanted posters," the human said.

"Like what? Reputation is everything you know."

"Like there are wanted posters at all, Mallory. They have stuck them everywhere," Duncan said in disbelief. "They are trying to find a dragon slayer who will work cheaper than I do. Why don't I just tell them I'll do it for the fifty coins?"

"Hush your mouth!" Mallory clicked his tongue. "Duncan, Duncan, Duncan, if you devalue yourself like that you'll never be able to make a hundred coins for slaying a dragon ever again. It's a skill few people have. Don't sell yourself short."

"It's a skill I don't have, either. It's all a big gag."

"I don't see why you're getting all worked up. It's not like someone is painting bad pictures of you."

"Hey, smarty pants, what if they get fifty people up in here hunting for you for the fifty coins? That's a lot of money to most people, and too many people for either of us to handle."

"No one's stupid enough to tangle with a dragon. I mean, look at me. I could tear a man from ear to ear. Of course you really can't tell that looking at this piece of crap picture."

"I can't believe the only problem you can see is that it's not a flattering picture of you."

"Ah ha, you admit it's a bad picture."

"That's not the point, Mal."

"Look, I know creature nature. No one is going to put their neck on the line for fifty coins. They'd have to be desperate, with no other income and...pretty sure they could kill me before I killed them."

"Hello! You wouldn't hurt a fly. You're a pacifist and a vegetarian. Most days you're about as scary as a caged gerbil."

"Have you ever been bit by a gerbil? They have sharp, pointy teeth...."

"Could you focus for a minute, dragon?"

"Admit it. I'm pretty scary when I want to be."

"Well you didn't scare these people enough to jump at the chance at hiring a real live dragon slayer like me. The last little town we did was a cinch. In and out in less than two days and a hundred coins richer. This one.... Well, they're more organized, and their mayor—while not as crooked—is every bit as shrewd as Earl was."

"You're worrying over nothing, Dunc. Look, you go on back to town and hang out looking available and dragon-slayer-ish. I'll come through town in about an hour and do some more terrorizing stuff. I didn't see anyone in that town that looked to me like they were getting ready to come after me, did you?"

"No not really. They were mostly running and screaming."

"Then don't lose your cool. This is easy money," Mallory said.

Duncan nodded, and Mallory watched him as he walked back towards Wart Haven town.

* * * *

Mallory ran into town gnashing his teeth, roaring, and mostly throwing trash cans around. People scattered in all directions in front of him. He threw some random fire balls around, careful not to do any real damage.

After all it wasn't really about trashing the town. They were in it for the money.

He had done enough roaring and thrown enough fire that his throat was sore, so he ran back out of town towards their camp.

Mallory had just run past the last house on the very edge of town when he caught the sound of a child crying. He turned and saw a little girl sitting under a window at the back of the house sobbing. She was obviously so terrified of him she couldn't even run, and he instantly felt like the world's biggest heel.

Instead of running into the woods to hide till his services were further needed, Mallory found himself walking up to the child. He hunkered down to her level. In the gentlest voice he could muster he said, "Hey kid, I'm not really a bad guy. I'm just pretending. I'm not really going to eat anyone or burn up anyone's house. You don't need to be scared of me."

The little girl looked up at him and managed to smile through her tears. "Oh, I'm not afraid of you."

"You aren't!?" Mallory was indignant.

"No. Let's face it, if you were going to do any of that stuff you would have done it already," she said with a shrug.

Mallory nodded. That made sense. He hoped the town's people weren't as smart as this kid. "Then what's wrong?"

"Listen." She pointed towards the window. When he listened it was easy to hear that the couple inside was fighting.

"Seriously, Jack, there isn't a scrap of food in the house," a woman's voice said.

"But dear...."

"You just took all our money and bet it on the dragon to win."

"But dear, it's a sure bet...."

"First off, if the dragon wins there is a good chance we'll all be dead. Second off, isn't that exactly what you said about the beans, Jack? Magic this and magic that. You traded our milk cow for a handful of beans and look how good that turned out. We had to move!"

"But honey, anyone who goes up against the dragon is bound to get killed. It's money in our pocket, I tell you. Our key to financial independence. We'll cash in and then we'll move to a town that doesn't have a dragon problem."

"And in the meantime what are we going to eat? Your pie-in-the-sky dreams of wealth and fame. We've got most of your worthless family living with us. We don't have two coins to rub together, and all of them are as allergic to work as you are. How about you get a real job and make some money to feed your family? That dragon slayer he looks like a big sort and you saw his armor—how it's all charred from dragon fire. They say he's killed a thousand dragons."

"But the mayor will never pay his fee. He's too tight fisted. And anyone else who fights the beast won't have a chance."

The little girl looked at Mallory with big tears in her eyes. "You *will* viciously and mercilessly kill anyone who comes against you, won't you?"

"I'm not going to kill anyone just so your father can cash in on his bet."

"But if he loses his bet we're all going to starve. There's no food in our house now."

"Look, come on, let's get out of sight."

As soon as the little girl had followed him a safe distance into the woods he turned to her and said, "What is wrong with you kid?! Didn't anyone ever tell you not to talk to strangers? And you should never, ever, ever follow a stranger into the woods! Are you crazy?"

The child shrugged.

"Can you keep a secret?"

She nodded.

"I'm a nice dragon, see? I don't even eat animals. I have trouble eating fish, though I think I've finally decided it's not like eating something cute and furry. But I digress. How about you and me be friends? I help you out; you help me out."

"My name is Christina. What's yours?" she asked.

He smiled. "Mallory. My name's Mallory. Christina is a nice name."

"Thank you. Mallory's a nice name, too."

"Why thank you. Wait here just a second." Mallory walked a bit away. He had fifty coins hidden in his cheek pouches, twenty-five on each side. He extracted ten from each to make sure he was still balanced then he walked back to the little girl. "Hold out your hand."

She did, and he put the twenty coins into her hand "They're sort of gooey," she said, making a face.

"Hey, kid, never look a gift dragon in the mouth," Mallory said. "Give those to your dad to go buy groceries. Tell him you found them in the street," Mallory said. He smiled. "Now remember it's our secret. Don't tell anyone that I'm really a nice guy, all right?"

"All right…. Can you tell me a story?"

"What?" Mallory asked.

"Can you tell me a story? Just a little one."

Mallory found a rock and sat down and was more than a little surprised when the child sat down on his lap. She wrapped her arms around his neck. He thought for a minute about a story then said, "Once upon a time there were these really good guys named Duncan and Mallory. Their boat broke down before the coldest winter ever. In the town nearest to the place that their boat broke down there was this bad, evil man named Earl…."

* * * *

"Like taking candy from a baby," Bilgewater said, shutting the door to the hotel room they were using as a temporary office. Sadie laughed and started counting all the money, double-checking their books.

"Odds are six to one against Duncan," she said.

"Love those odds. And of course the odds are ten to one against anyone else killing the dragon since Duncan is, of course, a licensed professional." Bilgewater chuckled.

"You think Duncan and Mallory know about the betting pool yet?"

"I doubt it. Duncan is about as observant as a box of rocks, and Mallory.... Well if he's smart—and I think we both know he is—he's nowhere near town. Except of course when he's running through making a racket reminding the town they have to be saved from him."

As if he somehow knew they were talking about him, suddenly screams, roars, and utter confusion rose from the streets. Bilgewater ran to the window, pushed back the curtains, threw up the sash, and looked out just in time to see Mallory run around a corner. The dragon set a hitching post on fire.

Sadie pushed in at his elbow to take a look. "He does a good job of looking really scary, doesn't he?" she said with admiration.

"Sadie, that dragon's gonna make us rich."

* * * *

It was a pretty little town with lots of two story buildings covered in gingerbread, each painted in several different colors. To Bilgewater they looked like fancy candies in a box, each one bright and ornate. It had boarded sidewalks and cobblestone roads. And except for the dragon attacks it was a quite peaceful place. He could get used to a town like this.

If he could ever get used to being stuck anywhere.

The mayor pushed onto the porch of the general store, shoving aside the town council to do so. The people in the street were all screaming and yelling. They wanted something done, and they wanted it done right now.

Bilgewater watched from the edge of the crowd as Duncan appeared in his armor with his sword on, and the crowd got quiet. Assuming the silence was for him Duncan stepped onto the general store porch in front of the mayor and started addressing not the mayor but the citizens.

"Fair err... Fear not, fair people, for I...for the nominal fee of one hundred coins...will gladly vanquish this foul beast."

"Pay the man what he asks!" one man screamed out towards the mayor. And then the whole group jumped in with a chorus of more of the same.

The mayor whispered to his right hand man then nodded his head, looked at Duncan and said, "The town will gladly pay your fee."

"Hold on just a minute there, sir." A man bigger even than Duncan walked out of the crowd, a crude spear in one hand and a flyer held high in the other. From the look on Duncan's face he recognized him almost as quickly as Sadie did.

"Damn, that's Humphrey," she said, and started backing up so quickly she ran into Bilgewater. He took hold of her elbow and moved them both into the shadows of the hotel porch where they were out of Humphrey's line of sight.

"I saw your poster and have come to slay your dragon. I will gladly do it for the price offered." Humphrey smiled at Duncan a daring, mean little smile. "Fifty coins seems a good fee to get rid of such a small and insignificant dragon. Why I have slain bigger dragons than him in my sleep."

Bilgewater watched Duncan's expression change from mere worry to open hostility. "I will lower my normal fee and do it for fifty just to save this poor, misguided man from a horrible death!" Duncan yelled out.

"Tell you what. Whoever kills the dragon first will get the fifty coins," the mayor said, and this seemed to make everyone happy except Duncan. Of course Bilgewater was none too happy, either.

"I think that idiot might actually kill Mallory."

"What should we do?" Sadie asked.

"Well, unless I'm wrong, Duncan will go to talk to Mallory. Though he may not be smart enough to figure out what to do about this sudden problem, he is smart enough not to let Humphrey follow him."

"I don't see how that helps," Sadie said, scratching her head.

"Here's what we're going to do...." Bilgewater whispered his plan to Sadie.

* * * *

Duncan sighed and looked behind him. He'd walked around town several times, through and around buildings. He'd even tried hiding in a garbage bin but he hadn't managed to shake Humphrey.

The only way this could have been worse was if Humphrey had just pointed right to him and told the town's people that Duncan and the dragon were friends. That it was all just a huge farce to pull coins from their pockets. Instead this guy wanted in on the action and he wasn't at all sure that Humphrey wouldn't kill Mallory for the money.

He had to get to Mallory and then they had to get out of here—just cut their losses and go—before the whole thing blew up in their faces. Unfortunately, it looked like he was going to have to find some other way to stop Humphrey from following him because he didn't seem to be able to lose him.

As he was hiding behind a tree on the outskirts of town trying to come up with a plan Humphrey just walked right up to him.

"Where you going in such a hurry, Duncan? Someplace you don't want to be followed? So I'm thinking you're going to warn your dragon friend, maybe."

"I don't know what you're talking about," Duncan said.

"Oh come on, your partner, the dragon. This is quite a sweet deal, and I just want in on it."

But there was something about his words that didn't match the way he was holding his body, the way he was clutching his spear.

"That dragon wasn't my partner. And this dragon here is the real deal. A big man eater he is, the…"

"…exact same dragon you were hanging out with when he cheated me out of all my money. You hit me in the head and knocked me unconscious so that you and he could make a clean get away. I don't forget things like that, my friend." Whatever act he'd been trying to put on had evaporated.

"You're no good at cards for the same reason I'm not. Everyone can see what you're holding on your face," Duncan hissed. "You're a bad card player and a sore loser. You came to our room screaming. What did you expect?" He wasn't about to tell him that he'd only knocked him out by accident.

"I *am* a sore loser. You best remember that. You and your scaly friend owe me money, and I'll get it back, one way or the other."

"Humphrey, old man!" someone yelled out and Humphrey turned.

Duncan took the opportunity to sneak away. He was almost gone when he recognized Bilgewater and Sadie walking towards Humphrey. Bilgewater caught his eye and winked at him, and Duncan ducked behind the corner of a house to watch.

"Bilgewater!" From the way he said it, Humphrey was no happier to see Bilgewater than Duncan was to see Humphrey. "I should have known you and your partner would be here. I knew you were working with the dragon and the idiot."

Duncan thought Humphrey calling him an idiot should be the definition of the pot calling the kettle black.

Bilgewater clicked his tongue. "And to think we were going to take you right to him. We've been taking bets for days on this fight. If someone who is not Duncan kills the dragon we make even more money than if Duncan kills him. We all know Duncan isn't going to kill his partner. Come on. I know right where he's hiding. I'll take you to him."

Bilgewater started leading Humphrey down the road. Since they were going in the direction he and Mallory had made camp Duncan was pretty sure they knew where he was. Duncan was starting to panic when

Sadie, who'd hung back from the men, turned around, caught his eye, picked up a small stick, and acted like she was hitting Humphrey in the head with it. Then she pointed at Duncan. Duncan nodded that he understood and started following at a distance. He picked up a big stick and started to close the distance.

Pretty soon Bilgewater had led Humphrey off the road and was leading him through the woods nowhere near Mallory.

"Are you sure you know where the dragon is?" Humphrey asked.

"He's around here close. I'm sure of it," Bilgewater said.

"How close?" Humphrey's asked suspiciously. Then he added, "Bilgewater, I swear if you're having me on, I will have your hide."

"Of course not, dear boy. We're very close now. As in we better keep our voices down. That dragon is tricky and he may seem civilized, but he'd just as soon kill you as look at you. We aren't friends with him, but he isn't unknown to us. You don't want to get on his bad side, so you better kill him quick and…."

Duncan's stick connected with the back of Humphrey head, making a sick, thudding sound, and Humphrey fell to the ground forming a sort of human puddle.

* * * *

Mallory looked from the unconscious, hog-tied man at his feet to the three people who had brought him in and shook his head. "Was this really necessary? Couldn't you have just talked to him?"

"He was going to kill you for fifty coins, Mallory!" Duncan said in disbelief.

"I abhor violence. It's so unnecessary," Mallory said, rolling the human at his feet around with his toe. "And messy. What are we going to do with him? He doesn't go with anything we have."

"It's not funny, Mal. You can complain about me hitting the poor creature later. What are we going to do with him now?" Duncan asked.

Mallory turned to Sadie and sighed. "Isn't that what I just said?" He looked at Bilgewater and Sadie and smiled. "I should have known you two were in town when I heard there was a betting pool." He frowned at them. "One poor man bet his family's food money and…."

"Mallory, what are we going to do about Humphrey?" Duncan demanded. "We have to cut our losses and go."

"You can't do that. We'll lose a fortune," Bilgewater said.

"He's tied up now. How much trouble can he be?" Mallory shrugged. "We go ahead, run our con, and take our piddling fifty-coin reward and go." Then he rubbed his clawed hands together, looked at Sadie and Bilgewater and said, "While you two take off with all the real money."

"Look, we did help you take care of Humphrey."

"They did," Duncan agreed.

Bilgewater swallowed hard and looked at Sadie. "I suppose we could cut them in for part of the action," he said, as if it were only slightly less distasteful to him than having his teeth pulled out with a rusty pair of pliers.

"That seems fair," Mallory said.

"I'm thinking…, If everything goes according to plan, we give you and Duncan fifty coins. After all, that's what Humphrey cost you when he showed up."

"Now see here, Bilgewater, there'd be nothing for these people to make book on without us, and that means no money for you, and we're doing all the work," Mallory said, letting just a bit of smoke come out his left nostril.

"But we aren't biting into your profits. Besides, if it wasn't for us you might be a dragon shish-kabob right now," Bilgewater said. "I wasn't just blowing smoke up Humphrey's pants. If he'd killed you we would have made a killing—excuse the pun. Most everyone is putting their money on you. A few are putting their money on Duncan, but no one is putting their money on anyone else. Someone besides Duncan kills you and all the money is ours."

"That's mighty big of you," Mallory said, though it was clear he wasn't feeling it.

"What are we going to do about Humphrey? We can't just keep him tied up," Duncan said, pointing at the man, who was starting to stir.

"Why not?" Mallory asked. "We can let him go when we're done and…." He smiled big. "I just had a great idea."

* * * *

Duncan stumbled back into town, being sure to be seen. A man ran up to him, and he made quite a show of using the fellow for support.

He could hear people shouting and then someone was ringing the town bell. By the time he reached the porch of the general store most of the town was there.

The mayor ran right up to him. "What…what happened man?"

He was expecting the question. After all, Mallory had coated him with mud and hit him with several pomegranates which had left splashes of what looked like blood all over him.

For answer Duncan pushed away from the man who was supporting him. He stood to his full height and held out Humphrey's tunic which was torn into shreds and coated in the pomegranate juice. He also held up Humphrey's spear which was broken in two. He cast his eyes towards the ground.

"I…I tried to tell him," Duncan said, working a lump into his throat. "I told him that you can't just run up on the dragon, but he wouldn't listen. He wouldn't and…. He charged right into the cave. I ran after him. He let out a horrible, blood-curdling scream and then I heard a sound I know all too well—the sound of human bones snapping as the dragon chewed. I tried to help, but the dragon hit me with his tail and knocked me out of the cave. I fell behind a clump of shrubs, and I guess I hit my head on a rock. When I woke up the dragon was gone, and all I found of Humphrey were these." He thought he said it with just the right amount of sadness for his fallen comrade. "If only he'd listened to me. You can't just run up on a dragon like that. You have to sneak up on them, get the upper hand. I knew he was no dragon slayer because I'd never seen him at any of the meetings. I guess I should have told you but…well, I knew you'd think I wanted the job for myself. He was a noble tinkerer, but only a tinkerer, not a warranted, licensed professional." He paused for effect. "A great elm has fallen in the forest. We are all less of what we once were because of this terrible loss."

Then he picked his head up looking at the mayor and said, "This dragon is a strong and tricky one. Never before have I faced such a horrible foe, but now I feel I must kill him or die trying, to avenge the blood of this good, brave man who died so stupidly, but valiantly as well."

"Son, if you kill this dragon for us we will gladly pay your fee of one hundred coins," the mayor said, patting him on the back. "A moment of silence for the stranger the dragon ate."

The town's folk all bowed their heads.

* * * *

"Oh, he's good," Sadie said.

"Come on. We better go open up for business. Something tells me that a whole lot of people are going to start making or adding to their bets," Bilgewater said. Together they walked back to their room, being careful not to skip with joy.

Bilgewater couldn't help a slight chuckle, "A great elm has fallen in the forest. Where does he come up with such absolute tripe?"

"I thought it was a beautiful sentiment, and if you think about it, it fits."

"How so?"

"Well Humphrey is as big as a tree and every bit as dense."

* * * *

Mallory was getting a little worried about the jerk, so he poured some water on his head to wake him up. The guy spit some and slurred a few word-like sounds. His eyes opened and then closed. Then he tried to roll over on his back, which he really couldn't do because they had him trussed up like a pig.

"What…what happened?" he finally got out.

"Sleeping off a drunk? Fell down a flight of steps?" Mallory said. The sound of his voice seemed to wake Humphrey all the way up and his eyes flew open.

"What? Who?"

"Humped and you."

When he could focus, Humphrey saw that Mallory was lying on his side just inches from him, so that their noses were almost touching.

"What a giant pain in the rear you turned out to be. My partner and I have a sweet deal going. First Bilgewater and Sadie have to push their way in and cash in on our con, and then you…. Well you show up and try to ruin everything—not to mention the whole killing me thing."

Humphrey did a good job of putting some distance between him and Mallory, considering how he was trussed up. "Where are Bilgewater and Sadie?"

"Ran off screaming, 'Please, please don't kill me!' right after I hit you in the head," Mallory said.

Bilgewater had asked Mallory to keep their conspiracy hidden from Humphrey, saying, "He's like a bad coin. He just keeps turning up. I'd just as soon he didn't know we double crossed him."

Mallory considered the frightened man in front of him. "I'll take care of them later. You on the other hand…. Frankly, you ruined my dinner. You know how hard it is for me to digest when I learn someone wants to kill me? And at a discount no less! Seriously, fifty coins to kill me? Why do I even try, what's the point? You work and work and work at scaring the crap out of people and for what? Fifty coins? It's an insult!"

Mallory stood up, dusted himself off, and walked over to throw some logs on the fire. Not because it was cool, just because he was sure where the human's mind would go when he saw him tending the fire. Seeing Humphrey swallow hard he knew he hadn't guessed wrong.

"Look, dragon, I know you aren't some stupid animal. Let's make a deal. You let me go, and I run away and never tell a soul about your con game."

"I'm not seeing what I get out of that deal," Mallory said, stirring the fire with a stick and then just for good measure throwing a ball of fire into it.

"You get me not telling the town's people what you're doing," Humphrey explained.

Mallory laughed the most evil laugh he could dredge up, and he'd been practicing. "They don't know what we're doing now, and as long as you stay right here they aren't going to find out. You can just stay tied up till Duncan has collected that reward money and we go."

"I can't stay tied up like this for days. How will I go to the bathroom?"

"Well I suggest you just don't eat anything, drink as little as possible, and move away from any puddle you happen to make."

"That's inhuman."

"Hello! Dragon."

"You can't do this!" Then, as if he had just thought of it, he started screaming at the top of his lungs, "Help! Help me! Help!"

"Seriously? Seriously? Do you really think we'd be close enough to town that they could hear you scream? Do you take me for a rank amateur? Besides which they'd just be even less likely to come up here figuring I'm torturing you or worse."

"Then I'll scream what you're doing." Humphrey drew a deep breath and started yelling again. "Duncan is in cahoots with the dragon! It's a swindle!"

"Yes, yes. Why don't you scream that a thousand times? You know what that sounds like to anyone close enough to hear any part of it?"

Humphrey shrugged, no doubt saving his voice for his message.

"'Help, help! Send Duncan! The dragon's killing me!' So knock yourself out."

The human screamed his message for about five minutes, and then Mallory jumped, landing with his feet just inches from Humphrey's head. He glared down at him. "Of course, if you irritate me enough I could always just eat you." Humphrey fell silent. "That's better, now you be a good boy. I've got a little errand to run." Mallory grabbed his vest, checked the pockets, and took off. The minute he left Humphrey started screaming again, but Mallory was right and long before he got close to the town even his sharp ears couldn't hear the man's voice any more.

* * * *

He found Christina waiting in the clearing for him. She waved big and skipped up to him with a bouquet of wild flowers. He handed her an apple he'd brought with him from camp.

"I was afraid you weren't coming," Christina said.

"Nonsense, I said I'd come, didn't I?"

"Uh huh. I like your vest."

"Why thank you." Mallory watched as the child devoured the apple greedily. "Have you been waiting long? You seem awful hungry."

Christina was quiet for a minute then she looked up at him. Her blond hair framed her tiny face and her blue eyes were swimming with tears. "I gave my daddy the money and he went to get groceries but…. Instead he bet all the money on you, so we still don't have any food and…."

"No offense, but your father is a fool."

"I know. That's what Mommy says," Christina said. She looked up at Mallory and smiled "I brought jacks. You want to play jacks?"

"You'll have to teach me how," Mallory said.

They'd been playing for a while and Mallory still couldn't think of any way to bet on jacks—at least not so you could cheat and win. "Christina, this just might be the fairest game I've ever played in my life. It's been fun, but I have to go. I've got work to do."

Mallory thought about it only a minute then he reached into one of the immense pockets in his vest and pulled out two bags of coins. It was in fact everything they had besides what was still in his cheek pouches and the twenty-five coins Duncan had in his pouch. "Can you do exactly what I tell you, Christina, without telling anyone at all about me?"

"Of course. We're friends," Christina said.

"Take this small pouch to your mother. Tell her you found it in the street. I assume your mother will actually buy groceries with it."

Christina nodded excitedly.

"Take the other bag—the big one—and take it down to the hotel. There are some people staying there, strangers from out of town. The man is called Bilgewater and the lady is called Sadie. They're the ones who people have been betting with. You go in and you bet all that money on Duncan to win."

"But he's not really going to hurt you because he's your friend, right?"

"That's right. You will win a lot of money. When you collect the money you bring it here and I will split it with you, and then your family will have lots of money. Do you understand?"

Christina nodded.

"You can't tell anyone about me and Dunc. You got that? No one can know."

She nodded again. "I won't tell no one, Mallory, 'cause we're friends." She hugged him and he hugged her back.

"I have to go. I'll meet you back here around this time tomorrow."

* * * *

"Where were you?" Duncan asked hotly as Mallory walked back into camp.

"I had an errand to run." Mallory shrugged.

"An errand to run. You aren't supposed to be doing anything but getting ready to attack the town tomorrow, let me kill you, and then hide while I collect the reward. You were supposed to be watching Humphrey so he didn't get away. When I got up here he had pulled himself over to the fire and was trying to burn the ropes off his hands. And he was screaming his head off."

Mallory looked at where Humphrey lay on the ground and frowned. "Look what you did now. You got me in trouble. Well I hope you're happy, young man."

"Where were you?" Duncan demanded.

"I wanted us to cash in on some of the action Bilgewater and Sadie are getting so I found someone to make a bet for me on you."

"You told someone. Someone in town knows you aren't really going to kill them and that it's all just an act!" Duncan was in a near panic. "Why would you do that, Mallory? Why would you do that without asking me?"

"Relax, Dunc. You'll give yourself an ulcer. You keep forgetting I'm the financial genius of this team. Don't worry. I got a little kid to make the bet for us."

"A kid? Are you insane? Mallory, kids can't keep secrets."

"They can if they think it might get them into trouble if they tell. It's perfect. No one's going to believe a kid. If she says I'm not a bad dragon and it's all a scam they'll just think she has a vivid imagination."

Duncan nodded. As usual, what Mallory said made perfect sense.

"Besides the kid's family is broke, and they need the money. It's in her best interest not to tell anyone what we're up to."

Then Duncan noticed Mallory's vest wasn't riding as low as it had been. "How much did you bet?"

"All of it," Mallory said, looking at his claws and flicking some dirt out from under one of them.

"All of it! All of it! Are you nuts?"

"Nothing ventured, nothing gained. Besides it's a sure thing, Dunc. Calm down, what could go wrong?"

"I can think of any number of things that could go wrong. Not the least of which is that Bilgewater and Sadie might skip town with the money and not pay anyone."

"I think not. They strike me as the kind who hedge their bets by not burning bridges behind them."

"They aren't going to pay on any bet we make."

"They won't know we're making a bet."

"They're going to let some little kid bet a bag of coins on me knowing I'm going to win?"

Mallory seemed to think on that for a minute, looking somewhat troubled.

"That's what I thought! You didn't really think about it at all." Duncan jumped up and almost hit his head on the roof of the rock overhang they'd made camp under. "You put the whole operation in jeopardy without asking what I thought, and let's face it, I'm the one who is out there not you." Duncan started stomping around. "I have a bad feeling, Mal, a real bad one." He looked to where Humphrey lay silent but smiling. He hadn't felt good about anything since Humphrey showed up.

"What are you grinning at, you jackal!" He stomped close to Humphrey, sending a plume of dust into his face.

"Nothing." Humphrey coughed and shrugged as best he could.

"Remember what you said about coincidences, Mallory?"

"Yes, and we already know it is no coincidence that any of these people are here. Look, the worst thing that happens is you're right and Bilgewater and Sadie won't let the kid make the bet. In which case you'll still get the reward money, and I'll get our money back from the kid." But Mallory didn't seem so cocky now, which bothered Duncan more than a little.

If Mallory wasn't sure things were going to go his way then Duncan was sure they were in for some huge calamity.

The dragon motioned for Duncan to follow him out of earshot of their prisoner. "As soon as you get the reward money…" Mallory knelt down and drew a crude map of the town with a stick in the dirt. "…meet me in the woods here. It's a small clearing about a hundred yards from the back of this house. We'll collect our winnings, if there are any, or just our money if Christina couldn't make the bet."

"I can't believe you gave all my money…."

"Our money," Mallory reminded.

"I can't believe you trusted all our money to some little girl. Did you take a hit on the head or something, Mal? Maybe eat some plant you shouldn't have?"

Mallory shrugged. "What can I say? I have a soft spot for kids."

"All our money, Mal. You've gone soft, soft in your head." He took his foot and rubbed out the map because he didn't trust that their prisoner wasn't going to escape. "I've got to get back to town. Make sure they know I'm there to protect them...."

"Protect them. Oh, that gives me a great idea. We could run a protection racket...."

"Don't even think about it. If we get out of this one alive and with any money at all, I say we head for home and put all of Winterhurst behind us for good."

Mallory nodded. "All right, partner."

Duncan grabbed his cloak and sword. "I'll be on the porch of the general store at high noon," he said in a whisper so that Humphrey couldn't overhear him.

"I'll be there," Mallory said, giving him a thumbs up with his opposable claw.

"Keep an eye on him," Duncan said, pointing at the hog-tied man, "He's not as stupid as he seems, and if he gets loose...."

"He won't," Mallory said. "I'll tie him good and tight just before I leave camp."

"You better sleep with one eye open, too. He'd just as soon kill you as look at you," Duncan added again in a whisper.

Mallory nodded his understanding and whispered back, "I abhor violence, Dunc, but that doesn't mean I have no sense of self-preservation. If it came down to me or him, have no doubt—he'd lose."

Duncan started for town, and the dread he was feeling as the darkness started to descend on him was as bad as if he were actually fighting a dragon the next day.

* * * *

"You want to do what?" Bilgewater asked the kid for a second time.

"I want to bet all this money on Duncan," the little girl said.

Bilgewater opened the bag, looked in, and didn't even dump it out to count it. He didn't have to count it to know that this was more money than any kid should be carrying around.

As if reading his mind Sadie smiled at the child, "Honey, where did you get all this money?"

"My daddy. Mommy won't let him bring the money himself because he…well, he is always losing all our money," the little girl said.

"And you're sure he wanted you to bet on Duncan, not the dragon?"

"That's what he said."

Sadie grabbed Bilgewater's arm and pulled him aside. "There is enough money there at the odds to seriously eat into our profits."

"I know," Bilgewater said, looking from the child to the bag in his hand. He smiled. "Of course we could always just mark it in the book wrong. Who's going to believe a kid got it right?"

"No, we absolutely could not do that, Bilgewater," Sadie said. "I don't often draw a line, but this is one you will not cross. You heard what she said. Her family is probably broke from her father's gambling and…."

Bilgewater sighed and half listened to all the reasons what he had said was totally and completely wrong. And why they made him the worst sort of person, and why if he wasn't very careful he was going to push things too far one day, and they were going to jump right back and bite him on the ass.

"Sheesh! If I'd wanted to hear a sermon I'd have gone to church. Well, what do *you* think we should do, Sadie?"

* * * *

Duncan went to the town bar and bought himself a beer. He watched the crowd as they kept their distance, but he could hear pieces of their conversations.

"He's very brave and a bit good looking," one of the saloon girls said.

But mostly he overheard things like, "He's a dead man."

"Not a ghost of a chance."

And even muttered chants of "Dead man walking" when he'd come in.

No one came near him to cheer him on. In the last two towns the people had near worshiped him. They'd all rushed around him to cheer him on.

Bilgewater and Sadie's betting pool had put a stop to all that. These people, most of them, had bet against him, so they felt guilty as they watched him. They wanted him to lose so that they could collect some money more than they wanted to be safe from the dragon.

Part of Duncan wished he could talk Mallory into killing a couple of them just so he'd seem like a bigger menace.

He wasn't getting the good feeling this con had given him before, and he was ready to get this over with and get back on the river. Ready to put a little distance between himself and this town filled with not-very-nice people, all hoping to cash in when he was eaten by a dragon. He left the bar early and went to the room he had rented for the night, but he didn't enjoy either his bath or his bed.

As he tossed and turned trying to go to sleep he started to wish he'd found some way to stay in Hellsbut. Be their new blacksmith, and just have a nice, calm, not-so-adventurous life surrounded by people who thought he was a hero.

When he finally got to sleep he had a dream that he was the black-smith in Hellsbut. It started out being a rather sweet dream. He had two little kids and their mother had a wart on her hand that foretold the weather.

Everything was nice, just how he thought it might be, and then his wife's wart looked right at him and said, "It's going to be a bad winter. The worst yet." And then he was freezing. He was trying to work metal, but the anvil was too cold, and no matter how much coal he put in the forge, no matter how hard he worked the bellows, he couldn't get warm. Then his feet, which were suddenly bare, turned blue and when he tried to walk they broke off and he fell. When he did the bucket went flying into the air and he was covered in crap from head to no toes.

He woke up screaming and sat straight up in bed. His breathing was coming heavy, like he'd walked uphill on a winter morning. When he looked down his feet were sticking out of the covers, and they were cold but still there so he started to calm down.

He heard knocking on his door. "What is it?"

"Complementary breakfast," a woman said.

"Give me a second," he said. He picked his pants up off the floor and put them on. Then he stood up and went to the door. As he opened it he could see a young woman carrying a tray laden with a pot of steaming coffee, pancakes, bacon, eggs and sausages. There was so much food that the tray was all but too heavy for the woman who carried it. She set it down on a small table by the window beside which stood a single chair.

"The manager wanted you to have a hearty breakfast."

"Since it's going to be my last meal and all," Duncan said with a half smile.

"You don't seem scared at all. The odds are six to one that the dragon will kill you." She was a pretty little thing, and there was a note of real concern in her voice.

"I know something they don't know. I have fought a dozen dragons, and though I've had bones broken and a few cuts and burns, I'm still very much alive. Did you," he picked up a piece of sausage took a bite and swallowed it before finishing his question, "bet against me?"

"Most certainly not," she said, a note of disgust in her voice. "A stranger with no ties to our community offers his services to fight a dragon that's terrifying our town. Why, to bet against you seems like a horrible wrong to me, and…no offense, but to bet against the dragon just seems foolhardy. I'm only a chambermaid. I don't make much money, and certainly not enough to make a bet when I might lose."

"There is too much food here for just me. Would you care to join me for breakfast?"

"The manager…. He would say he only pays me to work not visit with the guests."

"Then you tell the manager it was my wish that you have breakfast with me. Surely he wouldn't begrudge a man his last wish."

She nodded, and Duncan picked up the table and carried it over till he could sit on the bed. With a wave of his hand indicated she should sit in the chair. She carried it over and sat down across from him. She poured him a cup of coffee.

"Do you think it is your last day?"

"I know it's not," Duncan said, happy to talk to perhaps the only person in town—besides of course Bilgewater and Sadie—who wasn't hoping he was going to die.

"You are very brave," she said, buttering a piece of toast for herself.

"Yes, yes I am," Duncan said, realizing that what had been missing for him was playing the hero. This town had treated him like a mercenary from the start, trying to get him to take less money and then putting out wanted posters for Mallory.

They hadn't been playing by the rules Duncan had made for this con at all. Now suddenly everything seemed right because he was getting a free breakfast and a pretty girl thought he was a hero. "I also have faith in my skill as a warrior. I know what I'm capable of. They don't," Duncan added. The fact that he didn't choke on the piece of bacon he was chewing on told him that he really had become quite the actor.

In fact, here he was trying to eat as much of this food as he could, and he had been taught all his life to eat light before going into battle.

"Did you…did you always want to be a dragon slayer?" she asked him curiously.

"No, I thought I wanted to be a blacksmith once," Duncan said truthfully.

"Why didn't you?" she asked.

"What's your name, miss?"

"Lucinda."

"Well, Lucinda, the truth is that I'm a Romancer. I came from a family of great fighting men, and nothing would do but that I grow up to do as they had done. I wasn't allowed to make a decision about what I wanted to do or be," Duncan said, and thought *and once I got away from them, I found that the easiest way to make a living and do mostly what you want to do is to pretend to be something you never could be.* "What about you, are you happy to be a chambermaid?"

She laughed—a musical sound that made Duncan smile. "No one's happy to be a chambermaid, mister…."

"Just Duncan." He smiled.

"Anyway, Duncan, chambermaid isn't a career choice. It's what you get stuck with."

"What do you want to do?"

"You'll think it's silly."

Considering what I actually do for a living I'm hardly the man to pass judgment, Duncan thought. Then he smiled and said, "Try me. After all, I fight dragons for a living."

"I want to be a seamstress. Make clothes. You know, design them, sew them, maybe someday have my own shop where I sell what I make."

"That doesn't sound silly at all, and certainly it's not an unattainable goal."

"Are you kidding me? A sewing machine that will do what I want to do costs eighty-five coins. That's more than I make in six months. Katy Smith…she's the school teacher. She told me that I should save just a little money each time I get paid, and that eventually I'll be able to buy a machine. I don't think she knows what it costs me to live. By the time I pay room and board to the manager here I'm mostly working to pay my debt. I managed to save five coins in eight months, but then I had a toothache. It took everything I'd saved, and I still owe the dentist ten coins. Doesn't seem fair. Guy pulls one of my teeth, it takes him less than ten minutes to do it, and he charges me more money than I make in two months' time."

No, it didn't seem fair at all. Once again Duncan saw himself as not just a guy out to make a quick buck but as a great equalizer of sorts. He knew exactly what he was going to do, so he finished eating, enjoying the pleasant conversation and good food.

When he was done, Lucinda stood up and started to clean up the mess, loading everything onto the tray. She looked at him, smiled, and then said, "Now don't you go and get yourself killed today."

"I have no intention of it, and who knows, that varmint dragon may not even show up today. He may never come back, in which case I'll have to leave with my pockets light, but at least your town will be safe."

"You think that could happen? That he might just not come back?" Lucinda asked.

"Not for a minute." He smiled, wrestled his pouch from his belt, and dumped a bunch of coins into his hand. "You said the odds against me are six to one, right?" Lucinda nodded, staring at the pile of coins in his hand. "Well, I have no intention of dying and every intention of ridding this town of their dragon problem. So here are fifteen coins." He counted them out. "I will only give them to you if you promise to run right to the betting parlor and bet it all on me. Fifteen coins won't do much more than put you back where you were before you went to the dentist, but if you bet it on me and I slay the dragon…which I will…then you'll have ninety coins which ought to pay off the dentist and buy you that sewing machine you want."

"I…I can't take your money."

"Sure you can." He took hold of her wrist, gently opened her hand, and put the coins into it. Then he closed her fingers over them. "It will bring me luck and give me strength to know that one person in this whole town will not be cheering for my death."

She nodded. "I will place the bet right now, and when you beat this dragon I will put the money to good use. I will think of you often and fondly. Is there no way you can stay?"

Duncan wished there was if for no other reason than to get to know Lucinda better. He'd already told her the story of how he had to keep moving because the family of all the dragons he'd ever killed was after him. In fact he had shared the whole other list of lies he and Mallory had concocted, so that the things Duncan did, and the fact that none of them could see the body of the dead dragon, made perfect sense.

The people in the villages and towns of Winterhurst were extremely superstitious. Because of this they were gullible. As Mallory would say, they were an easy mark. Duncan once again felt a little guilty about what he was doing, but only a little.

As the dragon had pointed out they wouldn't be gullible if they weren't ignorant. And they were ignorant because they chose to learn only those things that were easy for them to understand, didn't take too much thought, and didn't go against anything they already believed.

Mallory had even explained that by taking advantage of these people's ignorance they were helping them to evolve. They would learn nothing about how to protect themselves from being swindled if they were never swindled, and they would never get any smarter.

Of course the dragon had a way of rationalizing anything away.

It didn't matter. It made Duncan feel better, and at the end of today they'd all think he was a hero. He'd collect his reward, and if nothing else he and Mallory would have shaken the boring out of the town for a few days. They'd put on a good show and leave the people with something to talk about for years to come.

As he watched Lucinda leave with the money and the tray he sighed. His only real regret was that he wouldn't get the chance for her to show her gratitude to him for all he'd done for her.

It was the price he paid for being a hero.

He packed all his gear into his backpack, put on the rest of his clothes and his armor and left the hotel. He walked to the general store, went in and started shopping. He got a section of rope and some vegetable oil.

"What you going to do with these?" the shop keeper asked as he rang up his purchases.

"This dragon is tricky, so I'm going to have to keep my wits about me. I'm going to try to set a trap for him, string the rope across the road just out of his line of sight—dragons have trouble seeing below their knees you know."

"I didn't."

"Well they do. It's all about where their eyes are in their head and because their knees bend backwards."

"Their knees bend backwards?"

"Yes, they do. Any way I figure I'll go find him, get him to chase me and trip him with the rope."

"What's the oil for?"

Because I have a new frying pan and I want to fry up some fish, Duncan thought. Just like he'd bought the rope because he'd used his last piece to tie up Humphrey and he always needed rope for something. Of course the idea was for him to appear to be shopping for items with which to kill the dragon so that he could be seen in public and appearing busy when Mallory came to destroy the town. "I, ah…I'm going to oil the rope so that when he hits it, it will be slick and he'll slide and trip. When he falls I'll chop off his head."

The shop keep got an "oh-you-poor-boy-you're-about-to-die-in-a-horrible-way" look on his face which Duncan figured worked for him.

Before Duncan could pull out the coins to pay, the shop keep shut the drawer of the cash register and the No Sale tab popped up.

"No charge, Duncan, and good luck to you son," he said.

"Thank you kindly." Duncan nodded, loaded the oil and rope into his pack and walked out on the porch. It shouldn't be long now. He walked off the porch slowly like a man on a mission but in no hurry to say hello to his death.

* * * *

Mallory checked the ropes on Humphrey where he'd tied him to a tree. He had decided after Humphrey tried to burn his ropes off that he'd best tie him to something so big he couldn't move it, just to be on the safe side.

"When I get loose, dragon, and I will get lose, I'm going to kill you and your little friend too!" Humphrey screamed.

"See, when you say things like that you don't leave much incentive for me to let you live," Mallory said, clicking his tongue and shaking his head. "This is all your own fault you know."

"What?"

"If you hadn't come in here trying to wreck everything we wouldn't have had to tie you up. You're a kill-joy, Humphrey, and nobody likes a kill-joy."

"So you're just going to leave me here tied to this tree, without food or water."

"Well I was going to come untie you as soon as we were ready to leave, but then you're going on and on about killing us and such."

This seemed to take all the wind out of the big man's sails and he started to actually cry. And then there was the pleading, "Please dragon. Please don't leave me here to die like this, please…."

"All right, all right! Geez, I'm embarrassed for you," Mallory said, shaking his head. "When we get done in town I'll send someone back to untie you. But if you come after us again, I have to tell you I'm not going to be this nice again."

Mallory started for town mumbling. "I'm just too nice that's my problem. It's my real undoing at the end of the day, I'm just too nice."

Twelve

If Duncan had walked through town any slower, snails and turtles would have run past him. He looked up in the sky. It was for sure high noon. He was starting to worry about Mallory when he heard the screaming start from the edge of town, followed by the roaring of his friend doing his best scary-dragon act.

He ran towards the noise saying, "No time to spring my trap. Everyone run for cover! He's in a killing mood this time."

As Duncan rounded a corner a fireball fell just at his feet. He jumped and glared at Mallory. That was a little too close for comfort. Duncan reached for his sword, had trouble getting it free, finally freed it—and tripped over the length of the blade and nearly fell. Mallory rolled his eyes, shook his head, and then ran at him.

Duncan raised the sword high and ran towards the dragon, hoping he didn't fall again. Mallory spit another fireball at him—this time not too close—and then he grabbed Duncan's sword arm with his tail. They fell to the ground and started to wrestle, all for the benefit of the watching town's people. Duncan pulled out a pomegranate he had hidden in his tunic and crushed it against Mallory's side. Mallory cried out in mock pain, got up, threw Duncan several feet then ran off.

Duncan jumped to his feet and chased Mallory out of town and into the woods. When they were well out of sight of the town's people, Mallory started throwing fire high into the air so that it could be seen in the distance, and Duncan grabbed a couple of pots and started banging them together.

"Die, demon beast, die!" Duncan thundered.

Mallory screamed out a painful, wailing cry.

"You'll beseech this town no more!" Duncan hollered.

"I think you mean *besiege* this town no more, beseech means…." Mallory started in a little more than a whisper.

"It's hardly time for a language lesson," Duncan whispered back as he knelt to the ground and started smearing his clothes with dirt and mud. Mallory hit him with a couple of pomegranates so that the red juice sprayed everywhere. "Ow! You don't have to throw them so hard."

Mallory picked up the pots and started banging them together. "Don't be such a baby. You're wearing chain mail, for heaven's sake. Besides, we all must suffer for our art."

"I don't see you suffering," Duncan whispered, rubbing at the spot on his chest where Mallory had hit him.

"Excuse me! I have to be the villain while you get to be the hero. Who was sleeping in a comfy bed while I was sleeping in a cold cave? I get no love, no admiration."

"All you care about is the money."

"Point taken."

"Aren't you dead yet?" Duncan asked.

"You getting tired already?"

"Yes," Duncan said.

Mallory nodded and lay down on the ground playing dead. This time it was a tree that would block anyone from seeing where the dragon's head had been "cut off." And of course, Duncan wouldn't let them get too close because it was for their own safety and all.

* * * *

Bilgewater and Sadie hung at the very back of the crowd.

"They aren't half bad," Sadie said of Duncan and Mallory's performance.

"Quite good actually." Bilgewater watched as the small gathering of those brave enough to follow—even though hanging well back—were suddenly elated at Duncan's apparent triumph over scaly evil. It didn't last long.

Bilgewater could see the change in their demeanor as each one seemed to realize they'd just lost a bundle of money. Because, of course, those brave enough to follow the brawling man and dragon were also those who had bet the most money on the outcome.

"Come on. There are a few people we'll have to pay, and then we best beat a retreat in case some of the rest aren't such good losers," he whispered to Sadie.

"Do we have to? I'd like to see how they're going to pull off the whole dead dragon thing," Sadie said.

"Come on." Bilgewater put a hand on her shoulder and propelled her along back towards town and their "office."

In all of town only three people had bet on Duncan. One, a young woman, was so excited about the new life she was going to buy with her winnings that Bilgewater found that he couldn't begrudge her huge payout at all.

As soon as they had paid the three people they owed money, they quickly packed their stuff and headed for the stables and their horses.

On the way they noticed a small group had gathered outside the general store, and they stopped to watch.

The mayor was standing on the porch and Duncan stood beside him. Considering how much money the mayor had bet against Duncan it was no wonder he seemed reluctant to let go of the small bag that no doubt held Duncan's "reward" money.

"Good people gather around! Duncan the dragon slayer has killed the dragon and we must all thank him."

Nearly the whole town appeared as if from thin air, but the muttering from the crowd didn't sound at all thankful. Then the young woman who had bet all her money on Duncan started to cheer. She jumped up and down and chanted Duncan's name until the crowd felt obliged to join in.

"Thank you, thank you, but that's not necessary. I was simply doing my job and…."

A big, filthy man with ropes hanging around his wrists and ankles broke through the crowd.

"Humphrey!" Duncan exclaimed before Bilgewater had even figured out who it was and obviously before Duncan had time to think about it. Then since he did have a chance to think about it he hollered, "Thank the gods you're alive, man!"

"Alive! Alive! You and your dragon friend nearly killed me. I've rubbed my arms and legs raw against that tree, but I'm free now—and just in time, I see. This man is no hero. He is a common grafter. The dragon isn't dead."

"We saw the dragon dead just before its carcass vanished," one man said and a bunch of others joined in.

Humphrey laughed. "They have played you for fools. Can't you see that nothing he has told you really makes sense? It's all a hoax."

Duncan was a quicker thinker than Bilgewater would have previously thought. A look of real concern entered his eyes as he said, "The poor man. I thought he had been killed, but obviously he has been in the dragon's lair all this time, tormented, torn, tortured. It's no wonder he is delirious…."

"Delirious!" Humphrey stomped forward. "*You're* delirious to think that even these dunder-headed imbeciles would believe that half-baked story you and that giant lizard came up with."

Bilgewater smiled and so did Sadie. Humphrey had just made a grand blunder. You didn't call people you wanted to be your allies dunder-headed imbeciles. "Come on. Let's get while the getting's good,"

Bilgewater whispered. Sadie nodded in agreement and started to follow him.

"Sir, I must protest. This man is a hero. He no doubt saved your life," the mayor said.

"Saved my life!" Humphrey laughed. "Saved my life! I'm telling you it's all a trick, a gag. He and that dragon are friends. Listen to me. He was never in any danger. *You* were never in any danger. Any fool could see that this man is no dragon slayer."

Bilgewater shook his head. Humphrey was digging himself a bigger and bigger hole.

"How dare you, sir! Why you went up against the dragon yourself, and it looks like he tied you up to eat you later. What seems clear to everyone is that you, sir, can't claim the reward money, so you don't want Duncan to have it, either," called out the woman who had cashed in on Duncan's success.

The mayor at that very moment put the bag of coins into Duncan's hand.

"Oh, come on, people," Humphrey said. Then his eyes caught and held Bilgewater's and he smiled. "You two tell them. You know it's all a trick. Tell them."

Bilgewater took his time turning around to face the crowd, collecting his thoughts at the same time. "Sir…" He stopped there, finding that for possibly only the third or fourth time in his life he couldn't think of anything to say. On the verge of panic he was saved by Sadie.

"My partner can not find the words, because what this man did earlier was so despicable," Sadie said.

"What did he do, miss?" the mayor asked. Bilgewater very much wanted to know himself.

"He came to us and said that he had tricked Duncan into believing he'd been eaten by the dragon because he had no intention of fighting the dragon himself. He had this idea that he would let Duncan kill the dragon, then show up and say he killed the dragon himself. But to make the lie believable, he needed us to back up his story. Then we could all split the money—he said that we'd make much more money if he, and not Duncan, killed the dragon. We were outraged and naturally refused. Clearly, this is a case of sour grapes because he can cheat no one."

"There is no end to the lies some people will tell to make a coin," Bilgewater said, getting back in the game. "But I never thought I'd ever in my life see someone who would stoop so low as to go out of their way to besmirch the name of such a fine, upstanding hero."

"The man is the worst sort of cad!" the woman who had won the money said.

The mayor turned to Duncan. "Didn't you say he was a tinkerer?"

"Yes, sir, but surely…."

"String him up!" some man yelled.

"We're not going to string a man up over a lie, but I think a good tar and feathering is in order, people," the mayor said.

Before you could say 'grab him,' half the town had fallen on Humphrey. While they were busy carting him away Bilgewater and Sadie made a break for it.

* * * *

Duncan stepped off the porch and started walking away, feeling forgotten. Then suddenly someone was hanging from his neck and kissing his cheek.

"Thank you, Duncan, thank you so much!"

Duncan smiled. "It was my pleasure, Lucinda."

"Are you sure…are you very sure you can't stay?"

"I can't. I wish I could."

"Maybe someday you could come back this way. When dragons stop chasing you and I have my own shop."

"Bet on it," Duncan said. "Good luck, Lucinda, with everything."

"Good luck to you, dragon slayer."

* * * *

Mallory had a good bit of trouble getting to the small clearing where he was supposed to meet Christina and Duncan without being seen. Even with his nifty cloak.

It was now more important than ever that he not be seen by anyone since he was supposed to be dead, and it would have been in bad form to get caught walking around.

Christina was sitting on a rock in the sun playing with a flower, spinning it around and around and counting. Mallory couldn't even guess at what she was counting. She didn't look happy. Her lips were turned down in a frown.

When she saw Mallory she smiled big and ran over to give him a big hug. She stuck the flower behind one of his ears as he picked her up.

"Now what were you so sad about?" Mallory asked.

"I'm not going to see you again, am I, Mallory?"

"No, I have to leave," Mallory said, feeling some sad himself now. "Did you make the bet?"

"The man wouldn't let me," Christina said with a shrug. "He said he couldn't let a little girl make such a big bet."

"Oh that crooked s.o...."

"What?"

"Nothing," Mallory said. "Oh well, give me the money back. I tried."

Someone walked up behind him. Whoever it was must have thought he didn't hear them, but of course he did. He grabbed them with his tail, the person let out a yelp, and he put the little girl down. He let go of whoever was caught up in his tail and turned quickly around. There was a woman standing there.

"I told you to tell no one, Christina."

"That ain't no one, silly." Christina laughed. "That's my mommy." She skipped up beside him and took hold of one of his clawed fingers.

Her mother looked plenty scared, too, but she held the sack of coins out towards Mallory just as Duncan came stomping into the clearing saying, "What? Did you just tell the whole town?"

"It's just my mommy," Christina said, looking up at Duncan.

"I didn't know where she was getting the money," the woman started with a bit of a stutter. "We needed it so badly, but I didn't want her stealing. And the story she told.... Well it was ridiculous, but I could tell she wasn't lying and I...I just wanted to thank you. That little bit of money may not seem like much to you, but it means we'll eat for the next week."

Mallory bowed his head humbly. "It was my pleasure. Well, Christina, I'll miss you but we have to be going...."

"Of course I don't know what we'll do after that," the mother continued. "My husband's an idiot really. Not a bad man, just a lazy dunderhead and a bit of a dreamer. Of course I guess we'll find a way. We always do."

"I'm sure you will...."

"Besides Christina we have twin babies, so no way that I can work. My mother-in-law lives with us, but she lost an eye playing darts at the pub last year and she's always running into something these days. Then there is my sister-in-law. Did I tell you she has five kids?"

"No, we really must be...."

"She does—and only one leg. My brother, well he has her other leg, but it doesn't work so good. My sister and her baby live with us, too, and the baby... Well I think it's coming down with something and my sister keeps losing her glass eye...those are expensive you know... I wish my mother-in-law would give up darts. Every time it rains my sister's baby get's a cold. It might be allergies, but frankly I think it's because her crib is under a drip. There's just no place else to put it...."

Thirteen

"I can't believe you gave them all our money!" Duncan groaned.

"Me? You're the one who gave them all our reward money," Mallory said, sweeping his claws through the air in dramatic gestures. "I didn't give away any more money than you did. Besides, I don't think we ever would have gotten out of there if we hadn't given them the money."

Duncan laughed in spite of himself. "Well it did seem they needed it more than we did. So do we have anything left from the last two jobs?"

"I have a little hidden away but not much," Mallory said truthfully.

"Are you ever going to tell me where you hide it?"

"I told you, if I told you I'd have to kill you." Mallory smiled back.

"Bilgewater and Sadie snuck away without giving us the fifty coins they promised us," Duncan reminded him.

"We got the full one hundred, so I imagine they decided they didn't owe it to us. They did save us more than once back there." He smiled. "I have the feeling it's only a matter of time till we run into them again, and when we do don't think for a minute I won't remind them they owe us fifty coins."

"So…. We did all this work and we have nothing to show for it, yet I don't really feel bad," Duncan said.

"I wouldn't say we have nothing to show for it. There are a few things we have learned, and the next time we do this…."

"Oh no!" Duncan shook his head and started walking faster down the road. "We're going home, and then we're putting some distance between this place and us before someone besides that numbskull Humphrey figures out what we did. We're going to go to a big city and dock our boat. You'll play cards, and I'll watch your back."

"Hah! You spend more time drinking and chasing skirts than you spend watching my back," Mallory said.

"That's my cover. It's how I keep people from knowing I'm covering your back." Duncan laughed.

"Yeah, yeah but someday when we come back this way we'll dust off this con and…."

"Nope. I'm done being a dragon slayer," Duncan said.

"But why? I thought you liked being a dragon slayer…the love and admiration of the people…"

"That I lie to over and over and over again. Then there's the constant fear of getting caught in one of those lies. We did all of that, and at the end of it we don't have any more money than we started with because we gave it all away."

"But wasn't it fun?" Mallory asked.

"What?" Duncan didn't understand.

"Come on. We aren't completely broke. It was exciting, and we actually helped some people."

"We mostly did it to help ourselves. Parts of it were fun, but parts were terrifying and again…we're mostly broke."

"Mostly only counts in fire breathing."

* * * *

Two days later they walked into the harbor where their boat was docked.

"My feet are killing me," Duncan complained. "I can't wait to get home, sit down in my new chair, and take a nap."

Suddenly Mallory stopped dead in his tracks. He backed up a step, looked down a street, and then started walking double time, taking hold of Duncan's arm. "Come on, man. Let's get going."

"What on Overlap! I'm not in this big a hurry to get home. Did you not hear me say my feet hurt?" Duncan said.

"I just saw Humphrey. He looks madder than a wet setting hen… Well, exactly like a setting hen, actually, since he's still mostly covered with feathers."

"So? I'm not afraid of Humphrey. The two of us can take him."

"First, must I remind you that I prefer to avoid violence? Second, you can't fight your way out of a paper bag. And third, he was talking to the city police. Now I don't know if what we did back in Wart Haven could get us in trouble here, or if they'd take a stranger's word for it, but I'd rather not find out."

"How do you even know he's seen us or that he was talking about us at all?"

"I don't know that he's not."

"Point taken," Duncan said. Mallory didn't have to say more than that. Duncan sped up, and by the time they reached Demon Home they were both practically running. The outside looked fine, and when they boarded, except for a little dust, it was just as they'd left it, so the demon had obviously done a good job protecting the boat.

That Fred hadn't decided to trash their new stuff in their absence was a happy surprise for Duncan. If there had been time he probably would have hugged the comfy chairs they bought for the main room just before they left.

"I'll get the boiler going. You cast us off." Mallory smiled suddenly. "I hear there's a city not far down stream called Purn, where the card tables are hot and they make the best vegetarian shish-kabob in three sectors. I think it's time for us to move on. What say you, partner?"

"I couldn't agree more, Mal."

Mallory ran to start the furnace as Duncan lifted the gangplank and started casting the boat off from the dock.

He was getting ready to throw off the last line when a familiar voice yelled out, "Hold up a minute! Wait for us!"

When Duncan looked up he could see Bilgewater and Sadie booking it down the dock.

"You guys owe us money," Duncan said, watching them through slitted eyes.

"Ah, that's what we're here for, to give you your money," Bilgewater said, and then he and Sadie jumped from the dock onto the deck of the boat.

"Don't try to con a con man, Bilgewater. We both know you're here for the same reason we're suddenly in such a big hurry to leave. You saw Humphrey talking to a cop," Duncan said.

Sadie sighed with relief then and said to Bilgewater, "And I thought we were running because that guy we 'got' our horses from said he was going to kill us."

Bilgewater cut Sadie a look, and she cringed a little. "Oops."

Duncan laughed and shook his head. "Sounds like you guys are in some deep horse crap there."

Bilgewater cut him a pleading look. "Come on, Duncan old man, you know how it is with issues of ownership. The lines can blur."

"Not really."

Bilgewater smiled appealingly. "Look, we had your back in Wart Haven. It's not like we hurt the horses. We just used them for a while. It's actually good for horses to be ridden…."

"Now you sound just like Mallory." Duncan laughed.

"We'll gladly pay you what we owe you, and of course we'll pay for passage on your boat to some place downstream…. Or up. It doesn't really matter where we go at this point. Away from here fast would be great."

"Demon Home isn't just a name, the ship is haunted by a demon," Duncan warned.

"We've lived with worse, right, Sadie?" Bilgewater said quickly.

"Well I've lived with you—that's pretty bad," Sadie said with a half grin.

"What are you waiting for?" Mallory walked out on deck and glared at Duncan. "Come on, let's get out of here before every cop and their dog is…." He saw Bilgewater and Sadie then, and as if he fully expected to find them there said quite calmly, "You two owe us money."

Bilgewater draped an arm over Mallory's shoulders and led him back in the boat saying, "And as I was telling your partner we're here to pay our debt to you and to pay you for the privilege of a trip in your fine boat."

Mallory cut Duncan a look and Duncan smiled and said, "They're horse thieves."

"Horse *borrowers*," Bilgewater said. "We returned them."

"I hear it's good for them to be ridden," the dragon said.

"And seriously can anyone really own a living thing?" Bilgewater added.

"Like peas in a pod," Duncan said.

"Rotten peas in a twisted pod." Sadie laughed.

He smiled at her, nodded in agreement and started for the bridge.

He heard screaming, turned to see Humphrey and a couple of cops running down the dock, and he doubled his pace up the stairs. "Start the boat!"

"Yes! By all means, start the boat," Mallory said in near panic.

"No, Mal, I wasn't asking! I mean *you* turn on the steam to the motor, and I'll go to the bridge and get us going."

"Gotcha," Mallory said, and ran for the boiler room as Duncan ran the rest of the way to the bridge.

* * * *

Mallory flipped the switch that sent steam to the engine and hoped they had enough pressure…. Which they did, just barely. He hit the boiler with a blast of fire to hurry the process, careful not to set the boat on fire.

The boat moved out of the slip slowly at first, then started to speed up.

Mallory hurried to the main room and looked out the door. He got there just in time to see Humphrey dive off the dock and start swimming after them. For a second it looked like he might catch them, too.

Suddenly Humphrey's arms started flailing in the air as if he were grasping at something that just wasn't there. Clearly his clothing and all those feathers had absorbed enough water that they were weighing him down.

He went under and came roaring back to the surface yelling for help. Just as they hit their head of steam and started rolling down the river in earnest, Humphrey went down for the third time.

The police, looking more annoyed than anything else, grabbed some boat hooks and pulled the struggling man from the water.

"I'm going to get you, dragon! If it's the last thing I do!" Humphrey screamed, waving his fists in the air and making it hard for his rescuers to fish him from the water. "You haven't seen the end of me by a long shot!"

"Jerk," Mallory said. He closed the door to the deck so that he couldn't hear Humphrey screaming and turned his attention to their "passengers."

"We will have to figure out a fair price for your passage."

"Of course," Bilgewater said.

"Accommodations are sparse, which is, of course, a pleasant way of saying that there are no beds in your rooms. There will be evening entertainment, which is a nice way of telling you that a small but very aggressive boat demon will be terrorizing you after dusk. Meals will be served at irregular hours, which means that, for a fee, I will cook whatever fish you can catch out of our toilet. Thank you for choosing Demon Home for your transportation needs."

As Mallory started up the stairs he could hear them laughing. Of course they had yet to meet Fred.

He walked up to the bridge to get a better look at the dock. He checked to see if the police were going to send boats after them, or if they really had made a more or less clean get away.

From the way Humphrey was jumping around and yelling, it was obvious he expected the police to make chase. It was just as clear by the way that the cops stood with their arms crossed that they had no intention of doing so.

"Well here's some good news," Mallory said. "It looks like they aren't going to come after us."

"You realize this is the first time we've actually had the boat in the Sliding?" Duncan said.

Mallory looked out at the massiveness of the river. "Seems silly now that we didn't know we weren't on the river, doesn't it?"

"You know, Mal, it's a little intimidating. There are boats everywhere and… Well, we were going to learn more about the boat and driving it, and the river and all that, but we didn't. We didn't even ever get that map we kept talking about. I wish I knew what I was doing instead of just guessing."

"Now what would be the fun of that? It seems simple. Don't run into other boats and don't run into the land." Mallory turned and started down the stairs.

"What are you going to do?"

"Someone has to entertain our guests." Mallory smiled and yelled down the stairs, "Anyone up for a game of cards?"